Ch



# Practical Photography on Glass and Paper

## Part 2

SALZWASSER
VERLAG

Charles A. Long

# Practical Photography on Glass and Paper

## Part 2

Reprint of the original, first published in 1864.

1st Edition 2022 | ISBN: 978-3-75259-452-2

Verlag (Publisher): Salzwasser Verlag GmbH, Zeilweg 44, 60439 Frankfurt, Deutschland
Vertretungsberechtigt (Authorized to represent): E. Roepke, Zeilweg 44, 60439 Frankfurt, Deutschland
Druck (Print): Books on Demand GmbH, In de Tarpen 42, 22848 Norderstedt, Deutschland

# PRACTICAL
# PHOTOGRAPHY

ON

## Glass and Paper.

# PRACTICAL PHOTOGRAPHY

ON

# Glass and Paper.

## PART II.

CONTAINING

CLEAR DIRECTIONS FOR THE PRACTICE OF THE VARIOUS DRY PROCESSES ON GLASS AND PAPER; THE MANUFACTURE OF COLLODION, &c.; ENLARGING PROCESSES; PERMANENT PRINTING PROCESSES, &c. &c.

TOGETHER WITH

VALUABLE RECIPES AND IMPORTANT FORMULÆ.

LONDON:

1864.

# PREFACE.

---

The favourable reception accorded to "Photography on Glass and Paper" as a First-Book, and the numerous inquiries from those whose initiatory steps in the art have been taken under its guidance for further and more advanced instruction, have suggested to the publishers the importance of issuing a Second Part, by which the student might complete his knowledge of the most important modifications and applications of all branches of Photography. A comprehensive statement of the dry processes in successful use has been thought especially necessary. And, in addition to details of many other applications of the art, such complete and careful instructions have been given for the manufacture, modification, and management of the various preparations required, as will enable the photographer, resident at places remote from sources of aid, readily to overcome difficulties and secure success. In order the better to secure this last purpose only those processes have been described which have been found in practice satisfactory and certain.

*November*, 1864.

# CONTENTS.

# PRACTICAL PHOTOGRAPHY.

## Dry Collodion Processes.

It is obvious that for landscape photography a dry process, that is, a process which permits the preparation at home of the sensitive plates, which may then be packed up and carried about conveniently, exposed in the camera when required, and then developed and finished at home, possesses many advantages over the wet process, which, if practised in the field, renders necessary a portable dark room of some kind. Various clever developing boxes, dark tents, &c., have been devised; but the best of these encumbers the photographer with a great deal of luggage, with which it is desirable, if possible, to dispense. This the various dry processes enable him to do. Their chief drawbacks are greater trouble in preparation, less sensitiveness, and uncertainty of the result until the negatives are developed, when the photographer is perhaps many miles from the spot at which they were taken.

Many theories have been put forward as to the principles upon which the preparation of dry plates should be based; but some uncertainty still prevails upon the subject, in this respect practice far outstripping theory. There are several processes very excellent in practice, and we shall not trouble the reader here with the vexed question of theory, simply contenting ourselves with stating, as clearly as possible, the details of those processes which have been found most successful in practice.

Before detailing the processes, we will make one or two preliminary remarks, which will apply with equal force to all the processes to be *described.* As you will be unable to determine the value of you results until you have returned from your trip, it becomes especially important that no failures shall arise from preventible causes. Give heed, therefore, to the following advice, which, for clearness, we shall divide into half a score of rules.

I. Select your glass with care; always using, for dry processes, good thin patent plate.

II. Always use new glasses, reserving those which have been once used for the wet process, in which you see your results at once. There is always some uncertainty about glasses which have once been used.

III. Grind your glasses at the edges, and clean them with scrupulous care. Use a broad camel's hair pencil to remove any dust the last thing before coating with collodion.

IV. Use a pneumatic holder for sustaining the plate, so that it may be as little handled as possible. This will also cause the plate to be covered up to every corner, and lessen the liability of the film leaving the glass during any portion of the operations.

V. Let the first washing water after the plate leaves the nitrate bath always be distilled, and the last also where a final wash is directed. If you have facilities for so doing, always wash in a series of vertical baths, say half-a-dozen; in which case it will never be necessary to touch the plate with the fingers whilst washing, the plate being retained on the same dipper throughout.

VI. Except where the bath or collodion require special conditions for the process, always see that they are such as work cleanly and satisfactorily in the wet process, before commencing the preparation of the plates.

VII. Always try one of a batch of plates before trusting them for important work at a distance.

VIII. Always pack dry plates so that they shall be impervious to air and moisture as well as to light.

IX. Never under-expose dry plates. It is easy by management in developing to produce a good negative from an over-exposed dry plate; but it is impossible to secure thoroughly good results from an under-exposed plate. It is a good maxim to expose for the deepest shadows, the lights in such case will rarely suffer.

. X. As a rule, develop slowly, using very little silver at first. If the plate show signs of over-exposure, then, by adding silver quickly, and stopping the development quickly, a good picture may be secured; but if the exposure be right, slow development will give the finest negative. If signs of under-exposure appear, then very slow development, and the use of very little silver, will largely remedy the defect. In all cases avoid over-intensifying, as the colour of most dry plates is very non-actinic, and a thin deposit will often resist light vigorously in printing.

---

## GENERAL CONDITIONS RELATING TO DRY PLATES.

To avoid repetition, we may state in one chapter a few of the conditions applicable to dry plate photography, and the materials required, generally.

### The Collodion.

The physical qualities of the collodion are of great importance in most of the dry processes. It is important to secure a collodion which gives a porous film readily permeable with liquids after it has been dried. Some samples, when once desiccated, become horny and hard, never again permitting the free permeation of water into their structure. Such collodions are not suited for dry processes. A permeable powdery film is desirable, and one which adheres well to the glass. A sample of pyroxyline made after the formula given as suitable for negative collodion in another chapter, but with the addition of half a drachm of water for each ounce of nitric acid, will give a suitable collodion. The negative collodion described in the chapter in question will generally give suitable film when it has been iodized a few months, but it will require the addition of more bromide.

As a rule, the presence of a bromide is indispensable to successful dry photography, and in much larger proportion than is necessary with wet plates, especially for subjects possessing strong contrasts, and where rapidity is required. In the latter case, the bromide may be used in equal proportion with the iodide.. For general purposes the following formula will give good results :—

| | | |
|---|---|---|
| Iodide of ammonium | ... ... ... | 2½ grains |
| „ cadmium | ... ... ... | 1½ „ |
| Bromide of cadmium | ... ... ... | 2 „ |

Added to each ounce of plain collodion. If an ordinary commercial sample of bromo-iodized collodion be used, from one to two grains of bromide of cadmium may with propriety be added to it for dry plate purposes.

A bromo-iodized collodion, which has been a few months made, and has acquired a little colour, will generally give the best results with dry plates; but if it be very old it will not be quite so sensitive as a newer sample.

## Preliminary Preparation of the Plate.

In many of the dry processes, especially those in which either albumen or gelatine is not used as a preservative, there is a frequent tendency in the film to leave the plate during the operation of developing, fixing, and washing. To obviate this it is found at times desirable to coat the plate with some substance which will adhere firmly itself to the glass, and also hold firmly the coating of collodion. For this purpose solutions of gelatine, albumen, and india-rubber are used, and have each their advocates. For the method of using gelatine, we refer to Major Russell's instructions given in the chapter on the tannin process.

Albumen has for many reasons, we think, the greatest advantage; to use it, proceed as follows :—To the white of one egg, with the germ removed, add three ounces of distilled water, and a drachm and a half of strong liquid ammonia. Beat thoroughly into a froth, and then allow it to settle for a while. After the plates have been clean washed and well drained, coat them, whilst still wet, with the solution of albumen, and then allow them to dry before a brisk fire, carefully avoiding dust.

This coating is found very valuable with the dry collodion plates without preservative to the negatives, on which it gives greater vigour. If it be found that the bath is injured by the preliminary coating of albumen, as sometimes is the case, this may be avoided by pouring over the dried film a saturated solution of protosulphate of iron; and after leaving it there about a minute, washing thoroughly, and drying, as before.

The objection which some photographers have to albumen for a preliminary coating is based upon the fact that it sometimes injures the bath, and moreover has some effect on the character of the image formed, as chemical combination with the albumen, and nitrate of silver, doubtless, being formed. A coating of india-rubber is free from the objection, and answers the purpose. India-rubber sliced very thin, one grain to each ounce, should be dissolved in benzole, or first softened with chloroform and then dissolved in benzole. Great care is required in its use to avoid unnecessary evaporation, and the stock should occasionally be diluted to make up for the loss by evaporation. After coating, each plate should be held before a fire sufficiently hot to slightly melt the india-rubber, or otherwise it will not adhere firmly to the glass.

The film of collodion adheres to all these coatings, and their presence prevents any slight unperceived want of perfect cleanness in the glass less likely to spoil a negative.

Where a preliminary coating is not used, and any tendency of the film to leave the plate is manifested, it is a good plan to apply a varnish with a camel's-hair pencil round the edge of the plate, covering about the eighth of an inch all round. Almost any kind of varnish will serve, or, what is better, bees-wax dissolved in benzole. This edging will generally prevent the loss of the film.

## The Nitrate Bath.

In many cases a nitrate bath, which will work well in the wet process, will also answer well for dry plates. A neutral bath is favourable to rapidity, but not always favourable to cleanliness. As a rule, a stronger bath is desirable for dry plates than for the wet process, and it works best when more or less freely acid, and acetic acid in the bath is better for dry plates than nitric acid. In some cases the presence of organic matter is recommended as a condition of success, as in Mr. Bartholomew's morphine process, where one grain of muriate of morphia to each eight ounces of bath solution, slightly acid with acetic acid, gives very excellent results with simply washed plates. In other cases, except where a special bath is described, the conditions necessary in a bath for the wet process will obtain in dry processes generally.

### Keeping Properties of Dry Plates.

It is often desirable to know how long dry plates will retain their good qualities after preparation before exposure, and how long they will keep after exposure, and before development, without deterioration. No absolute certainty exists on the subject; but it may be laid down as a general condition, that in proportion as they are sensitive, they are unstable, and easily deteriorate. As extreme sensitiveness depends upon the elements forming the sensitive compound being in what has been called a state of "tottering equilibrium," it follows that slight causes will disturb its condition; and as in photography it has been found that heat, time, and other causes sometimes have an effect similar to that of light, it will readily be seen that the more sensitive the compound the more easily it will be decomposed, and also that this decomposition will more readily take place after exposure, by which the molecules have been disturbed, than before exposure.

The best keeping plates we know are collodio-albumen plates, which have received a final wash of a solution of gallic acid after drying. These, if kept carefully, will keep for months. The same is true of Fothergill plates that have received similar treatment. Plates prepared by the tannin process, in its simplest form, keep well, and may be used weeks, and sometimes months, after their preparation. Tannin plates, with any admixture, such as honey, gum, malt, in the preparation, &c., keep less perfectly. All hygrometric preservatives are of uncertain keeping qualities, and plates with any trace of free nitrate of silver keep imperfectly. In all processes where the plate is desired to keep well, it is desirable that one of the washings should be in a solution of salt and water, so as to convert all free nitrate into chloride of silver.

To ensure the best keeping conditions, dry plates should be very carefully stored and kept air-tight as well as light-tight. If they are stored in parcels, packed face to face, with a strip of card at each end to prevent abrasion, and then wrapped in thin sheets of gutta percha, and a second wrapper of lead foil, they will keep well. If stored in boxes, a piece of gold beaters' skin may be run round the joint formed by the lid of the box. It is not well to put them into the dark slide of the camera until the day they are going to be used; and as a general principle, the sooner they are developed after exposure the better.

### Exposure of Dry Plates.

The time of exposure required by dry plates is very indefinite, and there is a frequent tendency to understate the true time. The most sensitive dry plates we know are the extra rapid plates of Dr. Hill Norris, prepared by a secret process. We have seen instantaneous pictures taken by these, but they have always been inferior to instantaneous pictures taken under similar conditions of light, &c., with good wet collodion. In all instances, we believe, they would require at least twice the exposure of wet collodion. As a rule, dry plates require from six to twelve times that exposure. Perhaps we may state generally, that simple tannin with ordinary development should receive from eight to twelve times the exposure of wet plates; that collodio-albumen and Fothergill plates, with ordinary treatment, from six to eight times the exposure of wet plates; tannin, with honey or malt, and suitable development, malt alone, resinized collodion, dry collodion without preservative, tannin with much bromide, or a bromide alone and alkaline development, and some others, from three to six times the exposure of wet collodion, and some of these under some circumstances with still less exposure.

### Development of Dry Plates.

Much licence in exposure, as well as excellence of result, depends on the management of development. The usual method is with pyrogallic acid. Where time is not an object, a saturated solution of gallic acid is safer, but more tedious. In very warm weather, the following should be employed for long developments :—

| | |
|---|---|
| Saturated solution of gallic acid ... | 1 ounce |
| Water ... ... ... ... | 1 „ |
| Acetic acid ... ... ... | 5 to 10 minims |
| Alcohol ... ... ... ... | 5 „ |

The picture can also, in some processes, be brought out by iron, and afterwards intensified by pyrogallic acid. Of course it is necessary that a drop or two of silver solution should be added to each application of the developer.

Where pyrogallic acid is used, and for ordinary exposures, the method recommended by Major Russell, and given in our chapter on the tannin process, is excellent. It consists in keeping a standard solution of pyrogallic acid, and another solution of equal part of citric and nitrate of silver, and mixing the required quantities of these with water for use, commencing with an infinitesimal proportion of the silver solution, and when the image is well out, intensifying rapidly by adding it freely if the picture appear over-exposed, or cautiously if it appear under-exposed. In some cases, Mr. Mudd's method may be adopted with advantage. Instead of commencing development in the usual manner with a solution containing pyrogallic acid, acetic or citric acid, and nitrate of silver, he applies to the plate a two- or three-grain solution of pyrogallic acid, without either acetic or citric acid, or nitrate of silver. With this solution the whole of the detail is fully brought out, and if the plate have been sufficiently exposed, this is effected in a few minutes. The plate now presents a thin phantom image, with less intensity than an iron-developed plate; but on treatment with the ordinary pyrogallic acid developer, containing citric acid and a few drops of nitrate of silver, rapidly acquires vigour and density. The process of development proper having already been effected, this process of adding intensity can be stopped at the moment the desired vigour is obtained.

Hot development, which has so long been used with albumen and collodio-albumen plates, has, more recently, been applied with advantage, in many cases, to tannin and other dry plates. The method recommended is to place the plate in hot water, various temperatures, from 100° to 200° Fah., being suggested. The film thus thoroughly softened and chemical action being accelerated by heat, the regular development with pyro and citro-nitrate of silver is carried out. The great difficulty is to prevent the plate drying rapidly and irregularly, and the great danger fog or surface reduction.

The use of an alkali in developing is found especially successful with tannin plates, the details will be found in the chapter on that subject.

In recapitulating, it is clear that water moderately hot, sufficiently to permeate the film thoroughly, may be in most cases used with advantage, as may also a solution of pyro, without free acid or silver, until the image is brought out; that intensity with detail is best obtained afterwards, by the use of pyro and the citro-nitrate of silver recommended by Major Russell, using little silver if detail be wanting, and applying it freely when any degree of over-exposure is manifest; and that the use of ammonia under proper circumstances is of great value. It should always be remembered that as with aids to sensitiveness there is greater danger of fog, stains, &c., so it is also with energetic developers which bring out an image with short exposure; whilst they rapidly bring out the image, they also readily produce fog and stains if any latent source of these evils be present.

---

## THE COLLODIO-ALBUMEN PROCESS.

This process, invented by Dr. Taupenot, and sometimes called by his name, is one of the oldest dry collodion processes; but, in certainty and excellence of results, it remains unsurpassed. Its only drawbacks are the trouble in preparation, and the long exposure required. Under some circumstances there is a little trouble arising from a tendency to blisters in the final processes of developing, fixing, and washing. We shall give the formula adopted by Mr. Mudd, who has been very successful with this process.

Any collodion may be used, but one which is thin and limpid, giving a powdery film, is least liable to blisters. A tough collodion may be made limpid and to give a powdery film by adding a few grains of carbonate of soda, agitating a while, and then decanting when well settled.

Now coat the cleaned plate with collodion in the usual way. After allowing the film to "set" well, sensitize in the ordinary nitrate of silver bath. If the collodion should give a very thick and creamy film, it must be reduced by adding ether. After sensitizing, the plate must be well washed, and then placed in a dish containing a weak solution of iodide of potassium and water (about one grain to the ounce of water) for two or three minutes, gently moving the dish the while. Rinse with tap water, and drain a minute.

Next, to the whites of 10 eggs, add:—

50 grains iodide potassium
10 ,, bromide ,,
100 minims liquid ammonia
2½ ounces water.

Dissolve the iodide and bromide in the water, then add the ammonia. Mix all together with the albumen, and beat the whole into a froth. Let it settle. It is then fit for use.

While the plate is still wet, pour over its surface the albumen. Pour off again. Repeat this twice. Now allow the plate to drain five or ten minutes; then dry it rapidly before a clear, bright fire, and make it quite hot.

To make the plate sensitive, it is only necessary to dip it for one minute into the aceto-nitrate bath:—

40 grains nitrate of silver
½ drachm glacial acetic acid
1 ounce water.

Warm the plate slightly, immerse it, drain a moment, and then wash as before in the dishes, and finally under the tap. The plates may be dried artificially, but will dry without heat in about ten minutes.

Plates so prepared will keep good, in cool weather, six or eight weeks; but, in July or August, it is better not to trust them longer than a fortnight.

The best method of developing is with a solution of pyrogallic acid alone, without free acid or silver. Take the exposed plate, and, after placing it upon the stand, pass over the surface a little distilled water; then take a plain pyro solution, without acid, say two or three grains to the ounce of water, and pour it on the plate. This mixture must be made just before use, as it does not keep without acid. The sky and high lights will appear almost immediately, and ultimately, without either silver or acid, the whole picture comes out. It now requires intensifying. Take—

Pyro ... ... ... ... ... ... ... 2 grains
Citric acid ... ... ... ... ... 2 „
Nitrate of silver 2 or 3 drops of 20-grain solution,

and pour on the plate. If necessary, add more silver, until sufficient intensity is gained.

A warm solution of pyrogallic acid may be used when the negative is under-exposed, and in the winter months, when the pictures will not appear with cold water.

During the development it is more than probable that the surface may be marked by streaks or stains; or a deposit may cover the whole plate. If this should occur, stop the development, wash with water, and, with a piece of fine cotton-wool, rub away these defects, and go on again with the development. The horny surface of the albumen allowing this to be done without fear of damaging the negative. This is the great advantage the process has over every other. The plate can be developed for hours or days, because, though this deposit falls, it can be wiped off again and again. This is an immense advantage when the picture is under-exposed, as it can be frequently brought out by long development.

To develop with gallic acid:—take the exposed plate and put it face upwards into a glass or other dish, with a sufficient quantity of a saturated solution of gallic acid to cover it. When it has remained five or ten minutes, add a few drops of 10-grain silver solution, and mix well in the dish; the picture will gradually appear. When all the details are out, add more silver till the development is complete.

Whichever process of development be adopted, great care is required to attain just the proper amount of intensity and no more. In all processes where albumen is used, the real printing intensity is much greater than it at first appears, owing to the light-resisting colour of the deposit. There is great danger of over-development, as some photographers are not content until the sky is quite black; at which time, in an artistic point of view, the picture is quite ruined.

Fix in hyposulphite of soda, about six ounces to the pint of water, with a few drops of acetic acid added. Cyanide of potassium should not be used for fixing these negatives, as it loosens the film and causes blisters.

---

## THE FOTHERGILL PROCESS.

This process, which used to be a great favourite, has not been so much practised of late. In careful hands, however, it yields very good results.

The collodion should be bromo-iodized, somewhat old, and giving a powdery adherent film. The nitrate bath is best strong, about 40 grains of nitrate to the ounce, with about a quarter of an ounce of acetic acid to a pint of nitrate solution. The plates, having been coated and excited, should be washed in three changes of distilled water two or three minutes in each. The plate is then to be covered with the following preservative solution:—

| | |
|---|---|
| Albumen ... ... ... ... | 1 ounce |
| Ammonia ... ... ... ... | 10 minims |
| Water ... ... ... ... ... | 3 ounces. |

Agitate the whole together in a large bottle, and filter through sponge just before using.

The first quantity applied should be made to flow over the plate in a continuous wave, and be poured off at once from the opposite corner; the second be permitted to remain thereupon not less than a minute. The plate is now to be washed freely, dried spontaneously, or by the application of a gentle heat, and is ready for use. After exposure, the dry plate should be moistened with distilled water, and developed with the following solution :—

| | | |
|---|---|---|
| Pyrogallic acid ... ... ... | 1½ | grain |
| Citric acid ... ... ... ... | ½ | ,, |
| Water ... ... ... ... ... | 1 | fluid ounce |
| Alcohol ... ... ... ... | 10 | minims. |

Add to each fluid ounce about half a drachm of a 15-grain solution of nitrate of silver, or less at the commencement of development. Fix with hyposulphite of soda, wash, dry, and varnish as usual.

After the Fothergill plate is fully prepared, it may be finally coated with a solution of gallic acid, and left to dry. Or the solution may be applied after the plate has dried. The strength of the gallic acid does not appear important: various strengths, from one to four grains, have been used with advantage. The result is an increase of vigour and brilliancy, and great immunity from fog and stains.

A method of preparing Fothergill plates, proposed some years ago, has been recently revived, and is said to give increased rapidity and fine results. It consists in adding 20 or 30 drops of a 30-grain nitrate of silver solution to the albumen solution; and, should any turbidity ensue, removing it by the addition, a drop at a time, of strong liquid ammonia. The plates, excited and washed as usual, thoroughly washed, the preservative poured over it once or twice, then drained, again thoroughly washed and dried. The plates so prepared will not keep long, but they are very sensitive and give good results. They are developed and fixed as usual.

## DRY COLLODION WITHOUT PRESERVATIVE.

On the first introduction of the collodion process it was thought that the excited collodion plate just sufficiently washed with distilled water, to prevent the free nitrate of silver from crystallizing on the surface, might, when dry, retain its sensitiveness. In practice, however, many difficulties were met with, which led to the employment of the various preservatives now in use. A certain method of using the simply washed still remains a desideratum, but very good results have, notwithstanding, been at times produced. The difficulty appears to fix the conditions which shall secure absolute certainty of success. We will describe the method which has, in our own hands, given the best results.

The collodion should have a porous powdery texture, so that having been dried it is readily permeated again by liquids. This powdery texture may be secured in three or four ways:—

*First*, By the use of weak acids and a high temperature in making the pyroxyline.

*Second*, By agitating the collodion with a little carbonate of soda, about a grain to each ounce at intervals during about twenty-four hours, and, after subsidence, decanting. A minute trace of caustic potash or ammonia may be used instead of carbonate of soda. To avoid the presence of any alkalinity, a little free iodine should afterwards be added, sufficient to make the collodion the colour of pale sherry.

*Third*, By the introduction of as much water into the collodion as it will bear without reticulation. This method can scarcely be regarded as producing a powdery film, nevertheless it tends to bring about the required condition, the film being spongy, cellular, and readily permeable by fluids.

*Fourth*, By age. When iodized collodion, especially if it contain an alkaline iodizer, has been kept a few months, a slight decomposition ensues, which produces a powdery film. Collodion in this condition, with the addition of a full share of bromide, often gives very excellent results with this process.

The collodion should always contain a bromide. The following iodizing formula will give good results :—

| | | |
|---|---|---|
| Iodide of cadmium | ... ... ... | 2 grains |
| „ of ammonium | ... ... ... | 2 „ |
| Bromide of cadmium | ... ... ... | 1 grain |

In each ounce of collodion.

A 30-grain nitrate bath slightly acid with acetic acid. Coat and sensitize the plate as usual, wash in three or four changes of water, and dry quickly.

After exposure, immerse in a 10-grain neutral nitrate bath, and develop with iron or pyrogallic acid in the usual way.

### Another Method.

A slight modification of this method has been found by some to give still better results. It consists in immersing the plate for about 30 seconds in a 4-grain bath of gallic acid after the last washing. The plate must not in this case be immersed in the nitrate bath, nor developed with iron, but after the method described under the head *Fothergill Process.*

---

## THE RESIN PROCESS.

All the instructions for dry collodion without preservative obtain here ; the chief difference consists in adding to the collodion about a grain of common resin to each ounce of collodion. It is important to avoid the use of nitric acid in the bath when using this collodion.

---

## THE GELATINE PROCESS.

This process was originated by Dr. Hill Norris. The plate, after being coated with a bromo-iodized collodion, is excited and washed well in the usual manner, is coated with a solution of gelatine made by adding 100 grains of transparent gelatine in a pint of distilled water, and dissolving by the aid of heat. When clear, two ounces of alcohol are added; it is then bottled for use. To apply it to the plate it requires heating, by placing the bottle in hot water. The plate is covered with this solution, which is allowed to flow backwards and forwards a little, and then poured off; another coating is then applied, and the plate is drained and dried. The plates are sensitive and keep well. Development may be effected either by means of an ordinary pyrogallic solution, or by gallic acid.

---

## THE META-GELATINE PROCESS.

The meta-gelatine process, originated by Mr. Maxwell Lyte, is as follows:—The plate, being coated with bromo-iodized collodion and excited, is *slightly* washed to remove part of the free nitrate of silver, in distilled water, and then coated with the meta-gelatine solution, which is prepared as follows: Dissolve one ounce of pure gelatine in a pint of distilled water, and add one drachm of oxalic acid, and boil until the quantity is reduced to nearly one half. Whilst the solution is still hot, neutralize with chalk. When it has settled, draw off the clear portion, and add to it the white of an egg beaten up with its own bulk of water. Again boil and filter. The addition of the albumen is to remove the remains of oxalate of lime, which render the solution milky and turbid. The particles of albumen combine with the oxalate of lime, and, when coagulated with the boiling, leave the solution, after filtration, quite clear.

The plate, when coated with meta-gelatine, is drained and dried. Development may be effected either with iron, pyrogallic acid, or gallic acid; or, the image may be brought out with the former and strengthened by the latter.

---

## THE MALT PROCESS.

This process is a great favourite with many, being very sensitive and gives fine delicate negatives. It is accredited to Mr. Macnair.

The process is as follows:—Mix 7 ounces of well-bruised or ground pale malt in about 24 ounces of hot water, so that the mixture, after being well stirred, should be at the temperature of 155° to 158°. Place the teapot containing the infusion before a moderate fire for about half an hour, when the heat will have fallen to about 138°, and the infusion has acquired a sweetish taste. It may now be cooled slowly, and filtered, when it should be quite fluid, bright, and of the colour of very pale sherry.

Coat the plate with bromo-iodized collodion, and excite in a neutral bath of 35 grains nitrate of silver per ounce of water; wash off all the free nitrate of silver at a tap, finishing with distilled water. Rest the plate for a few seconds on blotting paper, and before it begins to dry pour over the malt infusion in the same way as the collodion: then dry quickly.

After exposure wash off the preservative coating, letting the water flow from the centre of the plate towards the edges; then, using a plate-holder, dip the face of the plate in a solution of nitrate of silver, or in the bath; but for this purpose it is better to have a separate bath, and one of 20 to 25 grains nitrate of silver per ounce is strong enough. Develop with

| | |
|---|---|
| Protosulphate of iron ... ... ... | 20 to 30 grs. |
| Glacial acetic acid ... ... ... | ½ drachm |
| Alcohol... ... ... ... ... | ½ " |
| Water ... ... ... ... ... | 1 ounce. |

If more intensity is wanted, wash, and continue the development with

| | |
|---|---|
| Pyrogallic acid ... ... ... | 2 grains |
| Glacial acetic acid ... ... ... | ½ drachm |
| Alcohol ... ... ... ... | ½ " |
| Water ... ... ... ... ... | 1 ounce, |

adding a few drops of nitrate of silver solution.

---

## THE TANNIN PROCESS.

Perhaps the most certain, simple, and satisfactory of all the dry *processes is* the Tannin Process of Major Russell, which we shall therefore describe somewhat more in detail than the majority of those already stated, using, where it is necessary, Major Russell's own words, as given in his excellent little treatise on the subject, or in the photographic journals.

In various dry processes a difficulty is occasionally found in a tendency of the film to blister, tear, or leave the plate during the processes of development, fixing, and washing; and this tendency, more in tannin plates than some others, is perhaps the only drawback of the process. To prevent this, Major Russell, in all cases, recommends the using a preliminary coating of some kind, either gelatine or india-rubber. If the latter be used, one grain of india-rubber, sliced very thin, is to be dissolved in an ounce of benzole, and then filtered; and we may remark that we have found solution much more easily effected if just sufficient chloroform to cover the india-rubber be poured over it first. This readily dissolves the india-rubber, and the proper degree of dilution may be secured by adding benzole afterwards. The coating of india-rubber should be dried by the fire. If gelatine be used, the student cannot do better than follow the instructions of Major Russell, as follows:—"Soak twenty grains in eight ounces of distilled water and four drops of glacial acetic acid. When thoroughly swelled and transparent, dissolve by warming. Should the water be heated before the gelatine has had time to swell, the latter will adhere to the bottom of the vessel containing it, in a stiff glutinous state, and will dissolve with great difficulty. Dissolve three grains of iodide of cadmium, three grains of bromide of cadmium, and a small piece of iodine in a few drops of water, and mix with the solution; then filter two or three times through white filtering paper in a warm place. The acetic acid coagulates the white impurity, which then collects into filaments, and is removed by filtering, leaving the liquid very bright. This solution will keep well without alcohol, and it is better not to add it, as it tends to produce ridges in the film of gelatine, especially when present in large proportion."

In regard to the collodion, it is stated that "almost any collodion will produce good results with tannin, if properly managed, no *matter how new and horny*, or how old and rotten. Even should it be too old or too new to work well in the wet process, it will still succeed. Some difference will, however, be found in the character of the resulting pictures, though not so great as in the wet process, and there will be a great difference in the sensitiveness. A new collodion is the most sensitive, and in the writer's hands gives the proper red tone and vigour of negative perfectly. An old and powdery sample, on the other hand, even if rendered colourless by cadmium, besides being very insensitive, gives a pale grey image which will not develop with quite so much vigour and richness of tone, and the film, when varnished, is soft and liable to injury, whereas that produced by a new and horny collodion is, in hardness and durability, only inferior to albumen." In our own hands a collodion made after the formula given in the chapter on collodion has given excellent negatives. We prefer it for use when it has been made and iodized two or three months.

The nitrate bath may be used nearly neutral, or slightly acid with nitric acid, and should contain not less than 35 grains of pure nitrate of silver to the ounce of water. In winter it may be stronger. The plate should remain in the bath five minutes in summer and ten minutes in winter.

The excited plate should be washed very perfectly, in not less than half a dozen changes of water, being kept in motion for a few minutes in each.

The tannin solution may vary in strength from two grains to thirty to the ounce, according to the subject. A strong solution gives great vigour and richness of tone; but slightly impairs sensitiveness. In some cases it has another singular effect. If the subject have much contrast, and be very strongly lighted, a plate prepared with a strong tannin solution and iodized collodion, gives a blurring of the lights, which appear to encroach on the shadows. In such cases the use of a weaker solution of tannin is found to be a remedy. For well lighted landscapes a two-grain solution is recommended, with about half a drachm of alcohol to each ounce. The best proportion of tannin is to be decided by circumstances; as a rule, the feebler the image on the ground glass, the stronger should be the solution of tannin. "In no other process," Majo

Russell adds, "can the vigour and intensity of the picture be so easily regulated as in this, by varying in strength of the tannin solution."

After covering the plate with tannin, and allowing it to drive off all the moisture, drain and cover again with a fresh quantity, and leave it on for a minute, again drain, saving the second quantity for the first application to the next plate. Drain and dry quickly.

To develop the negative, first moisten the film with dilute alcohol, one part of methylated spirit to two of distilled water will serve. Then proceed as follows:—have prepared before hand a solution of 72 grains of pyrogallic acid in one ounce of alcohol, which will keep good for months; 30 minims of this is added to three ounces of distilled water. This is the developing solution. Make another solution of 20 grains of nitrate of silver and 20 grains of citric acid in one ounce of distilled water. From 10 to 20 minims of this are added to 3 drachms of the developing solution before applying it to the plate. If the plate appear under-exposed, the quantity of pyrogallic solution is to be increased and strengthened; if the plate appear over-exposed, then more of the citro-nitrate solution is to be added, to give vigour to the otherwise feeble image. It will be seen that the principle involved is that of securing development proper with the smallest quantity of free silver that can be used, and intensifying by the addition of more as soon as the image is fully developed.

Fix with hyposulphite of soda. The colour is warm and non-actinic, and gives a rich effect to Transparencies.

---

## MODIFICATIONS OF THE TANNIN PROCESS.

The tannin process in its original simplicity gives very fine negatives, but it requires a somewhat lengthy exposure. To obviate these, various modifications have been proposed both by Major Russell himself and by other gentlemen. We shall briefly notice the most important.

Major Russell's most recent modification consists in the use of a collodion containing bromide only, instead of a bromide in conjunction with an iodide. The collodion may be prepared as follows, using the pyroxyline described in the chapter on collodion as suited for positives :—

| | |
|---|---|
| Pyroxyline ... ... ... ... | 5 grains |
| Bromide of cadmium ... ... ... | 8 ,, |
| Alcohol ·805 ... ... ... ... | 4 drachms |
| Ether ... ... ... ... ... | 4 ,, |

Put the whole in a tall, narrow bottle, shake up until the solution of the pyroxyline and bromide is complete; then allow to settle, clear, and decant. If the alcohol is weaker, or if the pyroxyline is of a kind likely to give too little setting power, a larger proportion of ether should be used.

The bromized collodion should be excited in a 60-grain bath, and should be kept in for about fifteen minutes. If the formula given above is followed, the film will be very creamy. The collodion may be made much thinner by the addition of ether and alcohol, and it can then be excited in a weaker bath, and more quickly. The washing will be effected as usual, and a stronger tannin solution may be used than with a collodion containing an iodide.

In conjunction with the sole use of a bromide, or with the ordinary mode of preparation, it has been found that with tannin plates the use of pyrogallic acid and an alkali for development permits of a material reduction in the exposure. Liquid ammonia, carbonate of ammonia, carbonate of soda, or caustic potash is added in minute quantity to a solution of pyrogallic acid without silver or any free acid. With this developer a thin fully detailed image is readily developed, which may then be intensified by the usual application of a solution of pyrogallic acid, citric acid, and nitrate of silver.

We have found the following method successful: after moistening the film with alcohol and water, apply a solution of carbonate of ammonia, from one to two grains to the ounce, as soon as a trace of *an image* appears, or before, if it is very tardy, apply the same solution containing about two grains of pyrogallic acid to the ounce. This will bring out the image in all its detail red in colour but very thin. It may be intensified with pyrogallic acid and silver in the usual manner.

Major Russell gives very elaborately detailed instructions for this mode of developing. We condense his remarks as follows :—

" Dissolve six grains of carbonate of ammonia in two ounces and a half of distilled water and one ounce and a half of alcohol, sp. gr. about ·830 (1); this liquid may be kept ready mixed in a bottle. Dilute five minims of the following solution—pyrogallic acid, 96 grains; absolute alcohol, one ounce; ether, 3 drops—to two drachms, with the same proportions of alcohol and water as in the carbonate of ammonia solution (2). Measure out as much of (1) as will cover the plate (two drachms will be amply sufficient, if of stereoscopic size), and one-fourth the quantity of (2). Pour (1) over the dry plate on a levelling stand; it will flow freely, but still more so if a larger proportion of alcohol is used. Pour on and off two or three times, and watch the effect; if the tannin has been applied in weak solution, and especially if it has been washed off again, there will not be much developing action; but if the exposure has been sufficient, there will usually be enough to give an indication as to the kind of treatment likely to be required. Next pour off and mix with (2), pour on again immediately, at the far side of the plate, and tilt the plate quickly, so as to drive off all remaining moisture before the mixture into the measure; in this way the development will be started evenly all over the plate. Pour on and off quickly two or three times, then let the plate remain at rest, covered with the developer, and carefully observe the effect.

" If the appearance of the image indicates that the exposure has not been too great, the alkaline developer may be left to act for some time; but if the image shows symptoms of over-exposure, pour off and wash the plate quickly: in any case when the development with ammonia has been carried far enough, before intensifying with silver, the plate should be washed for several minutes under a stream of water, and then placed on a levelling stand, and left *covered with water for a* short time. After this the development may be completed with pyrogallic and acid silver, the proportions c which should be regulated by the appearance of the image, just a if the development had been commenced with the acid silve developer; by this means, and by varying the duration of the actio of the alkaline developer, any error in the exposure can be correcte within certain limits.

"The acid development will bring out nothing which failed t appear before, and, therefore, very strong pyrogallic solution wi not be needed; but by using at first a small quantity of silve solution which does not contain a very large proportion of acid, a the details faintly brought out by the alkaline developer will b established. By washing off quickly, and then intensifying wit weak pyrogallic and a large proportion of acid silver, over exposure can readily be corrected."

Various other modifications of the tannin process have been trie with success. A mixture of tannin and honey, from five to te grains of each to the ounce of water gives very good results, an may be treated in all respects as dissolved for tannin alone. mixture of tannin and gum in some hands gives good results, a also a mixture of tannin and a solution of malt. One method c using these additions, which gives good results, is as follows:—Afte sensitizing the plate, attach the holder, and pour over the film solution of one part honey to three parts water; let it flow thre times round the surface, and then off. Place on a levelling stan or level board, till next plate has been similarly treated, or unt half a dozen or more have been thus prepared. Wash off th honey solution thoroughly under a tap. Stand to drain for on minute, then apply the tannin solution, and dry. This plan c applying the diluted honey, before washing off the free nitrate, i applicable to all dry processes. Caramel may answer as well. I this process, it is preferable to mixing the honey with the tannin, a you get a cleaner plate, with less liability to stains, if the washin have been properly performed. The tendency of these additions i to give greater softness and decrease the exposure.

# The Calotype Process.

THE practice of negative photography on paper has, during the last few years, fallen considerably into disuse, as the results lack the delicacy of collodion. As this manual would be incomplete, however, without some instructions for those who desire to practice the processes, which, notwithstanding their recent neglect, have many advantages, and may probably again come into favour, especially in warm climates, we give a condensation of the chapters on the Talbotype and Waxpaper Processes, which appeared in the last edition of PRACTICAL PHOTOGRAPHY.

The process separates itself into the following divisions:—

Iodizing the paper.
Rendering the paper sensitive.
Exposure in the camera.
Development of the image; and
Fixing the picture.

TO IODIZE THE PAPER.—Make a solution as follows:—

| | |
|---|---|
| Nitrate of silver ... ... ... | 30 grains |
| Distilled water ... ... ... ... | 1 ounce. |

Add to this a solution of 30 grains of iodide of potassium in 1 ounce of water; a brilliant yellow precipitate will be the result. Allow this to settle, pour off the supernatant liquid, and treat the precipitate with a fresh 2 ounces of distilled water; let it rest once more, and again decant the clear liquid remaining above the powder. Now pour 1 ounce of distilled water on to the iodide of silver thus formed, and add one crystal at a time of iodide of potassium (continually stirring with a glass rod) until the whole of the precipitate is dissolved; the liquid may now be filtered through blotting paper, and preserved in a well-stoppered bottle for use. This solution is technically called "Double iodide of silver."

The paper best suited for the Calotype is that manufactured by "Turner, of Chafford Mill," or that by "Hollingworth, of Turkey Mill." Either of them allow of good pictures being produced on them. Having selected a sheet of paper, as free as possible from blemishes of any kind, pin it by two of its corners to a soft wood board (*a*, fig. 10), and laying it flat on a table, place a glass rod along its upper end, next the pins that retain the paper, holding it with the right hand; then with the left hand pour some of the double iodide of silver immediately in front of the glass rod (B), and move the same down the sheet of paper in such a manner that the liquid may follow the rod, and give an even coating. If this be not accomplished the first time the rod is passed over the surface, a repetition of the movement will generally secure this end. Care must be taken not to press too much on the rod, otherwise the surface of the paper is liable to become injured.

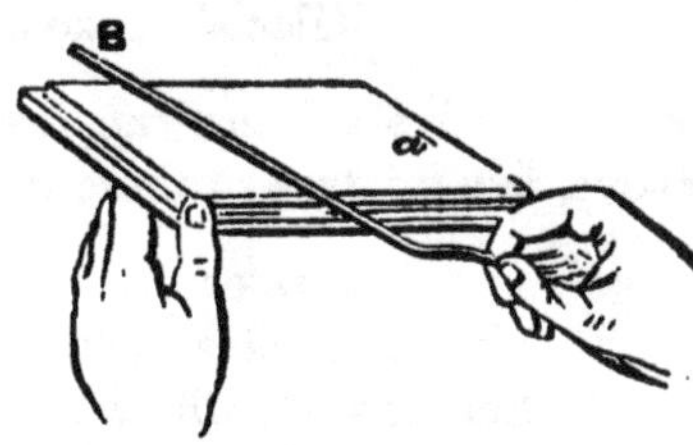

Fig. 10.

The paper being thus coated with an even layer of "Double iodide of silver," is to be removed from the board, and hung up to any convenient support, to become *surface dry*. It is then to be placed very carefully, prepared side downwards, on to the surface of water contained in a porcelain pan, and allowed to remain in contact with it for ten minutes. It is then to be removed to another pan of water, and to be totally immersed in it for the space of ten minutes more; and, finally, it is plunged into a large pan of water, and there soaked for thirty minutes, from which it is cautiously taken out, and hung up to dry spontaneously.

Care is required in floating the paper on the first bath, in order to prevent the intervention of air-bubbles between the surfaces of the water and paper. The paper being quite dry, will present a beautiful primrose tint, and is ready for the next operation, which is—

**Rendering the Paper Sensitive.**—The solutions required for this *purpose* are the following:—

| | |
|---|---|
| Nitrate of silver... ... ... ... | 50 grains |
| Distilled water ... ... ... ... | 1 ounce. |

| | |
|---|---|
| Gallic acid ... ... ... ... | 4 grains |
| Distilled water ... ... ... ... | 1 ounce. |

Glacial acetic acid—absolutely pure.

The sensitive solution applied to the iodized paper prepared as above, is a mixture of these in the proportions indicated below:—

| | | |
|---|---|---|
| Distilled water ... ... ... | 1 drachm | Gallo-nitrate of silver. |
| Nitrate of silver solution ... | 4 drops | |
| Solution of gallic acid ... ... | 3 drops | |
| Acetic acid ... ... ... | 3 drops | |

Thoroughly mix.

This solution is to be applied to the iodized paper in the same manner as the double iodide, as before described, namely, by means of the glass rod. After it has been allowed to remain on the paper for two minutes, the superfluous quantity is to be carefully removed by means of *perfectly clean* bibulous paper, and the paper, if not required to be used immediately, can be hung up to dry in a dark place. Paper prepared in this manner will keep good for 24 hours; that is to say, it may be prepared in the evening of one day, and the picture be developed in the evening of the next, without any detriment to its perfection.

Exposure in the Camera.—On a moderately bright day, with an average landscape, the time of exposure would vary from five minutes to ten; the exact amount depending on the nature of the objects, and their degree of illumination.

Bringing Out the Picture.—The paper is again pinned to the soft wood board, and by means of the glass rod the solution of gallic acid is spread over it, taking care that the whole of the paper is equally wetted. After a few minutes the latent image will begin to unfold itself in a most remarkable and beautiful manner. While *this is taking place,* the rod must frequently be passed over the paper, to equalize the action of the gallic acid, and also to prevent any part of the paper from becoming dry. When all the picture is developed, but is still of a light colour, a few drops of gallo-nitrate of silver may be added, and quickly spread over the paper; this will have the effect of deepening the tone of the impression, and of giving due preponderance and intensity to the dark parts of the negative. Judgment must be exercised so as not to carry the development too far, otherwise the light parts of the picture suffer.

If the paper has been too short a time under the influence of the light, it will be some considerable time before any appearance of an image will manifest itself when being treated with gallic acid, and the shadowy parts will, with great difficulty, come out, even if they do at all; but, on the other hand, if too long an exposure has been given, the picture will be visible on the paper before the application of the gallic acid, and on being subjected to the process of development as before described, will assume a red tinge, instead of the beautiful and intense black so characteristic of a negative that has undergone the correct time of exposure.

Fixing Bath—Composed of 4 ounces of hyposulphite of soda to 1 pint of water, in which it is to soak for about ten minutes, until the whole of the yellow colour disappears, when removal to a vessel containing an abundance of water will, after two hours' soaking, complete the operation of obtaining a negative by this process.

The Waxing Paper Negative.—Negative pictures on paper are much improved in transparency and definition by being saturated with white wax; the best mode of accomplishing which is, to soak the picture in boiling water for a few minutes to remove all the size from the paper, and then, after thoroughly drying it, to lay the picture face downwards on to a piece of blotting paper, and to pass over its back a flat iron that has been heated; at the same time a piece of perfectly pure white wax is to be held in contact with and made to follow the iron; the paper will by this means become impregnated with the wax, but on inspection it will be found that too large a quantity is on the surface; this is to be removed by placing the waxed picture between folds of perfectly clean blotting paper, and again passing a hot iron over the whole: by this operation the wax is again melted and the superfluous quantity absorbed by the super-imposed bibulous paper.

Pictures treated in this manner can be printed from with as much ease, and with almost as satisfactory results, as those taken on glass, the detail being brought out in a remarkable degree, the wax counteracting to a very great extent the unevenness of texture in the paper which militates so powerfully against the perfection of paper photographs.

---

## The Waxed Paper Process.

| | |
|---|---|
| Nitrate of silver ... ... ... | 400 grains |
| Glacial acetic acid, absolutely pure .. | 10 drachms |
| Distilled water ... ... ... | 10 ounces |
| Iodide of potassium ... ... ... | 4 grains. |

| | |
|---|---|
| Gallic acid ... ... ... ... | 1 drachm |
| Water ... ... ... ... | 40 ounces. |

| | |
|---|---|
| Hyposulphite of soda ... ... | 4 ounces |
| Water ... ... ... ... | 1 pint. |

Much has from time to time been written on this branch of the subject, and many are the plans recommended for obtaining photographic proofs on waxed paper. The following process will, however, be found to possess the great advantage of simplicity, compared with the original one as described by Le Gray, to whom the art is indebted for the invention of this beautiful method of producing *sun pictures.*

The natural divisions of the process are—1st, waxing the paper; 2nd, iodizing the same; 3rd, rendering it sensitive; 4th, exposure to the image in the camera; 5th, development of the latent picture; 6th, fixing the proof.

WAXING THE PAPER.—The paper most to be preferred for this process is of a uniform texture and very thin. A sheet of this is to be selected free from specks or blemishes of any sort, and treated in the manner following:—

Provide a flat tin dish about an inch deep (fig. 11), and fit this into an outer one that can contain water, which is to be kept at boiling heat by means of a lamp placed beneath; three or four cakes of the best white wax being placed in the inner vessel and melted, a sheet of the selected paper is to be immersed in it, and allowed to remain in this position until perfectly saturated with the wax. It may then be carefully raised by two of its corners and held over the vessel to drain, after which it is to be hung up to get cold: sheet after sheet may be treated in the same way. When a sufficient number is thus prepared, each sheet is to be placed between folds of blotting paper, and to have a hot iron passed over it; this will cause the wax to be re-melted, and the superfluous quantity absorbed by the blotting paper, thereby giving an uniform transparency to the paper. If all the superfluous wax be not absorbed, the surface of the paper will exhibit patches of undue brilliancy, owing to the outstanding of the wax. The paper, when properly prepared, should present a perfectly even and uniform surface, and the transparency ought to be without irregularity.

Fig. 11.

IODIZING THE WAXED PAPER.—This is accomplished by immersion in a bath prepared in the manner following:—

Dissolve 640 grains of iodide of cadmium, and 160 grains of bromide of cadmium, in two ounces of distilled water; next dissolve 6 grains of pure iodine in 2 ounces of alcohol of the specific gravity ·840: when the iodide and bromide of cadmium are dissolved, a them to 36 ounces, by measure, of skimmed milk, and thoroughly agitate; now add the alcoholic solution of iodine, and again shake the mixture.

It will be noticed that the caseine of the milk is by this means precipitated in the form of white curd: the mixture is to be thrown on a filter and the clear liquid preserved for use; this forms the iodizing solution for waxed paper, and consists of the whey or serum of milk impregnated with iodizing materials.

The patience of the operator will be somewhat taxed during the filtration of the iodized serum, owing to the slow rate at which it leaves the funnel; the best way is to set it aside for some hours, and when it has ceased to pass through the filter the precipitate may, with advantage, be washed with distilled water, which after filtering may be added to the iodized serum; this will make up for the waste caused by the bulky precipitate of caseine.

In order to iodize the waxed paper pour a sufficient quantity of the iodizing solution into a porcelain dish, and immerse the sheets in it one after another, taking great care that no air-bubbles are included between the surfaces of the paper and liquid; when a sufficient number have been immersed, they are to be allowed to soak for one hour, the whole mass of papers is then to be turned over in the liquid, in order to bring the sheet first immersed to the top; during the time of immersion the paper will have changed colour and will have assumed a purple tint, owing to the combination of the free iodine with the starch in the glaze of the paper. The sheets are now to be carefully removed from the bath, and hung up by the corners to dry.

The iodized paper when finished ought to be of a violet or purple tint, and should present rather a rough texture on the surface.

Should any drops form on the surface of the sheet of iodized paper while drying, it is an indication that some more alcohol must be added to the solution before a fresh quantity of paper is prepared. These spots are also apt to occur when the wax used in the preparation of the paper is contaminated with stearine or other fatty matter. The wax used should be perfectly pure, and should be obtained of some photographic house, as that usually considered pure by oilmen is not really so, and contains many impurities.

RENDERING THE PAPER SENSITIVE.—The sensitive bath is thus composed:—

| | | |
|---|---|---|
| Crystallized nitrate of silver | ... | 400 grains |
| Glacial acetic acid ... | ... ... | 10 drachms |
| Distilled water ... | ... ... | 10 ounces |
| Iodide of potassium | ... ... | 4 grains |

Filter a small quantity of this solution into a flat porcelain dish, as directed for iodizing, and float on to the surface a sheet of the iodized paper; allow it to rest for a few moments until the purple tinge is removed; then thoroughly immerse the sheet, and after waiting three minutes remove it by means of a pair of horn forceps (fig. 12) to a pan of distilled water for the space of five minutes, occasionally agitating during the immersion. The paper thus prepared is to be placed between folds of bibulous paper, and finally hung up to dry.

Fig. 12.

If the above operations have been skilfully carried through, the paper will present an even coating of iodide of silver, and will keep sensitive for ten or twelve days at the least. It should be preserved between leaves of clean blotting paper for use.

EXPOSURE IN THE CAMERA.—With a 3-inch lens, and a stop of ½-inch diameter, and an ordinary landscape, in bright weather from 5 to 15 minutes will be found sufficient, but if the weather be very dull, 20 minutes will not overdo the picture; this will convey only an idea of the time required.

DEVELOPMENT OF THE LATENT PICTURE.—Make a solution of gallic acid in water, of the strength of—

| | | |
|---|---|---|
| Gallic acid | ... ... ... ... | 1 drachm |
| Water ... | ... ... ... ... | 1 quart. |

Filter this into a porcelain pan, and float the paper on its removal from the dark slide of the camera, taking care to exclude all ai bubbles. The development will soon commence, if the right time of exposure has been given. When nearly all the picture is brought out, which may be seen through the back of the sheet, remove it from the pan, and add to the gallic acid solution some aceto-nitrate of silver—the same as used for rendering the paper sensitive—in the proportion of ½ a drachm of aceto-nitrate to 4 ounces of gallic acid solution; thoroughly mix, and immerse the partially developed proof; the details will soon begin to come out, and, at the same time, the dark parts of the picture will gather intensity; the degree of development may be judged of by holding the paper between the eye and the candle, or lamp, by the light of which we are operating. As in the Calotype process, we must guard against over-development, which will cause a deposit in the parts that ought to be transparent, thereby rendering the shadows in the resulting positive thick and muddy, instead of sharp and bright.

It is necessary to thoroughly mix the aceto-nitrate with the gallic acid as directed above, otherwise the proof will become marbled all over to such an extent as to be useless as a negative.

Fixing the Proof—Is effected by immersion of the paper in a solution of hyposulphite of soda, similar to that used for calotypes, and allowing it to soak until all the yellow colour is dispelled from the light parts; this will generally be the case in about ten minutes or a quarter of an hour, after which it is to be removed to a pan and well washed in abundance of cold water for about two hours, and finally it is to be hung up to dry. When perfectly dry, place the picture between folds of blotting paper, and pass a hot iron over it in order to re-melt the wax, and restore the transparency which has been partially lost during the various manipulations. This will complete the process of obtaining a negative picture on waxed paper.

# Various Processes.

---

## THE PREPARATION OF COLLODION.

THERE is little difficulty in the present day in procuring good samples of collodion with less trouble and cost than is involved in the manufacture by the amateur himself. Nevertheless, as occasions may arise when the photographer may desire to produce his own preparations, we subjoin simple and trustworthy instructions and formulæ, merely remarking at the outset that the most scrupulous care is required to avoid failure and danger in the manufacture of the pyroxyline.

Procure, in the first place, an earthenware jar, holding about a pint, and a deep earthenware dish, within which the jar can stand. Also procure a couple of stout glass rods about twelve inches long; a couple of glass spatulas the same length, and about an inch broad, will answer still better. Have also ready a kettle of boiling water and a pail of cold water. Now take of nitric acid, sp. gr. 1·420, three measured ounces, and of sulphuric acid, sp. gr. 1·840, three measured ounces, and put them into the pint jar which is standing in the larger dish. In this larger dish pour the boiling water so that it may surround the sides of the jar containing the acids. The temperature of the acids will rise when they are mixed, but probably not sufficiently, and it must be raised by means of the hot water in the outer vessel until it reaches 150° Fah. The cotton, which should be the best sample procurable, well carded and free from all impurities, should have been prepared previously; a quarter of an ounce is the proper proportion for the quantity of acids named. It should be separated into tufts, well pulled out, into about the size of a penny piece. These should be immersed in the acids, at the temperature stated, one at a time, and pushed quickly down into the acids, with the glass rod, and pressed against the side of the jar. The whole should be as rapidly immersed as possible, care being taken to prevent it rising above the surface of the acids, and so coming into contact with the atmosphere, which would endanger the formation of red nitrous fumes and the entire dissolution of the cotton. When all the cotton is immersed, a plate of glass may be placed on the top of the jar to prevent the acids from cooling, and the whole left for ten minutes.

Now seize the whole of the cotton between the glass rods, and pressing out as much of the acids as possible, quickly pass it into the pail of water which has been provided beforehand for the purpose, and quickly stir the cotton about so as to distribute it rapidly through the water. If care be not taken in this respect, the acids left in the cotton being diluted with the water, it occasionally happens that the whole of the cotton is dissolved at this stage. It should, therefore, be as rapidly as possible pulled from together, and distributed through the whole pail of water to stop as quickly as possible the effect of the acids. In a few minutes the water should be changed, and so for a quarter of an hour, giving not less than half a dozen changes of water during that time. It should then be placed under a stream of running water for a few hours, after which, if a piece of blue litmus paper remain unchanged in the water, the cotton is sufficiently washed. In some cases, where time is an object, a few drops of strong ammonia may be added to one of the final washing waters, after which wash well with rain water. Some authorities have objected to the use of ammonia for neutralizing any traces of acid remaining after long washing, but after considerable experience in its use, we have never found any disadvantage arising from it.

After the cotton is thoroughly washed it should have the water wrung from it, and be pulled out so as to be as open as possible, and spread upon a large sheet of paper to dry. This may be done spontaneously in a warm place, or it may be more quickly effected by the aid of a water bath. It should on no account be placed in an oven, on the hob, or, indeed, in any place near a fire, as we have in many cases known explosions, which might have been attended with serious consequences, result from such modes of drying. Where a small quantity for immediate use is required to be dried quickly, it may, after pressing as much water as possible, be immersed in alcohol, which will absorb the remaining water, and it will then, on pulling out, rapidly dry. When the washing is completed, the best mode of getting rid of as much water as possible, is to place the cotton in a clean napkin, and then wring it thoroughly until not another drop of water can be pressed out of it.

The pyroxyline produced by the formula we have just described ought to be somewhat short, but not rotten in texture. Not entirely explosive, but burning rapidly, just on the point of explosion, and leaving no ash. It should dissolve entirely in a mixture of equal parts of ether and alcohol, and give an even somewhat tough film, and thus present physical properties suitable for either positives or negatives.

For the convenience of those who may have difficulty in obtaining nitric acid of the strength we have named, we may state that the specific gravity of the nitric acid usually sold as "pure nitric acid," without any statement of its strength, generally contains more water than that we have named, and very commonly possesses a specific gravity of 1·360. With nitric acid of this strength, and the oil of vitriol of commerce as the sulphuric acid, the proportions should be in the ratio of six measured ounces of the latter to four measured ounces of the nitric acid. This, at a temperature of 150°, will give a very excellent cotton, perhaps a little shorter, and more suited to negative purposes than the former, but dissolving perfectly, and giving an even structureless film adhering well to the glass. In both cases the increase in weight will be from thirty to fifty per cent.

Where a pyroxyline solely for positive purposes is required, the temperature might with advantage be reduced to 130° or 135°. The result of which would be a little less intensity in the character of the image given, a little more transparency in the shadows, and more silvery whiteness in the image by reflected light.

Where pyroxyline is made with acid containing a little more water, or at a higher temperature, or with both conditions, the cotton becomes shorter and more powdery in texture, give thinner and more textureless film, which is somewhat porous in character, and at a certain stage acquires the quality of forming, to a certain extent, an organic compound with silver, which causes it to give a very intense image. It is to be understood that weaker acids, at the same temperature, or the same acids at a higher temperature, would in either case produce similar results. That is, weak acids at a moderate temperature, or stronger acids at a very high temperature, each tend to the production of a cotton giving, in collodion, a powdery film and somewhat intense image. The best mode of securing this end, therefore, is by a judicious combination of the two means thus presented. Thus with acids of the same strength, the temperature may be gradually increased up to 160° or even 180°, and at the same time additions of water, made at the rate of from half a drachm to a drachm at a time, for each fresh batch of cotton made, until a cotton of the desired quality, suitable for dry, or other purposes requiring the organic character, be obtained. The point to be guarded against when the maximum of water has been added, and the maximum of heat obtained, is the entire solution of the cotton in the acids, and the emission of red nitrous fumes.

Other substances besides cotton wool have been used for the manufacture of pyroxyline, such as linen, flax, paper, &c., but cotton wool has been found to answer general purposes much the best. Paper has, indeed, been frequently commended as giving a more fluid, structureless, and intense collodion than the pyroxyline made from cotton wool. Against this it has been very justly urged that paper is a mixed and uncertain compound, and can never be guaranteed to be twice exactly the same article. Notwithstanding this argument, many photographers prefer its use; and we are bound to add that in our hands many traits of its excellent character have been fully exemplified, and a pyroxyline, possessing all the most desirable characteristics for a negative collodion, has been the result of its use. Good white blotting paper, or that known as Swedish filtering paper, is the most suitable for the purpose. It should be cut into strips about half an inch wide, and crimped a little to cause it to lie loosely in the acids, and allow them to surround it properly. The formula and manipulations are, in other respects, the same as for cotton.

It is desirable for the amateur and novice not to work with too large a quantity of material at one time. The quantity we have mentioned, a quarter of an ounce of cotton, making nearly three drachms of pyroxyline, is quite sufficient for convenient manipulation, and when larger quantities are tried, the risk of failure from various causes is much increased.

It is desirable for the manipulator to wear, during these operations, india-rubber gauntlets, to protect the hands and wrists both from the fumes and splashes of the acids. The fumes alone are apt to colour the fingers and nails of a disagreeable yellow tint, which cannot be readily removed, whilst any splashes falling on the skin are very corrosive, and quickly produce serious wounds. Great care should be used to avoid splashes at all, as of course the clothes or any other fabric on which the acids may fall will inevitably be destroyed in such places.

It is always desirable that the operation be conducted under a chimney, where there is a good draught of air, so as to convey away any fumes which may arise; or, it may be conducted in the open air, the manipulator standing to windward. The ordinary vapours of the nitro-sulphuric acid are neither pleasant nor wholesome, and should be carefully avoided. Should the red nitrous fumes be evolved during the operation, the first effort should be to stop the progress, by punching down the part, from which they arise, into the acids. Should it be found impossible to arrest the progress, it will be better to leave the apartment at once, leaving open the door and window, risking the loss of the pyroxyline rather than the loss of life, which might be the consequence of breathing these deadly fumes.

Pyroxyline should be kept in a dry place, and in the dark, a tin box with a loose fitting cover answering the purpose for keeping it admirably.

The ether and alcohol for dissolving the cotton should be quite pure. Ether changes its properties when exposed to light and air, *and should* always be kept in the dark, and care should be used no to open a bottle near an uncovered flame, as the vapour is very inflammable and explosive. If by chance ether be spilled in a room where there is a candle, let the light be kept as high as possible as the vapour of ether falls. The use of an excess of alcohol will be found to dissolve a large amount of cotton, and give a more textureless film than when a large proportion of ether is used. Two parts of alcohol to one of ether has been found in practice to give good results; but in this case one part, at least, of the alcohol should have a specific gravity of ·805°. If this alcohol be difficult to obtain, equal parts of ether and alcohol, the latter of ·820 sp. gr., may be used.

The iodide of cadmium gives great sensitiveness and stability. The best results are obtained, however, by using it in connection with an alkaline iodizer, such as ammonium, sodium, or potassium. The proportion of mixed iodides should be about four or four and a half grains to each ounce of collodion.

The formula will stand as follows:—

| | | |
|---|---|---|
| Washed ether ... | ... sp. gr. ·725 | ... 1 ounce |
| Alcohol... ... | ... sp. gr. ·805 | ... 1 ,, |
| Ditto ... ... | ... sp. gr. ·820 | ... 1 ,, |
| Pyroxyline ... ... | ... | 15 to 18 grains |
| Iodide of ammonium ... | ... ... | 8 ,, |
| ,, cadmium ... | ... ... | 6 ,, |
| Bromide of ditto ... | ... ... | 2 ,, |

For some subjects having very violent contrasts, for instantaneous collodion and for dry plates, a much larger proportion of bromide may be used to secure softness and harmony. The tendency of bromides is to decrease contrasts, and secure detail. When the contrasts are great, and there is a tendency to hardness and over-intensity, the amount of bromide may be increased; when want of density is present the proportion of bromide may be decreased. A quarter of a grain or less per ounce will secure cleanness.

It sometimes happens that the collodion is working in some respects well, the right amount of intensity is present, and it is combined with sufficient detail, but is associated with a slight tendency to reduction of the shadows. This will most frequently happen when the collodion is new and newly iodized, especially if a large proportion of cadmium is present. The addition of an old coloured collodion will frequently remove this tendency; but if this cannot be conveniently done, or if the tendency to deposit be not removed without adding a proportion which would interfere with sensitiveness, then the addition of a few drops of tincture of iodine will frequently be found to answer the purpose; the amount should be proportioned to the state of the case, enough to make the collodion the colour of pale sherry will generally be sufficient. The addition of free iodine to collodion for positives, with a view to preserve clean shadows, is a practice of well-known value. In collodion for negatives its presence has generally been considered inimical to sensitiveness; but this will be found to be the case chiefly with pyrogallic acid development. Where bromo-iodized collodion and iron are used, and other things are in harmonious condition, free iodine will not be found to affect sensitiveness.

In some samples of collodion made with anhydrous ether and alcohol, it is difficult to obtain a dense creamy film; a thin opalescent effect, giving a feeble picture, only being obtained, even by prolonged immersion in a strong nitrate bath. When this effect is observed, and at the same time a disposition on the part of the film to repel the silver solution, it probably arises from the aqueous solution of silver penetrating the iodized film with difficulty. A few drops of distilled water to each ounce of collodion will at once open its pores sufficiently to allow the free permeation of the silver solution, and a dense creamy film, giving a brilliant image in place of the feeble picture before produced, may be at once obtained.

The best mode of preparing the collodion is to dissolve the iodide and bromide in the alcohol thoroughly first, and then filter. Next add the pyroxyline, and when it is well soaked with the alcohol add the ether. The pyroxyline will dissolve in a few minutes. It should then stand a few days to settle, and may be decanted off the sediment of undissolved cotton, or removed with a syphon. It is best used a week or two after it is prepared, and will generally keep good for a few months, and under favourable conditions, for years. *It is apt to grow* less sensitive by age and decomposition.

## COPYING AND ENLARGING.

In copying pictures of any kind, whether prints, drawings, or paintings, it is important to have the subject well lighted, and with a light as direct as possible; that is, the light should strike the picture at right angles, so as to prevent inequalities in the surface casting shadows, and so producing in the copy an appearance of roughness or texture altogether undesirable. The camera should be quite parallel to the picture, or the image will be distorted; a lens suitable to the purpose should be used, and with a small stop. Where the subject possesses straight lines, and entire absence of distortion is important, a triple lens, or a portrait lens well stopped down should be used. Where a little distortion or curvature of lines is unimportant, a single view lens may be used with advantage.

In copying, whether the image is to be the same size, or smaller or larger, the size is regulated by the distance at which the camera is placed from the object.

To obtain the image exactly the size of the original, the camera must be extended to just double the length of the equivalent focus of the lens, the object to be taken being at the same time placed at an equal distance to the amount of that extension from the lens. When an enlarged copy is required, the object is brought nearer to the lens, and the camera extended still more, and so just in proportion to the amount of enlargement required. When a small copy is required the reverse is the case.

The distances will, of course, vary with the focal length of the lens; and will be found by multiplying the focal length of the lens by the number of times of enlargement required, and adding to the product the length of that focus again. Thus, an object required to be enlarged four times, with a lens of ten inches focus, will require the camera extending fifty inches; being four times ten inches and ten inches added.

When a reduced copy is required with a similar lens, the object must be placed further from the camera, and the camera less extended. Thus, if instead of requiring the image four times larger, it were required four times smaller than the original, the object would be removed just four times and once the focal length of the lens, making fifty inches, whilst the ground glass would be brought nearer to the lens, the distance being just the focal length and one-fourth, or twelve inches and a half.

Where the focus of the lens is not known, it will be necessary in the first place to ascertain it. This, with a single lens, is very simple. It is only necessary to focus the sun, or some very distant object, quite sharply on the ground glass, and then measure the distance between it and the lens. With a portrait lens it is less simple. There are, however, various ways of doing it. One of the simplest, giving sufficiently accurate results, are as follows:—Take a map, an engraving, or sheet of letter-press, and fasten it flat against a well-lighted wall; now mark distinctly off a portion, say three inches. Proceed to draw out the camera and focus the subject accurately, taking care that the image is the exact size of the original, which will be ascertained clearly by observing that the three inches marked off in the original measure exactly those dimensions on the ground glass. *Now remove the lens altogether*, and measure the distance from the object focussed, to the ground glass; *one-fourth of that distance will be the equivalent focus of any portrait combination.*

The exact process to be used will depend much on circumstances. With oil paintings or subjects containing colour, a bromo-iodized collodion and iron development will give the best negative. With engravings or other subjects in black and white, a simply iodized collodion, with either iron or pyrogallic acid negative will give the best picture.

In producing enlarged copies of a photograph it is generally better to use the original negative than a print, and the enlarged print may either be produced by means of the solar camera, or by obtaining an enlarged negative from the original negative. This enlargement is effected by two operations; a transparent picture, the same size, or larger than the original negative, is first obtained, and from the transparent positive an enlarged negative. A camera capable of considerable extension is required, and either another camera or a long box made for the purpose. The negative of which an enlarged copy is required is placed in a groove at one end of the box; the lens of the camera is placed within the other end, and all light is excluded. The negative is then turned towards the zenith or the northern sky, and the image of the required size focussed, sharp, on the ground glass. A sensitive plate is then exposed, and the picture obtained is a transparent positive. If this transparent positive be placed in the groove originally occupied by the negative, and the operation repeated, the picture obtained is another negative.

A certain amount of enlargement may be effected at each operation. On the perfectness of this transparency the result largely depends. It should be very full of detail, and appear over-exposed according to the usual standard of transparencies for the stereoscope. The original negative should be very sharp and full of detail, not over intense, without blemish, and unvarnished. The lens best suited for the work is that which will give the flattest field. Bromo-iodized collodion and iron development will give the best results. The exposure will vary with the amount of enlargement, the size of the stop, the strength of the light, &c. By proper management of the collodion bath and developer, almost any quality of negatives may be obtained from a soft and delicate original image.

## ENLARGING BY THE SOLAR CAMERA.

For working the solar camera a room is required with a window facing south. The window must be provided with a shutter, in which an aperture is made so as to allow the reflector of the solar camera project outwards so as to receive the direct image of the sun. The condensing lens is placed with its convex side next to the mirror, the negative is then placed in its groove, collodion side, from the condenser. A good portrait lens, about half-plate size, is generally used for the enlarging lens. The mirror should be arranged to throw the image of the sun directly through the centre *of the condenser,* which should then be made to focus the sun's image sharply on the centre of the front combination of the enlarging lens. A screen, holding the paper, is then placed at a proper distance in the darkened room, the distance being regulated by the amount of enlargement, following the rule we have before laid down as to the multiplication of the focal length of the lens, thus: if the enlargement be required six times as large as the negative, and the lens have a solar focus of ten inches, the distance of the screen must be seventy inches, or six times the focus and ten inches added.

The negative should be very sharp and perfect all over, with a textureless film, free from stains or spots, delicate, and full of detail, merely developed with iron without intensifying, and should not be varnished.

It is necessary to have sunshine, and the print may be produced on ordinary sensitized albumenized paper, but this requires an exposure of an hour or two, during which time constant attention must be given to shift the mirror as the sun gradually travels. Printing by development is the method generally adopted, in which case the exposure is sometimes completed in a few seconds, and rarely requires more than a few minutes. The following formulæ for development printing will give vigorous fine-toned prints:

The salting solution is prepared as follows:—

| | |
|---|---|
| Chloride of magnesium ... ... ... | 4½ grains |
| Bromide of potassium ... ... ... | 7½ " |
| Gelatine ... ... ... ... ... | 4 " |
| Water ... ... ... ... ... | 1 ounce. |

On Turner's negative paper the bromide has a tendency to produce green in the tone of the finished print. On Towgood's small paper a more pleasant tone is produced by the above salting bath. On Towgood's small paper also the following salting solution gives very vigorous results:—

| | |
|---|---|
| Chloride of ammonium ... ... ... | 9 grains |
| Bromide of potassium ... ... ... | 3 " |
| Water ... ... ... ... ... | 1 ounce. |

The silver solutions vary with the paper, from 60 to 90 grains per ounce being used. On Saxe and Rive papers there is a tendency to excess of half-tone, and the paper is extremely rotten in washing. All the solutions, except the hypo, are brushed on. The salting solution is brushed on and allowed to remain until the paper lays flat, which, with most paper, is about three minutes. The silver solution is brushed on with Canton cotton, reserving the saturated piece to darken any of the shadows that may need it during development.

A faint trace of a visible image indicates sufficient exposure.

To develop, turn up the edges of the print so as to form a tray, and pour on a saturated solution of gallic acid, with a few drops of acetic acid added; the prints develop cleaner when acetic acid is used. Before fixing, wash very thoroughly, otherwise stains will be produced. The fixing solution is of the usual strength. The paper is most sensitive when exposed wet.

The tone is governed by the kind of paper, the salting solution, and the exposure and development. Over-exposure and short development produce a red print; if the exposure and development are right, and in harmony with the quality of the paper and the salting solution, the tone will be a warm rich black. If the exposure be short, and long development is required to bring out the image, the tone tends towards green.

## TRANSPARENCIES.

There are two modes of producing transparencies. They may be printed on dry plates in a pressure frame by contact, in a manner similar to prints on paper, or they may be produced on wet plates in the camera.

The first method is perhaps the most simple. Plates prepared by any of the dry processes may be used, but the tannin process will perhaps give the most satisfactory results as to tone and brilliancy. The use of acetic acid in the developer tends to give a reddish tone, and the use of citric acid a bluish tone; by a judicious mixture of the two acids almost any colour can be produced. The use of an *old and coloured collodion*, a bath acid with acetic acid, and a ten-grain tannin solution, developing with pyrogallic acid three grains, citric acid one grain, acetic acid thirty minims, in one ounce of water, will give excellent results.

In printing on dry plates, two or three points require especial attention. Both negative and dry plate must be perfectly flat, or there will be great risk of breaking one or both. The negative must be well varnished with a hard varnish, and perfectly smooth. The pressure frame used should be perfectly true and flat, and the pressure light and elastic. Unless these points receive attention, and great care be used throughout, the negatives will be soon scratched and spoiled, and will be in constant danger of breakage.

If the transparencies are for the stereoscope, and the negatives have been obtained in a binocular camera, as the reader knows, the sides will require to be transposed. There are three modes of doing this: the transparency may be cut after it is taken, and transposed in mounting; or the negative may be cut at the outset, and the sides transposed and fixed together again in the printing frame; or a printing frame may be used which permits the exposure of one half of the slide at a time, the plate being so moved between each as to transpose the two sides of the negative, and make them occupy the proper position on the dry plate.

The exposure will rarely exceed a few seconds, somewhat depending on the sensitiveness of the plate, the density of the negative, and the strength of the light. To good bright diffused daylight the exposure with a tannin plate may vary from five seconds to thirty seconds. To the flame of a gas-light the exposure must be a little longer. A single experiment at the time will generally determine the exposure necessary.

The class of transparencies which have been generally most admired are those on albumen, well known in connection with the name of Ferrier in Paris, and Negretti and Zambra in London. Amateurs have rarely succeeded in producing this class of work, as it involves much care and skill. We subjoin a brief abstract of the process, and we may add, that the plates so prepared may be used either for negatives or transparencies, merely aiming in the former to secure a *good* body of albumen.

To the albumen of ten fresh eggs add one per cent. of iodide of ammonium dissolved in twenty per cent. of distilled water: now beat up the albumen for about a quarter of an hour, till the whole is converted into a froth, so thick and hard that pieces may be pulled up bodily with a fork when plunged into it. The basin should now be carefully covered in with a sheet of paper to prevent the access of dust, and put aside for six hours. After the froth has subsided, a thick crust is formed at the top: this serves as a filter for the substratum of albumen, which has to force its way through the crust when being decanted from the basin on to the plate.

The dark room should be carefully freed from dust some two or three hours before it is used, the floor being watered and swept, and all shelves and ledges well wiped with a damp sponge, for dust is the principal cause of blemishes in the albumen film, and, to prevent disturbing it as much as possible, it is advisable to take in all material required at one time, just before commencing operations. It is desirable that the room should be kept at a moderate temperature, though this is not essential.

The plate-holder is a round tapering stick, about half an inch in diameter, and nine inches long, having at one end a small cup, about an inch in diameter. Round the edge of the cup, which is about a quarter of an inch thick, some gutta-percha is melted.

To coat the plate, warm the gutta-percha of the plate-holder in the flame of a spirit lamp, then press it on the centre of the back of the plate: in a few seconds it will have cooled sufficiently to adhere firmly to the glass, so that it may be turned and whirled in any direction. Now hold up the plate, and with a soft flat brush remove any dust that may have stuck to the plate. Pour the albumen from the basin on to the plate in the same manner as if coating with collodion, and, if necessary, assist the even flowing with a glass rod. Drain the albumen off, first at one corner then at the other; tilt the plate, so that the fluid may again pass over it; again tilt the plate, and when the albumen has reached half-way across it, impart a rotatory motion to the glass by means of the holder worked between the hands; continue this for seven or eight seconds, then place the hand close under the plate, and force it off the gutta-percha. If any dust fall upon the plate during the operation, draw a fine camel-hair pencil between the lips, and pick off any spots with the point. Place the plate in the drying box, in each alternate groove of which a board slides freely, so as to separate each plate one from the other. The inside of the box must be well dusted before use, and the boards cleaned and thoroughly dried before a fire or in the sun, so as to render them absorbent, otherwise the film will not dry easily.

The bath for sensitizing is a dish with a perfectly flat bottom, made of plate glass, about one-third longer than the plate employed. The solution is as follows:—

| | |
|---|---|
| Nitrate of silver ... ... ... ... | 10 parts |
| Acetic acid ... ... ... ... | 10 „ |
| Distilled water ... ... ... ... | 100 „ |

This is poured into the dish till it stands about a quarter of an inch high. The bath is then raised at one end so as to keep the solution at the other. The plate is placed in the empty part, albumenized surface upward, when by a dexterous movement of the hand the dish is brought level, and the solution allowed to pass quickly and evenly over the plate. The plate should now be raised and lowered several times by means of a flattened silver wire, bent at one end into a right angle; in about forty seconds the plate may be removed from the bath. The same care must be taken, as in sensitizing a collodion plate, that the solution passes evenly over the film, for wherever there is a stoppage there will be a sharp clear line.

The plate, when removed, presents a nice light blue tint. It must immediately be thoroughly washed, back and front, with distilled or rain water. The water should be allowed to flow over it till no greasy streaks are perceptible. The plate is now drained, and may be used moist, or, if intended for keeping, they should be thoroughly dried, and stored away in the dark. The sensitizing solution should be filtered back into the stock bottle, and may be used over and over again, even when quite black.

The development is effected by a saturated solution of gallic acid, which has been warmed to a temperature of 80° Fah.; spread it rapidly over the plate with the aid of a soft brush, the hair being about an inch long. There is no fear of using the brush freely, as it would almost require a knife to scratch the hardened albumen. After the solution has been on a minute or two, pour off a portion, and to that remaining on the plate add some of the following:—

| | |
|---|---|
| Nitrate of silver ... ... ... ... | 2 parts |
| Distilled water ... ... ... ... | 100 „ |

Rest the brush on the plate, pour the nitrate solution over the brush, and rapidly mix the two solutions together. In a few seconds the picture begins to appear, if the plate has been properly exposed; if, however, it is under-exposed, the image does not appear until the solutions have been changed, and the previous operation repeated several times.

Fix with hyposulphite of soda, and well wash.

Transparencies may be printed on wet plates as on dry plates; but it will be necessary to place a thin strip of card at each end of the negative, to prevent the wet plate coming into absolute contact with it, and this will interfere somewhat with the sharpness of the image. The wet plate should be very carefully drained, and the exposure will be very short.

In producing transparencies in the camera, the wet process is generally used, and an especial arrangement of apparatus will be necessary. The best arrangement for the purpose consists of a long box, into one end of which the part of the camera carrying the ground-glass, &c., may fit, and having at the other end a frame holding the negatives to be copied. The length of the box will be determined by the focus of the lenses to be used. Suppose the lenses to have an equivalent focus of six inches, the distance between the lenses and the ground-glass would require to be twelve inches, and the same between the lenses and the negative, the box would have to be, therefore, nearly twenty-four inches long. In the middle of the box there should be a sliding frame carrying the lenses, and it would be found of great advantage to have an adjustment in this for regulating the lateral distance of the lenses from each other. A longitudinal division to keep the two images separate will, of course, be required in the box.

The stereoscopic negative being placed in its frame at one end of the box, and the lenses in their places, &c., the whole should be pointed to a clear expanse of sky, and the transparent image focussed on the ground glass. The image should be just of the same size as the original if the negative be of the usual stereoscopic size; but if the negative have been taken a little larger than usual, as is sometimes done when it is produced with an especial view to the production of transparencies, a somewhat reduced image will be obtained by sliding the lenses a little further from the negative and nearer to the ground glass. The apparatus should be slightly elevated, so as to get the light from the sky uninterrupted by any objects. A piece of white paper may be made to project at right angles beyond the negative, so as to serve as a reflector.

It will be seen that as every object produced in the camera direct is turned round on its axis and inverted, this effects the same result as transposing the halves, and a camera transparency from a binocular stereoscopic negative does not require any further transposition.

The chemicals generally may be such as work well with wet process for negatives. A bath acid with acetic acid, a full exposure, and an iron developer with a large proportion of acetic acid, will give good results. Pyrogallic acid development may be used when a browner tone is required. The exposure will depend on the state of the light and the size of the stop used in the lens. Either a single or double lens may be used, but in either case a small stop is desirable, so as to secure good definition all over the transparency.

The purpose for which the transparency is required will regulate several points of practice. If the transparency be produced as a step in the production of another negative, very full exposure, so as to secure the greatest possible amount of detail, is necessary. If the transparency be intended for the magic lantern, whilst it will be necessary to secure detail, it will be still more necessary to secure clean lights and deep blacks: to this end the negatives may be a little more intense than for other classes of transparencies. The character of the transparency for the stereoscope will depend somewhat on the subject, but in all cases softness and delicacy are desirable. As a rule, the negative best suited for producing transparencies is one which is soft and full of detail, having scarcely sufficient vigour for paper printing.

The tone of transparencies is somewhat a matter of taste. For some subjects having much atmosphere the warm greyish tone given by iron development is very effective. Immersion for a few minutes in a two-grain bath of bichloride of mercury will give greater force and intensity. A more prolonged immersion in a stronger bath, followed by a solution of ammonia containing about three drops of the strong liquid ammonia to an ounce of water, will give a black tone. Immersion for a few seconds in a dilute solution of sulphide of potassium or sulphide ammonium, gives a brown tone. Immersion for a few hours in a bath of hyposulphite of soda one ounce, chloride of gold one grain, and water five ounces, will give a purple tone.

Transparencies should be varnished with a varnish giving a textureless surface. For the stereoscope they should be backed with finely ground glass, or with a glass coated with benzole varnish, in which a few grains of white wax to each ounce has been dissolved.

## INSTANTANEOUS PHOTOGRAPHY.

The term instantaneous photography is a somewhat indefinite one; it is generally applied, however, to all kinds of pictures including objects in motion, such as street views with moving figures, or marine views with flying clouds or beating waves, and in proportion to the rapidity of the motion must be the briefness of the exposure: but the term instantaneous is commonly applied to exposures ranging from the infinitesimal part of a second to one or even two seconds.

*The especial conditions* necessary for instantaneous photography are chemicals in good condition, good lenses, good light, and suitable subject.

*The Chemicals.*—A good bromo-iodized collodion, which has not been iodized more than a few weeks, will generally give good results. If the subjects possess much contrast, the proportion of bromide should be increased in order to secure harmony. The collodion, for which a formula is given in another chapter, using from one grain to two grains of bromide, according to the nature of the subject, will answer well. The nitrate bath should be a new one which has not been doctored at all, slightly acidified with nitric acid, of which the smallest proportion which will give clear results should be used. A strong solution of protosulphate of iron should be used, with no more acetic acid than is sufficient to preserve the shadows from a foggy reduction. In cold weather, a 50-grain solution may be used; in warm weather, about a 30-grain solution will answer, with from 20 to 30 minims of glacial acetic acid. The negatives may be further intensified, where they require it, by any of the various intensifying processes.

LENSES.—Various kinds of lenses may be used successfully for instantaneous photographs, but it is an important condition that they shall define pretty well with a large aperture. Where a lens requires the use of a very small stop to secure tolerable definition, it is of a little service for instantaneous photography. In some cases single view lenses may be used; but, as a rule, in such case the stop used should not be less than one-twelfth of the focal length of the lens. For instance, if the lens have a focus of six inches, the stop should not be less than half an inch. As a general rule, portrait combinations are used for instantaneous pictures, as securing greater rapidity. It is better then to work with the smallest stop which will give sufficient light for the subject, a point which experience only will determine.

*Subject and Light.*—It is useless to attempt instantaneous photography in a dull light. As a rule, it is desirable to have the object illuminated with direct sunshine. Moreover, in the most perfect light, it is imperative to use great judgment in selecting the subject. It is always desirable to avoid having any very near foreground object, especially if that object be dark. In the first place, because it is not possible to get a near object and distant ones in good focus with a large aperture; in the next place, because a slight movement of a near object is much more conspicuous to the definition than the same movement in a distant object; and in the next place, because, as a rule, it is impossible to get a dark foreground object sufficiently exposed in the same time as distant and lighter objects. In street photography, for instance, a moving object in the immediate foreground, say within twenty or thirty feet of the lens, will probably be under-exposed, if it be taken with sufficient rapidity to prevent blurring; and if exposed a sufficient time to secure detail, will probably be blurred by the palpable moving. Again, in marine views, green foliage or dark vessels immediately in the foreground are difficult to secure, and at the same time do justice to breaking waves and flying clouds; and it often happens that when an attempt is made to secure the former together with the latter, that whilst striving to bring out detail in the dark objects in front, all detail is buried in the water and sky, and a hard, chalky picture is the result. It will readily be seen, therefore, that one of the most important points in securing success in instantaneous photography is the judicious selection of a well lighted subject without dark foreground objects.

There are many modes of uncovering a lens so as to secure a very rapid, or so-called instantaneous exposure: a variety of instantaneous shutters have been devised, each of which possesses more or less of merit. In the absence of any of these, a skilful person may give a very rapid exposure by using a loose cap of black velvet for the lens, removing and replacing it as rapidly as the hand can move. By this means an exposure of a fraction of a second can be given, which, except for objects in very rapid motion, is generally sufficiently short exposure.

## PERMANENT PRINTING PROCESSES.

It is a fact to be regretted that many photographs produced by the ordinary methods of printing with salts of silver have faded. It is only necessary here to say, that there is good reason to believe that fading is generally the result of carelessness in performing some parts of the work of printing, or of the use of materials and processes known to be imperfect. If the processes described in this little work be conducted with care and with pure materials, there is every reason to believe that the prints, if properly kept, will be durable.

There have been, however, a great many methods of printing proposed for securing entire permanency. We shall briefly allude to those which have given promise of success.

Carbon Processes.—Carbon being one of the most unchangeable materials known, it has long been thought that if photographs could be produced in that material, they would be quite permanent. This aim has been successful, and there are now several methods of printing in carbon, the best of which are, however, patented. The principle upon which they are chiefly based is the tendency of gelatine and similar substances, when mixed with a bichromate, to become insoluble. A mixture of gelatine, indian ink, and bichromate of potash, dissolved together, spread on paper, and when dry exposed under a negative, is acted upon by light. Those parts upon which the light acts through the most transparent parts of the negative become hardened and insoluble. The paper being immersed in warm water, these parts remain attached to the paper and form the shadows of the picture, whilst the parts protected by the dense deposit of the negative, remaining soluble, are washed away, and the white paper forms the lights of the picture. But in following this method a difficulty arises: it is the surface first acted upon by light which becomes insoluble, the portion underneath still remaining soluble, and this during the soaking in water becomes dissolved, and takes away with it all the delicate half-tone. It becomes necessary, therefore, to make some arrangement whereby the gelatine may be exposed with one side in contact with t negative, and then the unaltered portion washed away, so as to develop the picture, from the other side. This is done in several ways. One method, known as Fargier's, is as follows:—

Prepare the following solution:—

| | |
|---|---|
| Water ... ... ... ... ... | 100 parts |
| Gelatine ... ... ... ... | 10 ,, |
| Bichromate of potassa ... ... ... | 1 part |

Indian ink, sufficient to give the depth of colour required.

The mixture is poured on glass plates and spread uniformly with a camel's hair pencil. Next day the plates are sufficiently dry to be exposed under negatives. The time of exposure is from one minute in sunlight to fifteen minutes in the shade.

Before development the gelatine film is covered with a thick film of collodion, and then immersed in hot water, which soon melts the gelatine on the opposite side. When the picture is detached a glass plate is applied above it; the film thus imprisoned between two plates is easily turned; it is reimmersed in the water, after removing the glass carrying the picture: then, after the washing in cold water to remove the last impurities, a sheet of gelatined paper can be applied to it and the picture attached without much difficulty.

In Mr. Swan's patented process a plate of glass is coated with plain collodion: this, when dry, is coated with a mixture of gelatine, indian ink, sugar, and bichromate of ammonia. When dry, the tissue is easily detached from the glass. It is then exposed under a negative, the collodion side in contact: the exposure must be ascertained by experience. When done, it is mounted on paper by means of a solution of india rubber in benzole, the collodion side in contact with the paper, which leaves uppermost the surface opposite to that which was exposed to light. It is now immersed in warm water, which removes all the gelatine, colour, &c., not acted upon by light, whilst every part on which light has acted, being insoluble, remains attached to the collodion. Where the negative is most transparent, light has acted to the greatest depth, and a thick layer of gelatine and colour remains undissolved, and this forms the deepest shadows; in the half-tones the layers are thinner just ir proportion to the degree of transparency in the negative. Th( thinner layers are semi-transparent, and allow the white paper t( be shown through, thus forming gradations in the picture. A modification of this consists in coating paper with gelatine pigmen and sugar, but without bichromate. When required for use, it i rendered sensitive by floating on a 10-grain solution of bichromat( of potash. It is then dried and exposed, gelatine side next th( negative, next mounted with the gelatine side downwards on t( another piece of paper with india rubber solution; then immerse( in warm water, which quickly removes the original paper on whicl the gelatine rested and permits the picture to be developed. I may either remain on the paper on to which it was last mounted, o: be transferred on to fresh paper. In the latter case, the imag( will be in its right relations as to right and left, but, in the former it will be reversed. The strength of the gelatine solution is abou one ounce of gelatine in five of water. It is not necessary to ente: into further details of a patented process.

Mr. Pouncy has patented a method similar in many respects, bu in which printing ink forms the image. This is rendered sensitiv( by the addition of bichromate of potash and asphaltum, and afte: exposure is developed with turpentine.

A variety of other processes with the salts of iron, uranium, &c. have been tried with various degrees of success, but have not com( into general use. A uranium process, recently perfected by Her Wothly, has been patented in this country, and promises mucl success.

---

## SAVING SILVER FROM WASTE SOLUTIONS, ETC.

Every photographer who makes the art either his profession or hi pastime should recover the large amount of silver which is generall wasted in washing waters, exhausted fixing solutions, &c. As it i computed that less than 2 per cent. of silver originally used goes t form the picture, it will be seen that with care an important savin can be made. There are three kinds of residues from which sil can be saved, each requiring different treatment. They are, firstly, Sensitive paper cuttings, filters, and any materials containing silver, which can be reduced to ashes; secondly, Hyposulphite fixing baths, waste developing solutions, &c.; and, thirdly, Washings from the prints before toning, and all solutions, such as old nitrate baths, which can be precipitated as chlorides.

Clippings of unfixed prints, discoloured, and waste pieces of excited paper filters, &c., are burnt out in the open air in a sheet-iron box about 3 feet deep by 2 wide, allowing the burnt waste to smoulder for a considerable time, to burn off the charred matter, that it may take up less space in the crucible in reducing.

The silver in the fixing baths, and used developing solutions, may be recovered in the form of sulphide by adding liver of sulphur or sulphide of potassium in solution, continuing to add it as long as any black precipitate is produced, but taking care not to add too much. When the precipitate has subsided, a little of the clear liquid may be taken from the top, and tested with a little further sulphide of potassium. If no further deposit fall, test another portion with nitrate of silver to see if too much sulphide has been added, as excess would dissolve a portion of the precipitate.

The washing water, &c., are placed in a large wooden vessel wider at the bottom than the top, like a precipitating jar, and it should have a tap a few inches from the bottom, to draw off from time to time the clear water. Common salt is freely added, and occasionally a little hydrochloric acid. The supernatant water is from time to time drawn off, taking care that no silver salt is left in the solution. When a sufficient quantity of the precipitated chloride of silver has accumulated, it is washed and dried for reduction.

All the residues must be quite dry before reducing them.

The various residues may be sent to a refiner to reduce to the metallic state, or they may be reduced by the photographer himself, in which case he ought to have a small furnace for the purpose. This may be produced ready for use, or may be built of firebricks, care being given to secure a good draught. Coke is used for heating, and with the natural draught thus secured, a white heat is easily obtained. A small Griffin's furnace, heated by gas, is sometimes used, and a small assay can be effected by it in about twenty minutes. A common fire might be used, if sufficient heat could be obtained; and many kinds of stoves in use are quite efficient. Crucibles of various sizes are required, the best being known as "London pots." Plumbago pots are less apt to crack, but they are acted upon by the flux. A pair of long iron pincers for lifting the pots in and out of the fire will also be required.

*To Reduce Ashes.*—Place a fire-brick or two at the bottom of the furnace, and upon that the lower half of a plumbago crucible, in which the other crucible is to stand. The object of this is to save the silver from going amongst the ashes if the pot break, which will happen sometimes, in spite of all precautions. Now build up the fire of coke around the fire-bricks and plumbago crucible, and whilst the heat is getting up, place the pot intended for use into the fire, inverting it at first, so as to get gradually heated and lessen the risk of fracture. Place the pot in its proper position, and build up the fire with pieces of coke all round up to the edge. Next, nearly fill the pot with the ashes, cover up the furnace, and leave it for a quarter of an hour, by which time the bulk of the ashes will be much reduced by the perfect combustion of the portions of carbonized paper. Now add an equal weight of dried carbonate of soda, or of a mixture of this with carbonate of potash, and stir, to mix intimately, with a piece of wood; place the cover on the pot, see that the fire is good, close the furnace, and leave it for half an hour. If the heat have been maintained the whole will now be melted, and of course reduced in bulk, leaving space for more ashes. It is now at the option of the manipulator either to pour out the melted mass into another vessel, previously warmed a little to prevent flying, where the silver, being the heaviest, will sink to the bottom, or to add more ashes and flux to that already melted in the pot, and proceed as before until it is full, leaving the pot then to cool gradually as the fire is suffered to die out. When quite cool, the pot is broken, and the silver found in an ingot at the bottom of the slag formed by the melted flux. From five ounces to six are considered a good average return from a pound of ashes.

*Sylphide of Silver* requires some time and care to reduce it, as the whole of the sulphur must be burned off. When the sulphide has been thoroughly dried, it must be mixed with an equal weight of nitrate of potash, and thrown a little at a time into a red-hot crucible. An iron ladle will be necessary for this purpose. Care must be taken not to put in too large a quantity, or the combustion which takes place will drive the metal out of the pot. When the crucible is full, the fire must be made up, and a good heat maintained for about half an hour, after which the cover may be removed, and a portion of the flux taken out with an iron ladle, to make room for more material, and the same process repeated; after which more flux should be taken out, and its place supplied with a small quantity of nitrate of potash and some carbonate of soda. This will ensure the complete combustion and removal of the sulphur. The fire should now be continued for about a couple of hours. When the pot is cool it may be broken, and the silver recovered as before.

*To reduce Chloride of Silver.*—Mix carbonate of soda and potash in equal quantities, add one pound to one pound of chloride of silver, mix well, and throw into a red-hot crucible small portions at a time; for, if the whole were thrown in at once, it would boil over, and cause a considerable waste of silver. When the crucible is full, or nearly so, cover and leave it for half an hour at a white heat. The silver will be found beneath the slag of flux as before.

# A Chapter of Recipes.

We have in the various processes treated of in this little work given the most approved methods of obtaining the best results; as, however, varying circumstances sometimes render modified operations desirable, we subjoin a series of recipes for obtaining good results by slightly varied results in different ways.

## VARIOUS IRON DEVELOPING SOLUTIONS.

With a highly bromized collodion a strong developer is an advantage, and permits very short exposure. A weak developer is slow in action, but increases density.

| | | |
|---|---|---|
| 1. | Protosulphate of iron ... ... ... | 5 grains |
| | Acetic acid (glacial) ... ... ... | 5 minims |
| | Water ... ... ... ... ... | 1 ounce. |

This should be made fresh and used in summer, with a collodion simply iodized, or containing very little bromide. It gives considerable density.

| | | |
|---|---|---|
| 2. | Protosulphate of iron ... ... ... | 8 grains |
| | Acetic acid (glacial) ... ... ... | 20 minims |
| | Water... ... ... ... ... | 1 ounce. |

This is suited for landscape work, with a collodion containing a little bromide.

| | | |
|---|---|---|
| 3. | Protosulphate of iron ... ... ... | 10 grains |
| | Acetic acid (glacial) ... ... ... | 30 minims |
| | Liq. ammon. fort. ... ... ... | 3 ,, |
| | Water ... ... ... ... ... | 1 ounce. |

This is best freshly mixed, and gives intensity.

| | | | | | |
|---|---|---|---|---|---|
| 4. Protosulphate of iron ... | | ... | ... | 11 grains |
| Acetic acid (glacial) ... | | ... | ... | 13 minims |
| Formic acid ... | ... | ... | ... | 10 „ |
| Water ... | ... | ... | ... | ... | 1 ounce. |

This is recommended as giving great detail in deep shadows of foliage.

| | | | | | |
|---|---|---|---|---|---|
| 5. Protosulphate of iron ... | | ... | ... | 15 grains |
| Acetic acid (glacial) ... | | ... | ... | 15 minims |
| Water ... | ... | ... | ... | ... | 1 ounce. |

This is a good portrait developer for summer use.

| | | | | | |
|---|---|---|---|---|---|
| 6. Protosulphate of iron ... | | ... | ... | 50 grains |
| Acetic acid (glacial) ... | | ... | ... | 30 minims |
| Water ... | ... | ... | ... | ... | 1 ounce. |

This is valuable with a highly bromized collodion for portraits in winter, and instantaneous pictures in summer.

The last mentioned will work best when a month or two old, and No. 5 when a week or two old. Alcohol sufficient to make each flow freely must be added; the amount will be regulated by the state of the bath. When the solution is about to be kept before use, the acetic acid should be added, but no alcohol until the time of use.

*Acetate of Iron.* — The protacetate of iron gives more intensity when used as a developer than the protosulphate; but it should be used fresh, as it does not keep. It is made by dissolving 12 grains of protosulphate of iron and 12 grains of acetate of lead in an ounce of water, then filtering out the white precipitate of sulphate of lead, and adding 10 drops of acetic acid. Or it may be made by adding 6 grains of acetate of soda to 12 grains of protosulphate of iron, and 12 drops of acetic acid. There will be no precipitate in the latter.

*Saccharo-Sulphate of Iron.*—This salt seems to favour density of image, and renders less acid necessary. It is prepared by dissolving 200 parts of pure protosulphate of iron in 100 parts of boiling distilled water, then dissolving 50 parts of crystallized sugar candy in 30 parts of boiling distilled water. The solutions are then mixed and crystallized. For photographic use the solution may be used without crystallizing the salts. A solution containing 40 grains of protosulphate, 12 of crystallized sugar, and 25 drops of acetic acid, gives good results.

*The Double Sulphate of Iron and Ammonia.*—This double salt is chiefly recommended because the crystals have little tendency to peroxidation. It is also said that it gives good results, with a shorter exposure, and that it yields very clean and dense negatives. It may be used in a manner similar to the ordinary sulphate, adding, however, a little less acetic acid. The following solutions will be found to give good results:—For ordinary work in summer,

| | |
|---|---|
| Sulphate of iron and ammonia ... ... | 25 grains |
| Acetic acid ... ... ... ... | 15 minims |
| Water ... ... ... ... ... | 1 ounce |
| Alcohol ... ... ... ... ... | *quantum suff.* |

For cold weather and ill-lighted subjects:—

| | |
|---|---|
| Sulphate of iron and ammonia ... ... | 35 grains |
| Acetic acid ... ... ... ... | 20 minims |
| Water ... ... ... ... ... | 1 ounce |
| Alcohol ... ... ... ... ... | *quantum suff.* |

A stronger developer for very rapid work is made thus:—

| | |
|---|---|
| Sulphate of iron and ammonia ... ... | 100 grains |
| Acetic acid ... ... ... ... | 30 minims |
| Water ... ... ... ... ... | 1 ounce |
| Alcohol ... ... ... ... ... | *quantum suff* |

## VARIOUS MODES OF INTENSIFYING.

*Iron and Silver.*—This method may be used either before or after fixing, with or without the previous application of a solution of iodine. In hot weather, the solution should consist of 10 grains of citric acid, and 5 grains of protosulphate of iron; in winter, 5 grains of citric acid, and 5 grains of iron, may be used. Or, a solution containing 10 grains of nitrate of silver, and 10 grains of citric acid, may be kept, and a few drops added to the ordinary developer for intensifying. Tartaric acid may be substituted for citric acid, but the tone of the picture is very blue, and allows actinic light to pass through. Or, after all the detail is brought out by the ordinary process of development, the plate is washed and flooded with silver solution from the bath, and the process of development again repeated with iron, by which sufficient density is obtained.

*Pyrogallic Acid and Silver after Fixing.*—This is chiefly useful where there is already some amount of intensity; but scarcely sufficient to produce brilliant prints. It consists in the application to the film of the following solution :—

| | |
|---|---|
| Pyrogallic acid ... ... ... | 2 grains |
| Citric acid, in winter 1 gr., in summer | 2 „ |
| Water ... ... ... ... ... | 1 ounce, |

with a few drops of a twenty-grain solution of silver added. It is applied to the plate, until the desired amount of intensity is obtained. There is not usually such an appreciable increase in the amount of additional deposit as in the former method, but the colour of the deposit is considerably deepened, and becomes very non-actinic. The effect of this process on a soft negative is sometimes very fine. With a picture in any degree under-exposed, hardness is apt to spring from this process. It is scarcely necessary to say in using this or other intensifying process after fixing, that great care is imperative in washing away the hypo or *cyanide fixing solution,* before applying the intensifying agent.

*Iodine, Pyrogallic Acid, and Silver.*—In this process a solution of iodine is applied prior to intensifying with pyrogallic acid and silver, as above. The solutions are applied after fixing, and may be used either whilst the negative is wet, or after it has been dried. Prepare a solution of iodine in water as follows :—

| | |
|---|---|
| Iodine ... ... ... ... ... | 1 grain |
| Iodide of potassium ... ... ... | 2 grains |
| Water ... ... ... ... ... | 1 ounce. |

Cover the picture with this solution, and leave it for five or ten minutes, then wash well. The process may be conducted by daylight, which is, indeed, desirable to act on the film of iodide of silver thus formed. Now develop afresh in a dull, or yellow light, by means of solution of pyrogallic acid and silver, as directed in a former paragraph. The alternate use of the iodine solution, and the pyrogallic acid and silver, may be carried to almost any extent, and any intensity gained. Instead of the iodine solution as above described, a few drops of strong alcoholic tincture of iodine added to water, until it is the colour of sherry, may be used; but it is more troublesome than the aqueous solution.

This is the most powerful of the intensifying processes, as it allows of an accumulating intensity almost without limit. It is under some circumstances very valuable, but is at the same time, unless judiciously used, very dangerous, as there is great danger by its means of producing hardness.

*Mercury and Iodide.*—This may be used either before or after drying the picture. If the latter plan be used, it is necessary that the collodion be one which adheres well to the glass, and that the plate be perfectly clean before the collodion is applied. The plate is first moistened with water, and then covered with a solution of bichloride of mercury, a strength of about six grains to an ounce of water is a safe proportion. The colour of the film will be changed to a grey, and must never be allowed to pass this stage. If it becomes at all white, the best result cannot be obtained. Immediately the dark grey tint is produced, the plate is to be well washed and then covered with a 1-grain solution of iodide of potassium. The effect of this is to change the bluish grey into a greenish grey, the colour of the deposit, by transmitted light, being very similar to that produced when gallic acid is used for development. The colour is very repellant to actinic light, and gives excellent results in printing. If the mercury be too strong, or its action continued too long, a yellow negative is obtained, the printing powers of which are much inferior, and the deposit on which is, moreover, so sensitive to light, that the negative is apt to change in the sun, and sometimes becomes quite transparent. The same process throughout may be used, before the plate has been dried, immediately after fixing and washing. Bichloride of mercury may be applied in the same way, and followed by a very dilute solution of hyposulphite of soda or of ammonia, in which case a brown or black deposit will be obtained in the negative.

Negatives thus intensified are apt to become harder whilst printing, and sometimes useless. Wherever mercury is used for intensifying, the negative must be varnished, to prevent any contact between the excited paper and the film.

*Other Modes.*—Sulphide of ammonium or of potassium, applied after fixing, blackens the deposit. A similar effect may be produced by allowing the plate to remain a few hours in an old hypo bath. A solution of chloride of gold produces a deep bluish-black tint. A solution containing tincture of iodine adds slight intensity, and gives a yellow tint. A solution of bichloride of palladium produces a black tint, which does not add much to the printing powers of the negative. A weak solution of bichloride of mercury, without any after-treatment, will give a little more decision to a negative already nearly sufficiently vigorous.

---

## TONING PROCESSES.

There is a variety of preparations for toning prints, in the whole of which, however, gold is the toning agent. The chief object of the various additions is, by rendering the solution of chloride of gold *neutral, or slightly* alkaline, to decompose the salt, the gold being *then thrown down* upon the silver image in a metallic state. As the degree of subdivision of any metal materially affects its colour, it is probable that the materials used in the various toning solutions have the effect of modifying the colour by modifying the degree of subdivision in which the particles are thrown down.

*Chloride of Lime and Gold.*—As commercial chloride of lime is not always of uniform character, it is sometimes necessary to experiment in order to get the best working solution. Take as a standard solution 1 grain of chloride of gold, 1 grain of chloride of lime, and 1 grain of carbonate of lime. If, when used 48 hours after mixing, this solution bleach excessively, there is too much chloride of lime; if there be difficulty in obtaining pure blacks and whites, add a little more chloride of lime and a little chloride of gold, and use in a few hours. When it is desired to hasten the ripening of the solution, hot water may be used; but it should be remembered that all the solutions containing chloride of lime are better kept a few days before use.

*Another Formula*:—

| | |
|---|---|
| Chloride of gold ... ... ... | 2 grains |
| Chloride of lime, from ... ... | 2 to 4 |
| Water ... ... ... ... | 1 pint. |

This bath used immediately, or soon after its mixture, gives poor results: the prints are always impoverished; if they remain long in the bath they become slaty and grey; if a short time, they are brown and red, and in each case are mealy and flat. The great secret of success consists in keeping the solution a proper time, after mixing, before using it for toning purposes. The shortest time in which it acquires the proper qualities is 24 hours, and it goes on improving for a month. The prints are a little over-printed. The results generally fine, black, vigorous prints.

*Chloride of Lime. Ommeganck's Formula*:—

| | |
|---|---|
| Chloride of gold ... ... ... | 15 grains |
| Carbonate of lime ... ... ... | 150 ,, |
| Chloride of lime ... ... ... | 24 ,, |
| Water ... ... ... ... | 7 pints. |

Preparation: dissolve in *aqua regia* (nitric acid one part, hydrochloric acid two parts), metallic gold 90 grains; after solution, add 30 grains of common salt to prevent decomposition during evaporation; evaporate by a gentle heat until the saline mass contains no excess of water. It is not necessary to push the evaporation to complete dryness; a trace of acid is not of much consequence. Dissolve the salt of gold thus obtained in three ounces and a half of rain or distilled water, and a solution results containing about 45 grains of chloride of gold to the ounce of water. It is not, with this preparation, necessary to weigh every time small quantities that are required, nor is it necessary to preserve it from moisture. Two drachms and forty minims of the solution are taken and triturated in a porcelain mortar with 150 grains of carbonate of lime. If it be intended for immediate use, the preparation should be kept in contact for one hour; if on the morrow—and this is best—ten minutes will be found sufficient. By this treatment the chloride of gold abandons its acid and a certain portion of its chlorine. The whole of the operations should be conducted by the heat of a water bath, in winter, at a temperature of between 70° and 80° Fah. Carbonate of lime being nearly insoluble, a slight excess of it is not so important as an excess of carbonate of soda. This reaction being completed, 23 grains of chloride of lime (hypochlorite of lime) are added; this latter salt should be specially prepared and preserved in closely-stoppered bottles, on account of its tendency to become humid and decompose in damp air. After that, add 35 ounces of water, filter, and then add 5½ pints more water, and preserve in stoppered bottles. When this bath loses its toning properties through age, without having been exhausted, it may be restored by the addition of about four drops to the pint of a ten per cent. solution of chloride of gold. When the bath has lost its smell, it may be restored by adding a few drops of a fresh solution of chloride of lime. Either this or a few drops of solution of chloride of gold will restore its action after it has been partially used, and has grown inert.

On immersing the print in the hypo bath, the tone of the proof *changes at once to a* violet brown; but, as soon as it has been pro*perly fixed, it returns* to a pure black. Finally, the prints are washed, as before described. The hyposulphite bath should only be used once.

*Phosphate of Soda.*

| | | |
|---|---|---|
| Water | ... ... ... ... | 10 ounces |
| Tribasic phosphate of soda | ... | 18 grains |
| Chloride of gold | ... ... ... | 1 grain. |

*Acetate of Soda.*—This is the most generally used of all gold-toning processes; it is easy to manage, keeps well, and gives rich, warm tones :—

| | | |
|---|---|---|
| Water | ... ... ... ... | 10 ounces |
| Acetate of soda | ... ... ... | 30 grains |
| Chloride of gold | ... ... ... | 1 grain. |

This bath should be made at least twenty-four hours before use, and may be used over and over, strengthening it with freshly made solution from time to time.

---

## THE NITRATE OF SILVER BATH.

The nitrate of silver bath, if properly made and kept, will generally keep in order a long time : but it is important to the photographer to be able to deal with the various disorders to which the bath is incident, so that he may not need to make a fresh solution every time the old one is a little deranged. It is important to use pure materials at the outset, and take care that the solution comes into contact with nothing which will contaminate it. Make it, to commence with, of a strength of thirty grains to the ounce for summer, and thirty-five grains, or forty, to the ounce for winter use. Iodize it, by leaving a large coated plate in for a few hours, or by the addition of two grains of iodide of potassium to each pint of solution. If it work foggy, neutralize with freshly precipitated oxide of silver, or carbonate of soda, and sun for a few hours. Then filter and try again, working it as nearly neutral as possible, adding, if acid be necessary, the smallest trace of nitric acid.

*Correcting the Bath.*—A bath which is constantly worked every day, will get out of order in a short time, from the same causes which deteriorate a moderately worked bath in a longer time. The defects of a deteriorated bath are various, and require different modes of treatment, which we shall notice.

*Streaks in the direction of the Dip, and Fog*, often proceed from the same cause—either alkalinity of the bath, or the presence of organic matter. If the addition of a little nitric acid do not remove the evil, the bath may be sunned. Sometimes the streaks arise from the accumulation of ether and alcohol, which seem to exercise a slightly solvent effect on the film of iodide of silver formed, and produce the streaks in the direction in which the plate moves. Evaporation by exposure in an open vessel, and gentle heat, or boiling down, is the remedy. Sometimes the presence of scum on the surface of the solution will produce streaks. Drawing a strip of paper across the surface of the solution most effectually removes such scum. Streaks will often be observed immediately after strengthening a bath with fresh silver or strong solution, and will disappear after working a few plates. The fresh solution, not being iodized, exercises a slight solvent action on the iodide of silver formed; and of course that action is shown in the direction in which the plate moves. The remedy is leaving a coated plate in the bath a short time.

*Pinholes and Spots.*—The causes of these annoying troubles are so numerous that they are not always easy to detect. The pinholes with tails to them may almost always be remedied by the use of a larger proportion of bromide in the collodion; but the small round holes, which seem most plentiful in the dense parts of the picture, are more difficult to deal with. Dust, either in the bath or camera, is a cause too obvious to be mentioned. Supersaturation with acetate of silver is an occasional cause, and one difficult to remedy; the best plan is to avoid adding acetic acid to the bath: continued exposure of the bath to strong sunlight is a partial remedy. The presence of oxalate of silver in the bath, arising from the use of old and partially decomposed collodion, is an occasional cause. When this is the case, the bath may be seen to be slightly turbid, and after standing a few hours, a precipitate will fall, and the bath will again give clean plates. The best remedy is to avoid the cause. The most common cause of pinholes is the well known accumulation of iodo-nitrate of silver in the bath from long use. The best remedy is to dilute the bath with an equal bulk of distilled water, which will cause a precipitate, which, being filtered out, the proper amount of nitrate of silver is added to make up the strength. There are probably some other causes not well understood. It is noticeable that these spots will often be troublesome in warm weather, and disappear in cold weather. They will sometimes appear chiefly in a bath with much accumulated alcohol, and disappear after evaporation. Rest will sometimes cure a bath; sunning frequently, and boiling down occasionally. In hot weather, keeping the bath in a vessel of cold water is often useful.

One remedy which has been found useful consists in the addition of a little pure cyanide of potassium in solution. Needle-like crystals, which were seen floating in the bath and clinging to the dipper, are dissolved, and impurities are carried down by the precipitate.

*Want or Excess of Density.*—Want of density, when caused by the nitrate bath, is generally accompanied by fog. It may be caused by excess of nitric acid; neutralizing is then the remedy. It may be from the formation in an old bath of acetic ether; carbonate of soda and sunning are the best remedies. It may be from impurities in the nitrate; for which neutralizing must be followed by sunning. Excess of density is often due to the presence of acetate of silver, or the accumulation of organic matter; sunning is a good remedy.

*Neutralizing an Acid Bath.*—Oxide of silver, made by adding a little of a solution of caustic potash to a solution of nitrate of silver, may be used. The brown precipitate, having been washed in two or three waters, is then added to the bath until it is decidedly turbid, the solution well agitated and left for a few hours before filtering. The addition of carbonate of soda, besides neutralizing the bath, produces another good effect; it throws down a precipitate which often takes with it any impurities present. A ten-grain solution of bicarbonate of soda should be kept ready as added, a few drops at a time, until a permanent turbidity or precipitate is formed, which is not redissolved on agitation.

*Adding Acid to an Alkaline or Neutral Bath.*—It is better to avoid the use of acetic acid as much as possible. Dilute nitric acid is the most convenient for use. A drachm of strong nitric acid in 4 ounces of distilled water is convenient for use, half a drachm of the dilute acid containing a fraction over a minim of strong acid. By the use of such a preparation acid can be conveniently added in infinitesimal proportions. After each addition of acid, the bath should be well stirred or agitated, and left to stand some time, as, if tried immediately after the addition, its full effect will not be perceptible.

*Sunning a Bath.*—The bath should generally be neutralized before sunning. If it can be done conveniently, it is best exposed in an open vessel, which permits evaporation at the same time. Where this is not convenient without danger to the solution, it may be exposed in a bottle: several hours' action of strong sunlight is desirable. The solution should be then filtered, and tried before adding acid, as it will frequently be found that, after neutralizing with carbonate of soda, and sunning, a bath will work well without any addition of acid.

*Evaporation and Boiling Down.*—The partial evaporation of excess of ether and alcohol may be effected by placing the solution, for some hours, in an open vessel, in a warm place, or over a water bath or sand bath, at a very low temperature. In order to effect the entire removal of all traces of spirit, or to remove acetic acid, it is necessary to boil down the solution to dryness. Many photographers rely on partial boiling down, as the best mode of removing almost all the ills a bath is heir to. The operation is one requiring great care. It may be effected in various ways. If partial boiling down only is intended, the solution may be placed in a well annealed flask, and supported in a retort stand; a spirit lamp with wire-gauze burner is then placed underneath, not too close at first. If boiling down to dryness be intended, the solution should be placed in an open glass dish, or evaporating basin, and placed over a water bath, the heat being raised gradually. A method may be improvised by placing the solution in the most convenient glass vessel which will stand in an ordinary open cooking vessel. The glass vessel must not stand on the bottom of the pan, but be supported by some means—if it rest on a piece of tile, it will do. The heat must be raised gradually. Well annealed vessels should always be used.

---

## MOUNTING PHOTOGRAPHS.

A THICK piece of plate-glass, cut to the required size and shape, is the best guide in shaping the picture, as it enables the manipulator to see exactly the position and amount of picture included. A sharp knife, or old razor, may be used to cut with; and a piece of glase to cut upon. The utmost neatness and skill in getting a clean cut edge, free from jaggedness, is imperative.

When the prints are very stiff and dry, it is difficult to cover them with the starch, without their curling up, and smearing the surface. To prevent this, take a clean sponge and damp a few dozen before pasting them, they will then lie perfectly flat, and cause no difficulty.

The qualities necessary in an adhesive material are that it should be easy to prepare, easy to use, efficient when used, and free from deleterious effect upon the photograph. Gum has the disadvantage, if thin, of sinking into the paper, and showing on the face of the picture. It has, moreover, the tendency to rapidly turn acid; and if used in this state, it injures the photograph. Making it with boiling water reduces the tendency to acidity or decomposition; and if made thus, and used sufficiently thick, it may be used without disadvantage. Of the various kinds of paste, that made of starch is preferable, and, if used fresh, is perfectly safe. The patent starch, in powder, and without the blue tint, is best. Take a teaspoonful of the powder, and put it into a common marmalade jar; this is then mixed with the smallest quantity of water, which will make it into a thick paste. When it is rubbed perfectly smooth, boiling water is poured on it, the whole being rapidly stirred

Sufficient boiling water is used to make a thick transparent jelly and one good teaspoonful of the powder will make a jarful of paste This will keep good a few days in summer, and longer in winter It is easily made, easily used, efficient, and will not, if used properly injure the photograph. Glue, gelatine, isinglass, &c., are used by some. Of these, good Scotch or Russian glue will be found best This, for persons only mounting occasionally, will be found troublesome to prepare and use, but it is very efficient and safe. The prints should be rolled after mounting to make them perfectly flat and give them a good surface.

## A CONCLUDING HINT.

Remember that cleanliness is the most important element in successful photography. Every dish, bottle, and vessel of any kind should be washed when it is done with. Never use the same vessels indiscriminately for various solutions; but keep each to its own use. Never keep dishes or bottles standing with old and useless solutions; throw them away at once, and wash the vessel Never keep bottles of anything unlabelled. Never let an accumulation of useless rubbish get gathered into the operating room Always dust the dark room a few hours before it is necessary to use it. Never keep a bad negative, but clean it off at once Never leave negatives in a printing frame, or standing about when not in use. Never use a dirty plate. In short, let cleanliness, order, care, and taste govern every operation; failure will then be impossible.

# PRICE LIST

AND

# ILLUSTRATED CATALOGUE

OF

## APPARATUS AND CHEMICAL PREPARATIONS

USED IN THE ART OF

# PHOTOGRAPHY:

COMPRISING THE

WET AND DRY COLLODION PROCESSES,

WAXED PAPER, CALOTYPE,

ALBUMEN, AND POSITIVE PAPER PROCESSES.

---

1863.

# PREFACE.

---

## MESSRS. BLAND & CO.,

In submitting the following Catalogue of Instruments, Apparatus, and Chemical Preparations used in the beautiful Art of Photography, to the notice of Amateurs and Photographers in general, would take this opportunity of stating, that nearly the whole of the Apparatus therein described is manufactured on the premises, under their own immediate superintendence; thereby insuring instruments with all the most recent improvements, and at very moderate prices.

They would further state that, for the better carrying out of experiments in Photography, and the testing of Photographic Lenses during the manufacture, they have erected a spacious Glass Room, in which every requisite for the illustration of the various processes, and trial of Lenses, will be found.

Purchasers of Apparatus, and others desiring information, will receive every instruction and explanation as to the manipulations and scientific principles involved in the various Photographic processes, either by letter or personally, at the establishment, No. 153, Fleet Street, London.

Orders from abroad, which should be accompanied by an order for payment in London, executed in the best manner and in the shortest possible time.

# Price List

OF

# PHOTOGRAPHIC APPARATUS.

Messrs. BLAND & CO. would mention with respect, that it is necessary that all orders be accompanied by a remittance, or order for payment in London, otherwise they cannot be forwarded. Attention to this particular will obviate delay and inconvenience. BLAND & Co. suggest that it is desirable when orders are sent from Abroad to them through an Agent, that the climate for which the Instruments are intended should be specified, in order that suitable Apparatus may be ensured, and also that the Agent be definitely instructed to procure the same from

## BLAND & CO.,

153, FLEET STREET, LONDON.

## International Exhibition, 1862.

No Medals were awarded in this Class for Photographic Apparatus.

HONOURABLE MENTION: BLAND AND CO.

AWARD OF JURORS: BLAND AND CO.;

For very excellent workmanship and arrangements, especially adapted for INDIA and FOREIGN CLIMATES.

"Bland and Co. attest what the English can do as makers of apparatus."—*Times*, *August* 8th, 1862.

# LENSES.

**Single Achromatic Lenses,** unmounted, suitable for taking views by Calotype or Collodion processes :—

| | Diameter. | Focus. | | £ | s. | d. |
|---|---|---|---|---|---|---|
| No. 1. | 1¼ inches | 4 to 6 inches | | 0 | 6 | 0 |
| 2. | 1½ „ | 6 to 7 „ | | 0 | 8 | 0 |
| 3. | 1¾ „ | 6 to 8 „ | | 0 | 10 | 0 |
| 4. | 2 „ | 8 to 10 „ | | 0 | 14 | 0 |
| 5. | 2¼ „ | 8 to 10 „ | | 0 | 17 | 0 |
| 6. | 2⅝ „ | 12 to 14 „ | | 1 | 5 | 0 |
| 7. | 3 „ | 12 to 15 „ | | 1 | 16 | 0 |
| 8. | 3½ „ | 12 to 16 „ | | 2 | 10 | 0 |
| 9. | 4 „ | 16 to 20 „ | | 3 | 10 | 0 |
| **Stereoscopic Lenses—** | | | | | | |
| No. 10. | 1¼ „ | 4½ & 6 „ | each | 0 | 6 | 0 |

## BLAND & CO.'S ACHROMATIC LANDSCAPE LENSES.

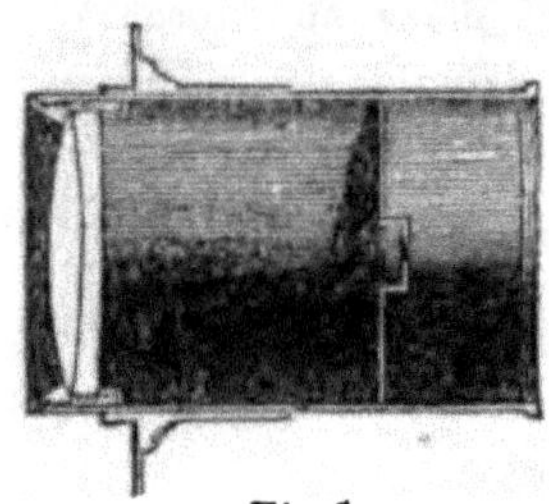

*Fig.* 1.

*Fig.* 2.

Mounted in handsome brass fronts, with rings for adaptation to Camera :—

| | Diameter. | Simple sliding Tube (*Fig.* 1). £ s. d. | For Pictures. | Rack and Pinion (*Fig.* 2) £ s. d. |
|---|---|---|---|---|
| No. 1. | 1¼ inches | 0 16 0 | 5 in. by 4 in. | 1 1 0 |
| 2. | 1½ „ | 1 1 0 | 5 in. by 4 in. | 1 6 0 |
| 3. | 1¾ „ | 1 5 0 | 6 „ by 5 „ | 1 11 6 |
| 4. | 2 „ | 1 12 0 | 6 „ by 5 „ | 2 2 0 |
| 5. | 2¼ „ | 1 15 0 | 7 „ by 6 „ | 2 7 0 |
| 6. | 2⅝ „ | 2 5 0 | 9 „ by 7 „ | 2 14 6 |
| 7. | 3 „ | 3 15 0 | 11 „ by 9 „ | 4 10 0 |
| 8. | 3½ „ | 4 12 6 | 12 „ by 10 „ | 6 0 0 |
| 9. | 4 „ | 6 10 0 | 15 „ by 12 „ | 7 7 0 |
| | Diameter. | Stereoscopic sliding Tube. | | Rack and Pinion. |
| No. 10. | 1¼ „ | 0 16 0 | | 1 1 0 |

*Fig.* 3.
Sectional view of Compound Achromatic Lens.

*Fig.* 4.

# BLAND & CO.'S

## COMPOUND ACHROMATIC LENSES FOR PORTRAITS,

*Fitted with set of Waterhouse's Central Diaphragms.* (*Fig.* 5.)

These combinations are particularly recommended for the qualities they possess of giving a flat field, and having their optical and chemical foci coincident, producing an image on the sensitive surface in an extremely short space of time.

Waterhouse's Stops. (*Fig.* 5.)

**Combination Achromatic Lenses,** mounted in handsome brass front, with rackwork adjustment, and adapted for either portraits or views:—

| FOR PICTURES | £ | s. | d. |
|---|---|---|---|
| No. 1. 4½ by 3¾ in. (*Fig.* 4.) . . | 2 | 15 | 0 |
| 2. arranged for views, 6 by 5 in. and portraits, 4¼ by 3¼ „ | 3 | 0 | 0 |
| 3. 5 by 4 in. . . . . . | 4 | 4 | 0 |
| 4. arranged for views, 7 by 6 „ and portraits, 5 by 4 „ | 4 | 10 | 0 |
| 5. 6 by 5 in. . . . . . | 5 | 10 | 0 |
| 6. arranged for views, 9 by 7 „ and portraits, 6 by 5 „ | 6 | 0 | 0 |
| 7. 8½ by 6½ in. . . . . | 11 | 16 | 0 |
| 8. arranged for views, 12 by 10 and portraits, 8½ by 6½ „ | 12 | 12 | 0 |

The arrangement of the above lenses for views consists in the removal of one lens in the combination, and placing the other in a different position in the sliding tube, with the requisite stops or diaphragms for regulating the amount of light.

# BLAND & CO.'S

## COMPOUND ACHROMATIC PORTRAIT LENSES,

*For Stereoscopic Portraits or Views, or for Carte de Visite Pictures.*

| | £ | s. | d. |
|---|---|---|---|
| No. 1. **For Stereoscopic Portraits and Views,** or Carte de Visite portraits, singly, fitted with Waterhouse's Central Stops . . . . . | 2 | 15 | 0 |
| No. 1 A. The above in pairs, with adjusting bar for caps of lenses, warranted of equal foci . . . | 5 | 12 | 6 |
| *** This lens is suitable for taking Carte de Visite pictures in an operating room of ordinary length, say from 12 to 14 feet. | | | |
| No. 2. Of larger size, suitable for a room 16 to 18 feet long, singly . . . . . . . . | 4 | 4 | 0 |
| No. 2 A. The above in pairs, warranted of equal foci, and connecting bar for caps . . . . | 8 | 10 | 0 |

---

## COMPOUND ACHROMATIC LENSES FOR PORTRAITS,

*With Rack and Pinion.*

*Fig.* 6.

| | | | £ | s. | d. |
|---|---|---|---|---|---|
| No. 1. For pictures, 4¼ by 3¼ inches (*Fig.* 5) | . | 14s. & | 1 | 1 | 0 |
| 2. " 6½ by 4¾ " . . . . | . | £2 & | 2 | 12 | 6 |
| 3. " 8½ by 6½ " . . . . | . | £5 & | 6 | 0 | 0 |

BLAND & CO. supply Lenses of all the most eminent British and Foreign manufacturers at the makers' prices, the list of a few of whom are subjoined:—

LIST OF

# ROSS'S PHOTOGRAPHIC PORTRAIT LENSES.

*The whole of these glasses give fine and correct definition, both at the centre and margin of the picture, and have their visual and chemical acting foci coincident.*

| | £ | s. | d. |
|---|---|---|---|
| No. 1. **Portrait lens,** consisting of two achromatic combinations, mounted in tubes with rack-and-pinion movement, the lenses 1¾ inch diameter, and 4½ inches focal length from the back glass, producing pictures on plates 4 by 3 inches and under. . . . . . . . . . | 5 | 0 | 0 |
| A set of Waterhouse's Diaphragms in morocco case, for ditto . . . . . . . . . . . | 0 | 15 | 0 |
| No. 2. Ditto, ditto, the lenses 2½ inches diameter and 6 focal length, for pictures on plates 5 by 4 inches and under . . . . . . . . . . | 8 | 0 | 0 |
| A set of Waterhouse's Diaphragms in morocco case, for ditto . . . . . . . . . . . | 1 | 0 | 0 |
| No. 2 **A.** Ditto, ditto, the lenses 2½ inches diameter and 7½ inches focal length, for pictures on plates 5 by 4 inches and under. This lens produces *larger portraits* than the above . . . . . . | 10 | 10 | 0 |
| A set of Waterhouse's Diaphragms in morocco case, for ditto . . . . . . . . . . . | 1 | 5 | 0 |

☞ *Either of the above lenses is suitable for "Cartes de Visite" portraits.*

| | £ | s. | d. |
|---|---|---|---|
| No. 3. Ditto, ditto, the lenses 3½ inches diameter and 10 inches focal length, for pictures on plates 6 by 5 inches and under . . . . . . . . . | 16 | 0 | 0 |
| A set of Waterhouse's Diaphragms in morocco case, for ditto . . . . . . . . . . . | 1 | 10 | 0 |
| No. 3 **A.** Ditto, ditto, the front lens 3½ inches diameter, the back lens 4 inches diameter, 12 inches focal length, for pictures on plates 8½ by 6½ inches and under. . . . . . . . . . . | 25 | 0 | 0 |
| A set of Waterhouse's Diaphragms in morocco case, for ditto . . . . . . . . . . . | 1 | 15 | 0 |

ROSS'S LIST (CONTINUED.)

| | £ | s. | d. |
|---|---|---|---|
| No. 4. Ditto, ditto, the lenses 4½ inches diameter, 15 inches focal length, for pictures on plates 10 by 8 inches and under . . . . . . . . | 36 | 0 | 0 |
| A set of Waterhouse's Diaphragms in morocco case, for ditto . . . . . . . . . . . | 2 | 0 | 0 |
| No. 4 A. Ditto, ditto, the front lens 3½ inches diameter, the back lens 5 inches diameter, 20 inches focal length, for pictures on plates 16 by 14 inches and under . . . . . . . . . . | 30 | 0 | 0 |
| A set of Waterhouse's Diaphragms in morocco case, for ditto . . . . . . . . . . . | 2 | 5 | 0 |
| A Portrait Lens, 5 inch diameter, 20 inches focal length, for pictures on plates 18 by 16 and under, with set of Waterhouse's Diaphragms in morocco case | 42 | 10 | 0 |
| A Ditto, ditto, 6 inches diameter, 24 inches focal length, for pictures on plates 22 by 18 and under, with set of Waterhouse's Diaphragms in morocco case | 54 | 0 | 0 |
| A Portrait lens producing with the whole aperture pictures of a size for Locket plates 1½ by 1 inch, and with the diaphragm 3¼ by 2¾ inches . . | 6 | 0 | 0 |
| A set of Waterhouse's Diaphragms in morocco case, for ditto . . . . . . . . . . . | 1 | 0 | 0 |

## ROSS'S QUICK-ACTING "CARTES DE VISITE" LENSES.

These Lenses are constructed to give the flattest possible field *consistent with good marginal definition*, and have their chemical and visual foci coincident. They also reproduce the images of objects in their true perspective places.

| | £ | s. | d. |
|---|---|---|---|
| No. 1. **"Cartes de Visite" lens,** consisting of two actinic combinations, 1¾ inches diameter, 4¼ inches focal length, with rack-and-pinion movement, and Waterhouse's Diaphragms. This lens requires from 13 to 14 feet between the subject and the focusing-screen of Camera . . . . | 5 | 15 | 0 |
| No. 2. Ditto, ditto, 2$\frac{1}{16}$ inches diameter, 4¾ inches focal length, with rack-and-pinion movement and Waterhouse's Diaphragms. This lens requires from 15 to 16 feet between the subject and the focussing-screen of Camera . . . . . | 6 | 10 | 0 |

ROSS'S LIST (CONTINUED.)

| | | £ | s. | d. |
|---|---|---|---|---|
| No. 3. | Ditto, ditto, 2½ inches diameter 6 inches focal length, with rack-and-pinion movement and Waterhouse's Diaphragms. This lens requires from 19 to 20 feet between the subject and focussing-screen of Camera . . . . . | 11 | 10 | 0 |

The following table, shewing the greatest distance required between the subject and the focussing screen to produce figures 2¾ inches and 3 inches with each of the Lenses (the standard being 6 feet), is given as a guide to Photographers in their selection of a lens suitable for the length of their operating rooms:

| | For 2¾ in. | For 3 in. |
|---|---|---|
| No. 1 Lens ... ... | 14 feet ... ... | 13¼ feet. |
| No. 2 Lens ... ... | 16 feet ... ... | 14¾ feet. |
| No. 3 Lens ... ... | 20 feet ... ... | 18¾ feet. |

In order that the whole image may be in focus, the Camera should be placed level and midway of the subject, or thereabout; however, some little latitude may be allowed, and the Camera placed somewhat higher, when it will require tilting a little. But if the Camera be put at an elevation of about 5 feet, it must be tilted considerably, and a swing-back to the Camera will be indispensable to get the picture all in focus.

---

## ROSS'S PHOTOGRAPHIC LANDSCAPE LENSES.

| | | £ | s. | d. |
|---|---|---|---|---|
| No. 1 A. | **Landscape lens,** consisting of one achromatic combination, mounted in tubes, with rack-and-pinion movement, the lens 2 inches in diameter and 9 inches focal length, for producing pictures 6 by 5 inches . . . . . | 4 | 0 | 0 |
| No. 1. | Ditto, ditto, without rack-and-pinion movement. | 3 | 0 | 0 |
| No. 2. | Ditto, ditto, 2½ inches diameter, 12 inches focal length, for pictures 8½ by 6½ inches . . . . | 5 | 10 | 0 |
| No. 2. | Ditto, ditto, without rack-and-pinion movement. | 4 | 10 | 0 |
| No. 3. | Ditto, ditto, 3 inches diameter, 15 inches focal length, for pictures 10 by 8 inches . . . . | 6 | 10 | 0 |
| No. 3. | Ditto, without rack-and-pinion movement . . | 5 | 10 | 0 |
| No. 3 A. | A ditto, ditto, 3½ inches diameter and 18 inches focal length, for pictures 12 by 10 inches . . | 8 | 0 | 0 |
| No. 3 A. | A ditto, without rack-and-pinion movement . | 7 | 0 | 0 |

ROSS'S LIST (CONTINUED.)

| | | £ | s. | d. |
|---|---|---|---|---|
| No. 4. | Ditto, ditto, 4 inches diameter, 20 inches focal length, for pictures 15 by 12 inches. In consequence of the length of the Camera, this requires an universal joint handle to rack-and-pinion movement . . . . . . . | 12 | 0 | 0 |
| No. 4. | Ditto, ditto, without rack-and-pinion movement | 10 | 0 | 0 |
| No. 5. | Ditto, ditto, 5 inches diameter, 25 inches focal length, for pictures 18 by 16 inches, without rack-and-pinion movement. . . . . | 14 | 0 | 0 |
| No. 6. | Ditto, ditto, 6 inches diameter, 30 inches focal length, for pictures 22 by 20 inches . . . | 22 | 0 | 0 |
| No. 7. | Ditto, ditto, 7 inches diameter, 35 inches focal length, for pictures 24 by 22 inches . . . | 28 | 0 | 0 |
| No. 8. | Ditto, ditto, 8 inches diameter, 40 inches focal length, for pictures 26 by 24 inches . . . | 32 | 0 | 0 |

## ROSS'S STEREOGRAPHIC LENSES.

| | £ | s. | d. |
|---|---|---|---|
| A Stereographic Double Lens for Portraits, Groups, Views, and Interiors, Diameter of front combination 1 3/16 inch, of back ditto 1 7/16 inch, 3½ inches focal length. This lens has a rack-and-pinion movement, a set of Waterhouse's Diaphragms. and works INSTANTANEOUSLY . | 4 | 0 | 0 |
| Ditto, ditto, without rack-and-pinion . . . . . | 3 | 8 | 0 |
| An extra back combination can be supplied to the above for producing small "Cartes de Visite" pictures | 1 | 2 | 6 |
| A Stereographic Single Lens for Views, &c., 4½ inches focal length, 1 inch diameter . . . . . | 1 | 8 | 0 |
| Ditto, ditto, ditto, with rack-and-pinion. . . . . | 2 | 0 | 0 |
| A ditto, ditto, 6 inches focal length, 1 3/16 inch diameter . | 1 | 8 | 0 |
| Ditto, ditto, ditto, with rack-and-pinion . . . . | 2 | 0 | 0 |
| A pair of ditto, ditto, of either 4½ or 6 inches focal length, with combined rack motion and connecting bars to caps . . . . . . . . . . . | 4 | 5 | 0 |

*** Larger and smaller Photographic combinations to order.

## ROSS'S ORTHOGRAPHIC LENSES,

*With complete set of Waterhouse's Diaphragms,*

FOR

GROUPS, LANDSCAPES, AND ARCHITECTURAL SUBJECTS.

*The interiors exhibited by* Mr. Bedford, *which have been so highly eulogised by the* Times *and other leading Journals, were taken by the Orthographic Lens, with the whole aperture, on plates of the full dimensions which this Lens is advertised to cover.*

| Size of Picture. | Size of Group. | Diameter of Front Lens. | Back Focus. | PRICE. Rigid Setting. | | | PRICE. Sliding Tube Adjustment. | | | PRICE. Sliding Tube with Rack and Pinion. | | |
|---|---|---|---|---|---|---|---|---|---|---|---|---|
| in. in. | in. in. | in. | in. | £ | s. | d. | £ | s. | d. | £ | s. | d. |
| 6 × 5 | 4 × 3 | $\frac{9}{16}$ | 8 | 3 | 15 | 0 | 4 | 5 | 6 | 4 | 17 | 6 |
| 8½ × 6½ | 6 × 5 | 1¼ | 10½ | 4 | 12 | 6 | 5 | 4 | 6 | 6 | 0 | 0 |
| 10 × 8 | 7½ × 5½ | 1½ | 14 | 5 | 15 | 5 | 6 | 10 | 0 | 7 | 10 | 0 |
| 12 × 10 | 8½ × 6½ | 1$\frac{3}{16}$ | 16½ | 7 | 0 | 0 | 7 | 18 | 6 | 8 | 18 | 6* |
| 15 × 12 | 10 × 8 | 2¼ | 19½ | 8 | 0 | 0 | 9 | 5 | 0 | 10 | 5 | 0 |
| 18 × 16 | 12 × 10 | 3 | 26 | 12 | 12 | 0 | | | | | | |
| 22 × 20 | 15 × 12 | 3$\frac{6}{16}$ | 31½ | 17 | 0 | 0 | | | | | | |
| 25 × 21 | 18 × 16 | 4 | 34 | 21 | 0 | 0 | | | | | | |

* Hook's universal joint handle, for 12 × 10 and 15 × 12 lenses, price £1 0 0.

## SUTTON'S PATENT PANORAMIC LANDSCAPE LENSES AND CAMERAS,

(*Fig.* 7.)

| | £ | s. | d |
|---|---|---|---|
| Lens Camera, with screw adjustment, plate-holder and focussing-screen, water-tight gutta-percha bath, dipper, frame for holding plates while cleaning, box for one dozen curved plates, printing press and tripod stand, in varnished pine case, for pictures on plates 10½ by 5 inches (see page 15) | 22 | 0 | 0 |

| | | | | £ | s. | d. |
|---|---|---|---|---|---|---|
| Ditto, ditto, for pictures | 14 by 6½ inches | . . . | | 30 | 0 | 0 |
| Ditto, ditto, | „ 17 by 8 „ | . . . | | 40 | 0 | 0 |
| Ditto, ditto, | „ 20 by 10 „ | . . . | | 60 | 0 | 0 |

**These Lenses include an angle of 100 degrees, or about three times the usual amount of subject,**

**Water-tight Porcelain Baths, in Mahogany cases, may be had for above.**

---

## ROSS'S NEW ACTINIC TRIPLETS,

***For Architectural Subjects, Copying, and Landscapes.***

**These Lenses produce undistorted images, and have the central and marginal pencils most carefully corrected.**

**Photographers will find these Lenses invaluable for copying maps, charts, prints, architectural and other subjects, where straightness of marginal lines is imperative.**

**The Combination is so constructed that GROUPS may be taken with the *whole aperture* on a plate the next size smaller than that tabulated below.**

**The diaphragms are arranged in a closer series than has hitherto been the case, so that the time of exposure is more under the command of the operator; thus, with each diaphragm the exposure is to be half as long again as with the diaphragm of the next larger size.**

**The prices quoted below are for Triplets in sliding tubes, with complete set of Waterhouse's Diaphragms. For rack-and-pinion movement to Triplets from 6 by 5 to 15 by 12, inclusive, 15s. additional will be charged; larger sizes, £1. Hook's joint handle, £1.**

| Size of Plates. | Back Focus. | Price. | | |
|---|---|---|---|---|
| 6 by 5 and 7¼ by 4½ | 7 | £4 | 0 | 0 |
| 8 by 4½ | 8 | 4 | 5 | 0 |
| 8½ by 6½ | 10 | 5 | 0 | 0 |
| 10 by 8 and 11 by 9 | 12½ | 7 | 0 | 0 |
| 12 by 10 | 15 | 8 | 10 | 0 |
| 15 by 12 | 18 | 10 | 10 | 0 |
| 18 by 16 | 22 | 12 | 10 | 0 |
| 22 by 20 | 28 | 16 | 0 | 0 |
| 25 by 21 | 30 | 20 | 0 | 0 |
| 30 by 24 | 34 | 25 | 0 | 0 |

1. Panoramic Lens and Camera on Folding Tripod Stand.
2. Grooved Box for one dozen Curved Plates.
3. Holder for Plates while being cleaned.
4. Water-tight Bath, with Dipper.
5. Printing Frame.

*Fig.* 7.

LIST OF

## LEREBOUR'S COMPOUND ACHROMATIC PORTRAIT LENSES.

| | | | £ | s. | d. |
|---|---|---|---|---|---|
| No. 1. | For portraits, | 3¼ by 2¾ inches . . . . | 1 | 10 | 0 |
| 2. | „ | 4¼ by 3¼ „ . . . . . | 2 | 10 | 0 |
| 3. | „ | 6½ by 4¾ „ . . . . . | 4 | 0 | 0 |
| 4. | „ | 8½ by 6½ „ . . . . . | 9 | 0 | 0 |
| 5. | „ | 8½ by 6½ „ extra quick, diameter of lenses, 3½ inches . . | 15 | 0 | 0 |
| 6. | „ | 10 by 8 in., diameter of lenses, 4 inches . . . . . . | 25 | 0 | 0 |

---

## LEREBOUR'S SINGLE ACHROMATIC VIEW LENSES,

*With Sliding Tube Adjustment.*

| | | | £ | s. | d. |
|---|---|---|---|---|---|
| No. 1. | For landscapes, | 5 by 4 inches . . . . | 1 | 5 | 0 |
| 2. | „ | 7 by 6 „ . . . . . | 1 | 15 | 0 |
| 3. | „ | 9 by 7 „ . . . . . | 3 | 10 | 0 |
| 4. | „ | 11 by 9 „ . . . . . | 6 | 0 | 0 |
| 5. | „ | 12 by 10 „ . . . . . | 9 | 0 | 0 |

---

LIST OF

## JAMIN'S COMPOUND ACHROMATIC LENSES,

*With Rack-and-Pinion Adjustment.*

| | | | £ | s. | d. |
|---|---|---|---|---|---|
| No. 1. | For portraits, | 4¼ by 3¼ inches . . . . . | 1 | 5 | 0 |
| 2. | „ | 6½ by 4¾ „ . . . . . | 4 | 4 | 0 |
| 3. | „ | 8½ by 6½ „ . . . . . | 7 | 0 | 0 |
| 4. | „ | 10 by 8, with centralizing cone and focal variations of coincidence for portrait and landscape, lenses 4 inches diameter. with 2 sets of racks and pinions | 25 | 0 | 0 |
| 5. | „ | 14 by 12, lens 5 inches diameter . | 37 | 10 | 0 |

# REDUCED PRICE LIST

OF THE

# NEW PHOTOGRAPHIC LENSES

## FOR PORTRAITS AND VIEWS,

WITH

COINCIDENCE OF THE VISUAL AND CHEMICAL FOCI,

MANUFACTURED BY

## VOIGTLÄNDER & SON,

VIENNA AND BRUNSWICK.

| | | £ | *s.* | *d.* |
|---|---|---|---|---|
| No. **A.** | Consists of a combination of Achromatic Lenses $1\frac{13}{16}$ in. and $1\frac{7}{8}$ in. diameter, the combined focus being, with regard to the size of the picture, the same as a simple Achromatic Lens of $6\frac{5}{8}$ in. focus, in brass mounting, with central stops, and rack-and-pinion adjustment, adapted for taking pictures on $4\frac{15}{16}$ in. plates . . . | 7 | 2 | 6 |
| No. **B.** | Consists of a combination of Achromatic Lenses $2\frac{1}{8}$ in. and $2\frac{3}{16}$ in. diameter, the combined focus being $6\frac{5}{8}$ in., in brass mounting, with central stops, and rack-and-pinion adjustment, suited for taking pictures on $4\frac{15}{16}$ in. plates. This combination commands great power of light. It is a very quick acting instrument, and is particularly adapted for taking portraits of Children. . . . . . . . . | 8 | 17 | 6 |
| No. **C.** | Consists of a combination of Achromatic Lenses $2\frac{9}{16}$ in. and $2\frac{5}{8}$ in. diameter, the combined focus being $9\frac{5}{8}$ in., brass mounting, with central stops, and rack-and-pinion adjustment, adapted for taking pictures up to $7\frac{1}{4}$ in. . . . . . | 12 | 0 | 0 |

The Lenses marked **A. B. C.** are specially constructed for taking "**Carte de Visite**" pictures, and will be found to answer better for that purpose than any hitherto in use. These Lenses will of course take portraits as well.

VOIGTLÄNDERS' LIST (CONTINUED.)

Nos. **A.** and **B.** will take perfect pictures of the "**Carte de Visite**" size in a glasshouse of 17 feet.

Specimens (to be returned) will be forwarded on application.

Any of the above Lenses may be had in sets of two, four, or six, all of exactly the same foci.

---

| | | £ | s. | d. |
|---|---|---|---|---|
| No. **1.** | Consists of a combination of Achromatic Lenses $1\frac{3}{16}$ in. and $1\frac{5}{8}$ in. diameter, the combined focus being $5\frac{3}{4}$ in., in brass mounting, with rack-and-pinion adjustment, adapted for taking pictures on $\frac{1}{6}$ in. and $\frac{1}{4}$ in. plates, or up to $4\frac{1}{4}$ in. by $3\frac{1}{4}$ in. . . . . . . . . . | 4 | 15 | 0 |
| No. **1a.** | The above, with central stops . . . . | 5 | 10 | 0 |
| | These Lenses can be had in pairs of precisely the same focal length for taking Stereoscopic Portraits and groups of figures from life, and are the best that can be obtained for that purpose. | | | |
| No. **2.** | Consists of a combination of Achromatic Lenses, $2\frac{1}{8}$ in. and $2\frac{3}{16}$ in. diameter, the combined focus being $7\frac{1}{2}$ in., in brass mounting, with rack-and-pinion adjustment, suited for taking pictures on $\frac{1}{2}$, $\frac{1}{4}$, $\frac{1}{6}$ in. plates, or up to $6\frac{1}{2}$ in. by $4\frac{3}{4}$ in. . | 7 | 7 | 6 |
| No. **2a.** | The above, with central stops . . . . | 8 | 2 | 6 |
| | This Lens takes very beautiful "**Carte de Visite**" portraits, but it requires a glasshouse 21 feet long. | | | |
| No. **3.** | Consists of a combination of Achromatic Lenses, $3\frac{1}{8}$ in. and $3\frac{3}{16}$ in. diameter, the combined focus being $11\frac{1}{2}$ in., brass mounting, with rack-and-pinion adjustment, adapted for taking pictures 8 in. by 6 in. This is the most useful Lens that a photographer, whether amateur or artist, can possess . . . . . . . . | 14 | 0 | 0 |
| No. **3a.** | The above, with central stops . . . . | 15 | 0 | 0 |
| No. **4a.** | Consists of a combination of Achromatic Lenses, $3\frac{1}{8}$ in. and $3\frac{3}{16}$ in. diameter, the combined focus being $8\frac{7}{16}$ in., in brass mounting, with rack-and-pinion adjustment, and central stops, suited for pictures up to $6\frac{1}{2}$ in. by $4\frac{3}{4}$ in. This combination commands an immense power of light, and works *in a third* less time than Nos. 1, 2, 3 . . | 22 | 0 | 0 |

VOIGTLÄNDER'S LIST (CONTINUED.)

| No. | Description | £ | s. | d. |
|---|---|---|---|---|
| No. 5a. | Consists of a combination of Achromatic Lenses of the respective diameters of $3\frac{1}{8}$ in. and $2\frac{9}{16}$ in., the combined focus being $2\frac{5}{16}$ in., in brass mounting, with rack-and-pinion adjustment, and central stops, suited for taking pictures up to $3\frac{1}{4}$ in. by $2\frac{3}{4}$ in. This short focus, combined with the large aperture, enables it to command an intensity of light four times greater than any other. It is admirably adapted for taking portraits in private rooms not generally suited for the purpose, as also portraits of children. Good pictures can be taken with it in very dull weather . . . . . . . . | 22 | 0 | 0 |
| No. 6. | Consists of a combination of Achromatic Lenses of the respective diameters of $4\frac{3}{16}$ in. and $4\frac{1}{4}$ in., the combined focus being $14\frac{5}{8}$ in., in brass mounting, with central stops, suited for taking portraits and pictures from life, on plates of 12 in. . . . . . . . . . | 33 | 0 | 0 |
| No. 7. | Consists of a combination of Achromatic Lenses of the same diameter as No. 6, and mounted in a similar manner, but the combined focus of the Lenses being longer, viz., equal in effect to a single lens of $18\frac{3}{8}$ in., is suited for taking portraits on $13\frac{1}{2}$ in. plates . . . . . | 33 | 0 | 0 |
| No. 8. | Consists of a combination of Achromatic Lenses of the respective diameters of $5\frac{1}{4}$ in. and $5\frac{7}{16}$ in., mounted in brass. The combined focus is equal to a single lens of $22\frac{5}{8}$ in.; it will, therefore, take portraits on plates of 16 in. For small portraits this Lens can be used with its full aperture; but for larger ones or for groups, it is advisable to employ one or other of the stops . | 62 | 0 | 0 |
| No. 9. | This new combination consists of an arrangement of Achromatic Lenses of $6\frac{3}{8}$ in. and $6\frac{5}{8}$ in. diameter, the combined focus being 27 in. in brass mounting, with central stops, adapted for taking pictures on $19\frac{1}{8}$ in. plates . . . . . | 87 | 10 | 0 |

## LENSES OF THE LATEST CONSTRUCTION OF LONG FOCI.

| No. | Description | £ | s. | d. |
|---|---|---|---|---|
| No. 10. | Consists of a combination of Achromatic Lenses of $3\frac{1}{8}$ in. and $3\frac{3}{16}$ in. diameter, the combined focus being $14\frac{5}{8}$ in. in brass mounting, without rack and pinion, and without central stops, adapted for taking pictures on 12 in. plates . . . | 11 | 0 | 0 |

VOIGTLÄNDER'S LIST (CONTINUED.)

| | £ | s. | d. |
|---|---|---|---|
| **No. 11.** Consists of a combination of Achromatic Lenses of $4\frac{3}{16}$ in. and $4\frac{1}{4}$ in. diameter, the combined focus being $22\frac{5}{8}$ in. in brass mounting, without rack and pinion, and without central stops, adapted for taking pictures on 16 in. plates . . . | 27 | 10 | 0 |
| **No. 12.** Consists of a combination of Achromatic Lenses of $5\frac{1}{4}$ in. and $5\frac{7}{16}$ in. diameter, the combined focus being 27 in., in brass mounting, without rack and pinion, and without central stops, adapted for taking pictures on $19\frac{1}{8}$ in. plates . | 50 | 0 | 0 |
| **No. 13.** Consists of a combination of Achromatic Lenses of $6\frac{3}{8}$ and $6\frac{5}{8}$ in. diameter, the combined focus being 35 in., in brass mounting, without rack and pinion, and without central stops, adapted for taking pictures on $23\frac{3}{4}$ in. plates . . . | 67 | 10 | 0 |

*** The focus given in all the above Lenses must be understood as measuring from the centre of the combination.

A separate mounting can be furnished for using the front Lens of any of the portrait combinations, for taking views and objects of still-life; though the Orthoscopic Lenses are very much better for the purpose.

---

## The attention of Photographers is directed to the following Observations, which may serve to Guide them in the selection of Portrait Lenses:—

Voigtländer & Son's Lenses, Nos. 1 to 6 inclusive, as well as Nos. A. B. and C. have much more light, on account of their short foci, than common Lenses of the same diameters, and for this reason do not produce as large pictures. This apparent disadvantage will, however, to the greater part be remedied by the application of central stops, by which at a proportionately small loss of light, a larger picture, and greater depth is obtained.

All acquainted with the subject know, that the greatest difficulty in constructing a Lens, is to obtain a large, flat, and well-lighted picture, and it is this latter quality which the Lenses of Voigtländer and Son are known to possess to so great an extent, that is most appreciated by thoroughly practical Photographers.

To meet the wishes of those, however, who desire large pictures, Voigtländer & Son have constructed a new series of Lenses of long foci, Nos. 10, 11, 12, and 13. The foci of these Lenses being longer than the others of the same diameter, *a larger picture* and *greater depth* is obtained, certainly at some sacrifice of light, but yet these Lenses will be found to possess more light and greater sharpness of definition, than any other Lenses of the same diameter and foci.

The Lenses with long foci being much more easily constructed than the ordinary kind, are offered at a very much reduced price, to which the notice of Photographers is particularly called.

The relative power of light of Voigtländer's Lenses may be stated thus, Nos. A. C. 1, 2, 3, and 6, have the same amount of so-called normal light; Nos. B. and 4 have one-third more; No. 5, four times the amount; Nos. 7 and 8, one-third less; and Nos. 10, 11, 12, and 13, about one-half.

---

THE

# ORTHOSCOPIC PHOTOGRAPHIC LENSES

## FOR VIEWS, ETC.

These newly constructed Photographic Lenses, to which Voigtländer and Son have given the name Orthoscopic (correct showing), are especially intended for taking views, copying maps, plans, pictures, and works of art, and all other inanimate objects. With a good light and sensitive chemicals, Portraits may be taken; but this is not the purpose for which the Orthoscopic Lenses are intended.

This new combination consists, like the Portrait Lenses, of two Achromatics, but it differs from them in this particular, that both the Lenses are not Collecting Lenses, but the back or smaller one is a Dispersing Lens. The great advantages gained by this improvement over the simple Achromatic Lenses hitherto employed for taking inanimate objects, views, &c., are the larger field, the increased amount of light, better perspective in the picture, and a greater degree of sharpness of the various objects placed at different distances.

The putting together and mounting of the Lenses is similar to the portrait combinations, but without any rack and pinion. The aperture of the front Lens is never stopped, as is the case with the usual View Lenses, but left perfectly open. The small back Lens is provided with stops of four different apertures, increasing more or less the sharpness of the picture at the sacrifice of light, consequently increasing the time of exposure.

## SIZES AND PRICES OF THE ORTHOSCOPIC VIEW LENSES.

| No. | Front Lens. | Focus. | Size of Picture. | Price Complete. | | | Price without Front Lens. | | |
|---|---|---|---|---|---|---|---|---|---|
| | | | | £ | s. | d. | £ | s. | d. |
| 1 | 1$\frac{9}{16}$ in. | 11½ in. | 10 × 8 | 4 | 5 | 0 | 2 | 17 | 6 |
| 2 | 2$\frac{1}{8}$ in. | 15 in. | 15 × 11 | 6 | 5 | 0 | 3 | 15 | 0 |
| 3 | 3$\frac{1}{8}$ in. | 24 in. | 21 × 15 | 11 | 0 | 0 | 6 | 10 | 0 |
| 4 | 4$\frac{3}{16}$ in. | 32½ in. | 26 × 21 | 20 | 10 | 0 | 9 | 5 | 0 |
| 5 | 4$\frac{3}{16}$ in. | 40 in. | 33 × 26 | 20 | 10 | 0 | 9 | 5 | 0 |
| 6 | 5¼ in. | 50 in. | 42 × 33 | 31 | 10 | 0 | 13 | 0 | 0 |

| | £ | s. | d. |
|---|---|---|---|
| Orthoscopic Lenses, constructed expressly for taking Stereographs, combined focus 4½ in. with two Achromatics of $\frac{5}{8}$ and $\frac{13}{32}$ in..; mounted in such a manner that, when used in pairs for one and the same Camera and focussing screen, they may be adjusted to coincide perfectly | 3 | 7 | 6 |

These new Lenses are made of six different sizes,—the front Lens corresponding with the front Lens of the following Portrait combinations:—No. 1, 1$\frac{9}{16}$ in. diameter; No. 2, 2$\frac{1}{8}$; No. 3, 3$\frac{1}{8}$; No. 6, 4$\frac{3}{16}$; No. 7, 4$\frac{3}{16}$, long focus; No. 8, 5¼. The screws also agree. By this arrangement, those parties possessing either of the portrait combinations can be supplied with the brass mounting and small back Lens, only using their own front Lens, and thereby saving a very considerable cost.

## OBSERVATIONS.

The two glasses of the back Lens are not fixed in the mounting, in order to be able to clean them when necessary; but great care must be taken to replace them in their respective positions. The double concave Lens, with its flatter side downwards, first, then the concave convex Lens, the concave side down; the ring must not be screwed down too tight.

To focus with these Lenses when there is a want of light, it should be done with the full aperture; then the focussing screen of the Camera is lifted up, and the cap with an appropriate stop, is pushed on to the mount of the back Lens.

With regard to the size of the pictures as stated in the foregoing List of Prices, it must be understood that the smaller sizes can be obtained for objects very near, for instance, when copying prints, &c., whilst for views it will be possible to get the larger sized picture.

As each Lens is examined and tested under the personal superintendence of Messrs. Voigtländer & Son, just previous to the instruments being packed for this country, the possibility of any *(however slightly)* imperfect Lenses being received is quite *precluded.*

*Fig.* 8.

## TRUNK CAMERA FOR OPERATING ROOM.

*Fig.* 8.

Best Spanish mahogany or teak wood French-polished rigid square trunk Camera, with long-screw adjustment, enabling the operator to use lenses of different focal lengths; and for copying, with swinging back, for bringing objects at various distances into correct focus. 1 Single back, inner loose frames, and focussing screen.

| | | Plain. | | | Framed and Panelled. Extra. | | | Brass Bound. Extra. | | |
|---|---|---|---|---|---|---|---|---|---|---|
| | | £ | s. | d. | £ | s. | d. | £ | s. | d. |
| No. 1. for plates | 8½ by 6½ | 11 | 0 | 0 | 3 | 3 | 0 | 1 | 10 | 0 |
| No. 2. „ | 11 by 9 | 12 | 10 | 0 | 3 | 13 | 6 | 1 | 15 | 0 |
| No. 3. „ | 12 by 10 | 14 | 10 | 0 | 4 | 4 | 0 | 2 | 0 | 0 |
| No. 4. „ | 14 by 12 | 17 | 10 | 0 | 6 | 6 | 0 | 2 | 10 | 0 |
| No. 5. „ | 18 by 16 | 25 | 10 | 0 | 8 | 8 | 0 | 3 | 10 | 0 |

*Fig*, 9.

## SLIDING BODY OR EXPANDING CAMERA FOR OPERATING ROOM.

*Fig*. 9.

Best Spanish mahogany or teak wood, French-polished, square, sliding body Camera, with inner body panelled, and screw adjustment working from side of Camera. Swing back, rising front. 1 single back, 3 inner loose frames, and focussing screen.

| | | Plain. | | | | Brass Binding. Extra. | | |
|---|---|---|---|---|---|---|---|---|
| | | £ | s. | d. | | £ | s. | d. |
| No. 1. | for plates 8½ by 6½ . | 11 | 10 | 0 | . | 1 | 8 | 6 |
| No. 2. | „ 10 by 8 | 13 | 10 | 0 | . | 2 | 0 | 0 |
| No. 3. | „ 11 by 9 | 15 | 0 | 0 | . | 2 | 7 | 6 |
| No. 4. | „ 12 by 10 | 17 | 10 | 0 | . | 3 | 0 | 0 |
| *No. 5.* | „ 15 by 12 | 21 | 0 | 0 | . | 3 | 10 | 0 |

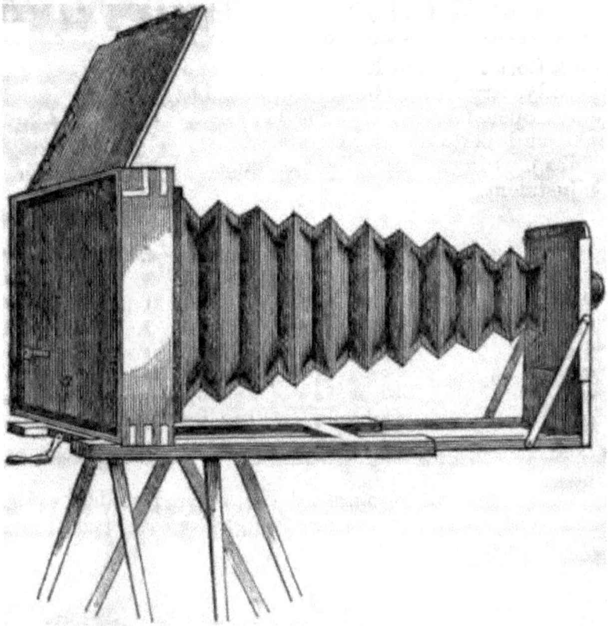

*Fig.* 10.

*Fig.* 11.

# BLAND & CO.'S IMPROVED KINNEAR'S CAMERA.

ANY OF THE LENSES IN THE FOREGOING LISTS CAN BE ADDED TO THIS CAMERA.

BLAND & Co.'s improved Kinnear's form of Camera with conical bellows' body, very light, strong, and portable, *Fig.* 10, represents the Camera open for use; and *Fig* 11, when closed up, forming a very light and portable package (a 10 by 8 Camera, weighiug about 7 lbs.). Single back, 2 loose frames, focussing screen, and screw adjustment.

| | | | Plain. | | | Brass Binding. Extra. | | |
|---|---|---|---|---|---|---|---|---|
| | | | £ | s. | d. | £ | s. | d. |
| No. 1. | for plates | 7 by 6 | 4 | 15 | 0 | 0 | 15 | 0 |
| No. 2. | " | 9 by 7 | 5 | 10 | 0 | 1 | 0 | 0 |
| No. 3. | " | 10 by 8 | 6 | 10 | 0 | 1 | 2 | 6 |
| No. 4. | " | 11 by 9 | 7 | 7 | 0 | 1 | 7 | 6 |
| No. 5. | " | 12 by 10 | 8 | 15 | 0 | 1 | 10 | 0 |
| No. 6. | " | 15 by 12 | 10 | 0 | 0 | 1 | 15 | 0 |
| No. 7. | " | 18 by 16 | 16 | 0 | 0 | 2 | 5 | 0 |

The above Cameras can be supplied with swing backs at an extra rate.

For India, B. & C. recommend the bellows to be of Russia leather to resist ravages of insects, though the cost is considerably increased thereby.

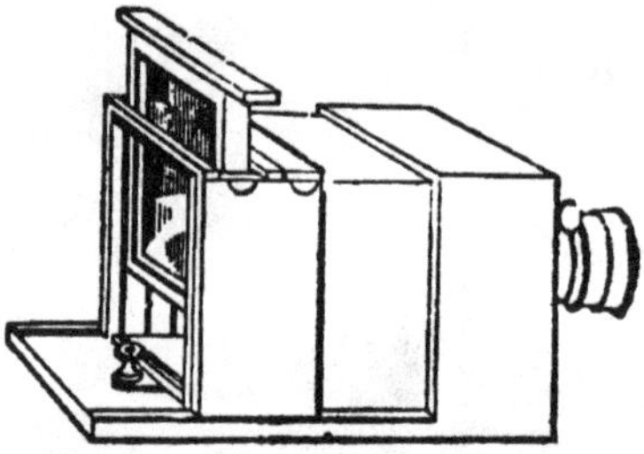

*Fig.* 12.

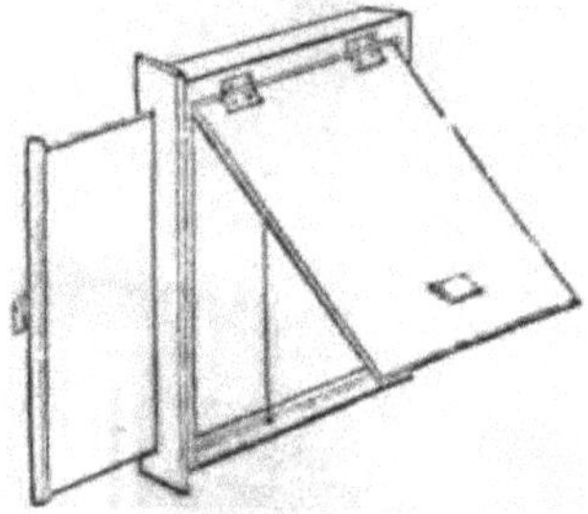

*Fig.* 13.

## SLIDING BODY OR EXPANDING CAMERAS,

*Of ordinary Construction, for Portraits by the Collodion Process.*

| | | £ | s. | d. |
|---|---|---|---|---|
| No. 1. | **Square sliding body Camera** (*Fig.* 12), of French-polished Honduras mahogany, with 1 single back (*Fig.* 13), 5 inches square, with 2 loose frames, for pictures 4¼ by 3¼, and 3¼ *by* 2¾, and focussing screen | 1 | 5 | 0 |

| | | £ | s. | d. |
|---|---|---|---|---|
| No. 1A. | Ditto, ditto, ditto of best Spanish mahogany, with rising front of superior make . . . | 1 | 14 | 0 |
| | Brass binding above Cameras . . . . . | 0 | 15 | 0 |
| | BLAND & Co.'s compound achromatic lens, No. 1, page 7, with Waterhouse's stops, for above Cameras . . . . . . . | 2 | 15 | 0 |
| | French lens of best kind . . . . . . | 1 | 1 | 0 |
| No. 2. | **Square sliding body Camera,** of best French-polished Honduras mahogany, with 1 single back 6 inches square, and 2 loose frames, for plates 5 by 4, and 4¼ by 3¼, with ground focussing screen . . . . . . . | 1 | 11 | 0 |
| No. 2A. | Ditto, ditto, ditto, of best Spanish mahogany, with rising front, of superior make . . . | 2 | 8 | 0 |
| | Brass binding above Cameras . . . . . | 0 | 17 | 6 |
| | BLAND & Co.'s compound achromatic lens, No. 3, page 7, fitted with Waterhouse's stops, for the above . . . . . . . | 4 | 4 | 0 |
| | French lens of best kind . . . . . . | 2 | 0 | 0 |
| No. 3. | **Square sliding body Camera,** best French-polished Honduras mahogany, with 1 single back 8 inches square, and 2 loose frames, for plates 6 by 5, and 5 by 4, and focussing screen . . . . . . . . . . | 2 | 5 | 0 |
| No. 3A. | Ditto, ditto, ditto, of best Spanish mahogany, and rising front, of superior make . . . | 3 | 10 | 0 |
| | Brass binding above Cameras . . . . . | 1 | 0 | 0 |
| | BLAND & Co.'s compound achromatic lens, No. 5, page 7, fitted with Waterhouse's stops, for the above . . . . . . . | 5 | 10 | 0 |
| | French lens of best kind . . . . . . | 2 | 10 | 0 |
| No. 4. | **Square sliding body Camera,** of best French-polished Honduras mahogany, with 1 single back 10 inches square, and 3 loose frames, for plates, 8½ by 6½, 6 by 5, and 5 by 4, and focussing glass . . . . . . . . . | 3 | 15 | 0 |
| No. 4A. | Ditto, ditto, ditto, of best Spanish mahogany, with rising front of superior make . . . | 5 | 15 | 0 |
| | Brass binding above Cameras . . . . . | 1 | 10 | 0 |

| | | £ | s. | d. |
|---|---|---|---|---|
| | BLAND & Co.'s compound achromatic lens, No. 7, page 7, fitted with Waterhouse's stops, for the above . . . . . . | 11 | 16 | 0 |
| | French lens of best construction . . . | 6 | 0 | 0 |
| No. 5. | **Square sliding body Camera,** of best French-polished Honduras mahogany, with 1 single back 14 inches square, 3 loose frames, for plates 12 by 10, 10 by 8, and 8½ by 6½, and focussing glass . . . . . . . . . . | 7 | 0 | 0 |
| No. 5A. | Ditto, ditto, ditto, of best Spanish mahogany, with rising front, and of superior make . . | 10 | 0 | 0 |
| | Brass binding above Cameras . . . . . | 2 | 5 | 0 |
| No. 6. | **Square sliding body Camera,** of best French-polished Honduras Mahogany, with 1 single back 18 inches square, 3 loose frames, for plates, 16 by 14, 14 by 12, and 12 by 10, and focussing glass . . . . . . . . . . | 12 | 0 | 0 |
| No. 6A. | Ditto, ditto, ditto, of best Spanish mahogany, with rising front, and of superior make . . | 17 | 10 | 0 |
| | Brass binding above Cameras . . . . . | 3 | 0 | 0 |

*** BLAND & Co. supply lenses to above Cameras of any other makers, as may be ordered.

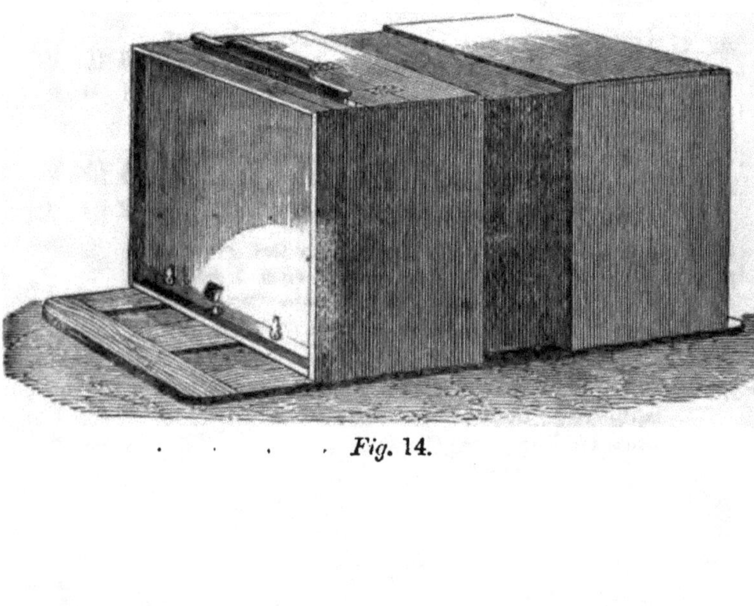

*Fig.* 14.

## SLIDING BODY OR EXPANDING CAMERAS,

*Adapted for Portraits and Views by the Collodion, Calotype, or Waxed Paper Processes. (Fig. 14.)*

| | | £ | s. | d. |
|---|---|---|---|---|
| No. 1. | **Sliding body Camera**, of French-polished Honduras mahogany, with 2 single (*Fig.* 13) dark slides, for plates, or paper for portraits 4¼ by 3¼, and views 6 by 5, and focussing glass . . | 2 | 6 | 0 |
| No. 1A. | Ditto, ditto, ditto, of best Spanish mahogany, with rising front, and superior make . . | 3 | 0 | 0 |
| | Brass binding above Cameras . . . . . | 0 | 16 | 6 |
| | Bland & Co.'s best compound achromatic lens, of best construction, with Waterhouse's stops (No. 2, page 7), adapted for either portraits 4¼ by 3¼, or views 6 by 5 inches . . . | 3 | 0 | 0 |
| No. 2. | **Sliding body Camera**, of best French-polished Honduras mahogany, with 2 single backs, for glass plates, or paper, and focussing glass for portraits 5 by 4, or views 7 by 6 . . . | 2 | 16 | 0 |
| No. 2A. | Ditto, ditto, ditto, of best Spanish mahogany, with rising front, and superior make . . | 3 | 15 | 0 |
| | Brass binding above-sized Cameras . . . | 1 | 0 | 0 |
| | Bland & Co.'s compound achromatic lens, of best construction (No. 4, page 7), fitted with Waterhouse's stops, for portraits 5 by 4, or views 7 by 6 . . . . . . . . . | 4 | 10 | 0 |
| No. 3. | **Sliding body Camera**, of best French-polished Honduras mahogany, with 2 single backs, for glass plates, or paper, and focussing glass for portraits 6 by 5, or views 9 by 7 . . . | 3 | 10 | 0 |
| No. 3A. | Ditto, ditto, ditto, of best Spanish mahogany, with rising front, and superior make . . | 4 | 15 | 0 |
| | Brass binding above-sized Cameras . . . | 1 | 5 | 0 |
| | Bland & Co.'s compound achromatic lens, of the best construction (No. 6, page 7), fitted with Waterhouse's central stops, for portraits 6 by 5, and views 9 by 7 . . . . . | 6 | 0 | 0 |
| No. 4. | **Sliding body Camera**, of best Honduras mahogany, French-polished, with 2 single backs, for glass plates, or paper, and focussing glass for portraits 8½ by 6½ inches, and views 11 by 9 inches . . . . . . . . . . | 5 | 0 | 0 |

| | £ | s. | d. |
|---|---|---|---|
| No. 4A. Ditto, ditto, ditto, of best Spanish mahogany, French-polished, and with rising front, and of superior make . . . . . . . . . | 7 | 7 | 0 |
| Brass binding above-sized Cameras . . . . . | 2 | 0 | 0 |
| BLAND & Co.'s compound achromatic lens (No. 8, page 7), of best construction, for portraits $8\frac{1}{2}$ by $6\frac{1}{2}$ inches, or views 11 by 9 inches, with Waterhouse's central stops . . . . . . . | 12 | 12 | 0 |

*Fig.* 15.

*Fig.* 16.

## BLAND & Co.'S PORTABLE FOLDING CAMERAS FOR LANDSCAPES.

This form of Camera will be found of great convenience where portability is a desideratum, and consequently most efficient for the purposes of the tourist and traveller.

These instruments are of the best workmanship, and are so constructed as not to warp nor lose their figure when exposed to the sun and weather in any climate.

| | £ | s. | d. |
|---|---|---|---|
| No. 1. **Portable folding Camera,** (*Figs.* 15, 16, of best Spanish mahogany, French-polished, with one double back, for holding two pieces of glass or prepared paper, sliding front for adjusting foreground and sky, focussing glass, &c., for pictures 7 by 6 inches . . . . . . | 4 | 0 | 0 |

| | | £ | s. | d. |
|---|---|---|---|---|
| No. 2. | Ditto, ditto, fitted with single Achromatic lens, mounted in brass sliding tube, for pictures 7 by 6 inches. No. 5, page 6 . . . . . . | 6 | 7 | 0 |
| No. 3. | **Portable folding Camera,** with one double back for holding two pieces of glass or prepared paper, sliding front for adjusting foreground and sky, focussing glass, &c., for pictures 9 by 7 inches . | 5 | 10 | 0 |
| No. 4. | Ditto, ditto, fitted with single Achromatic lens, 2⅝ inches diameter, mounted in brass sliding tube, taking pictures 9 by 7 inches. No. 6, page 6 . . . . . . . . . . | 8 | 4 | 6 |
| No. 5. | **Portable folding Camera,** with one double back for holding two pieces of glass or prepared paper, sliding front for adjusting foreground and sky, focussing glass, &c., for pictures 10 by 8 inches . . . . . . . . . . | 6 | 10 | 0 |
| No. 6. | Ditto, ditto, fitted with single Achromatic lens, 3 inches diameter, mounted with rackwork adjustment, taking pictures 10 by 8 inches . | 11 | 0 | 0 |
| No. 7. | **Portable folding Camera,** with one double back for holding two pieces of glass or prepared paper, sliding front for adjusting foreground and sky, focussing glass, &c., for pictures 11 by 9 inches . . . . . . . . . . | 7 | 10 | 0 |
| No. 8. | Ditto, ditto, with single Achromatic lens, 3 inches diameter, mounted with rackwork adjustment, taking pictures 11 by 9 inches. No. 7, page 6 . . . . . . . . . . | 12 | 10 | 0 |
| No. 9. | **Portable folding Camera,** with one double back for holding two pieces of glass or prepared paper, sliding front for adjusting foreground and sky, focussing glass, &c., for pictures 12 by 10 inches . . . . . . . . | 8 | 10 | 0 |
| No. 10. | Ditto, ditto, fitted with single Achromatic lens, mounted with rackwork adjustment, producing pictures 12 by 10 inches. No. 8, page 6 . . | 14 | 10 | 0 |
| No. 11. | **Portable folding Camera,** with one double back for holding two pieces of glass or prepared paper, sliding front for adjusting foreground and sky, ground focussing glass, &c., for pictures 15 by 12 inches . . . . . . | 10 | 0 | 0 |

| | £ | s. | d. |
|---|---|---|---|
| No. 12. Ditto, ditto, fitted with single Achromatic lens, mounted with rackwork adjustment, for producing pictures 15 by 12 inches. No. 9, page 6 | 17 | 7 | 0 |

Lenses of any other makers can be supplied to order for the above Cameras.

Larger sizes made to order.

---

*Fig.* 17.

## BLAND & CO.'S PORTABLE FOLDING CAMERAS FOR PORTRAITS AND VIEWS.

*Fig.* 17.

**Bland & Co.'s portable folding Cameras,** fitted with compound achromatic lenses, in handsome brass mounting, with rackwork adjustment, and capable of being altered for both portraits and views. *Figs.* 3 and 4, page 7.

| | £ | s. | d. |
|---|---|---|---|
| No. 1. **Portable folding Camera,** of French-polished mahogany, sliding front for adjustment of foreground and sky, one double back for glass or paper, and one single back with two loose frames for plates, fitted with compound lens of best construction, capable of producing portraits 5 by 4 inches, and views 7 by 6 inches . . | 7 | 10 | 0 |
| No. 2. **Portable folding Camera,** as above, of French-polished mahogany, fitted with compound achromatic lens, of best construction, capable of producing portraits 6 by 5 inches, and views 9 by 7 inches . . . . . . . . . . | 11 | 10 | 0 |
| No. 3. **Portable folding Camera,** as above, of French-polished mahogany, for producing portraits 8½ by 6½ inches, and views 12 by 10 inches . . | 22 | 0 | 0 |

*Fig.* 18.

## SLIDING BODY FOLDING CAMERA.

Best Spanish mahogany, French-polished, sliding body folding Camera, with one single back, two loose frames, focussing glass in frame, and with vertical and horizontal sliding front for adjustment of foreground and sky (*Fig.* 18).

| | | Plain. | | | Brass Binding, Extra. | | |
|---|---|---|---|---|---|---|---|
| | | £ | *s.* | *d.* | £ | *s.* | *d.* |
| No. 1. for plates | 7 by 6 | 4 | 10 | 0 | 0 | 15 | 0 |
| No. 2. ,, | 9 by 7 | 5 | 0 | 0 | 1 | 0 | 0 |
| No. 3. ,, | 10 by 8 | 6 | 0 | 0 | 1 | 5 | 0 |
| No. 4. ,, | 11 by 9 | 7 | 10 | 0 | 1 | 7 | 6 |
| No. 5. ,, | 12 by 10 | 8 | 5 | 0 | 1 | 10 | 0 |
| No. 6. ,, | 15 by 12 | 11 | 0 | 0 | 1 | 15 | 0 |
| No. 7. ,, | 18 by 16 | 17 | 10 | 0 | 2 | 5 | 0 |
| No. 8. ,, | 24 by 22 | 24 | 0 | 0 | 3 | 10 | 0 |

The above can be had of BLAND & Co., framed and panelled, or with fine screw focussing adjustment at an additional cost.

BLAND & Co.'s lenses, as per list (pages 6 & 7, *Figs.* 2 & 4), can be supplied with the above Cameras, or those of other makers, to order.

**Sliding Fronts** adapted to Cameras for the adjustment of foreground and sky, price according to size—6 by 5, or 7 by 6 inches, 7s. 6d. each; 9 by 7, 10 by 8, and 11 by 9, 10s. 6d. each, &c.

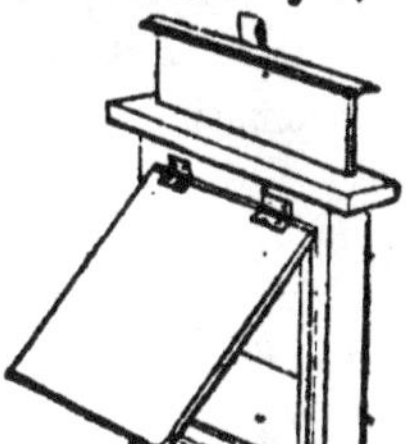

*Fig.* 19.

*Fig.* 20.

D

**Single** or **Double Backs** for Cameras:—(*Figs.* 19 and 20.)

*For Stereoscopic Pictures.*

| | Single Backs and 2 inner Frames (*Fig.* 19). £ s. d. | Double Backs (*Fig.* 20). £ s. d. | Brass Binding, Extra. |
|---|---|---|---|
| For plates 6¾ by 3¼ | 0 12 0 | 0 15 0 | 4s. and 5s. |
| " 7 by 6 | 0 18 0 | 1 2 0 | 4s. 6d., 5s. 6d. |
| " 8½ by 6½ | 1 1 0 | 1 5 0 | 5s., 5s. 6d. |
| " 9 by 7 | 1 2 6 | 1 7 6 | 5s., 6s. |
| " 10 by 8 | 1 6 6 | 1 10 6 | 5s. 6d., 6s. 6d. |
| " 11 by 9 | 1 9 6 | 1 15 0 | 6s., 7s. |
| " 12 by 10 | 1 12 0 | 2 0 0 | 6s., 7s. |
| " 15 by 12 | 2 5 0 | 2 15 0 | 7s., 8s. |
| " 18 by 16 | 2 15 0 | 3 10 0 | 8s., 9s. |
| " 24 by 20 | 3 5 0 | 4 0 0 | 9s., 10s. |

**Extra Openings** to Cameras, according to size of Camera, from 5s. upwards.

## FRENCH CAMERAS IN WALNUT WOOD,

OBLONG, UNPOLISHED.

| | £ | s. | d. |
|---|---|---|---|
| No. 1. ¼-plate **Walnut Camera** | 0 | 10 | 0 |
| No. 2. Ditto, fitted with compound lens, for portraits | 1 | 4 | 0 |
| No. 3. ½-plate **Walnut Camera** | 0 | 14 | 0 |
| No. 4. Ditto, fitted with compound lens, for portraits | 2 | 14 | 0 |
| No. 5. Whole-plate **Walnut Camera** | 1 | 0 | 0 |
| No. 6. Ditto, fitted with compound lens, for portraits | 6 | 0 | 0 |

## FRENCH WALNUT-WOOD CAMERAS, SQUARE.

| | £ | s. | d. |
|---|---|---|---|
| No. 1. ¼-plate square Camera, walnut wood | 0 | 14 | 0 |
| No. 2. Ditto, ditto, fitted with compound Achromatic lens, for portraits up to 4¼ by 3¼ inches | 1 | 8 | 0 |
| No. 3. ½-plate walnut Camera, square | 1 | 3 | 0 |
| No. 4. ½-plate walnut Camera, square, fitted with compound Achromatic lens, for portraits up to 6½ by 4¾ inches | 3 | 3 | 0 |
| No. 5. Whole-plate square walnut Camera | 1 | 10 | 0 |
| No. 6. Ditto, ditto, fitted with compound Achromatic lens, for portraits up to 8½ by 6½ inches | 6 | 10 | 0 |

*Fig.* 21.

## SOLID LEATHER CASES,

*For Folding Cameras, or Sliding Body Folding Cameras.*

(*Fig.* 21.)

| | | £ | s. | d. |
|---|---|---|---|---|
| No. 1. For a Camera, for plates | 7 by 6 | 1 | 10 | 0 |
| 2. „ | 9 by 7 | 1 | 14 | 0 |
| 3. „ | 10 by 8 | 1 | 16 | 0 |
| 4. „ | 11 by 9 | 2 | 5 | 0 |
| 5. „ | 12 by 10 | 2 | 12 | 6 |
| 6. „ | 15 by 12 | 3 | 13 | 6 |

---

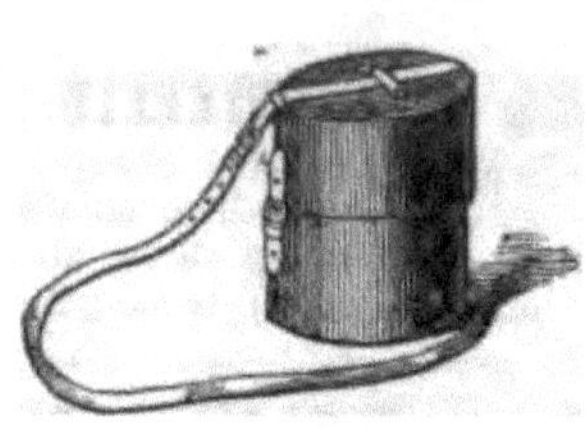

*Fig.* 22.

## LEATHER SLING CASES FOR LENSES.

| | £ | s. | d. |
|---|---|---|---|
| No. 1. For a Lens 2 inch diameter | 0 | 10 | 0 |
| 2. „ 2½ | 0 | 12 | 0 |
| 3. „ 3 | 0 | 13 | 0 |
| 4. „ 4 | 0 | 15 | 6 |
| 5. „ 5 | 1 | 2 | 6 |

# STEREOSCOPIC CAMERAS.

*Fig.* 23.

*Fig.* 24.

## SINGLE LENS STEREOSCOPIC CAMERAS.

| | | £ | s. | d. |
|---|---|---|---|---|
| No. 1. | **Stereoscopic Camera,** of most simple construction, fitted with compound lens for portraits or views, mounted on sliding front to take the stereoscopic pictures at two exposures; one single back for plates and ground glass (*Fig.* 23) | 2 | 15 | 0 |

The picture taken with this Camera requires to be reversed when mounted, in order to obtain the proper stereoscopic effect.

| | | £ | s. | d. |
|---|---|---|---|---|
| No. 2. | Stereoscopic Camera, of best construction, mounted on boards, with parallel adjustment, on Latimer Clarke's principle, steel-adjusting screw, long shifting back for stereoscopic plates, and ground focussing glass (*Fig.* 24) . . . . . . | 3 | 0 | 0 |
| | Single back, adapted to the above, with loose frame for portraits . . . . . . . . | 0 | 10 | 0 |
| | Brass binding above Camera . . . . . . | 1 | 5 | 0 |
| | BLAND & Co.'s compound Achromatic Lens, with *Waterhouse's* Central Stop for use with the *above,* for portraits or views . . . . . | 2 | 15 | 0 |

*Fig.* 25.

## STEREOSCOPIC TOURISTS' CAMERA.

This Camera is admirably adapted for working with the Dry Process; it is constructed on Latimer Clarke's principle, and has six dark slides for prepared plates or paper. It is fitted with a compound achromatic lens, which, with the Camera, backs and top of stand, pack into the mahogany box, the outside measurement being 11 by 9 by 9 inches, £7 7s.; or, with portable stand, £8 8s. (*Fig.* 25.)

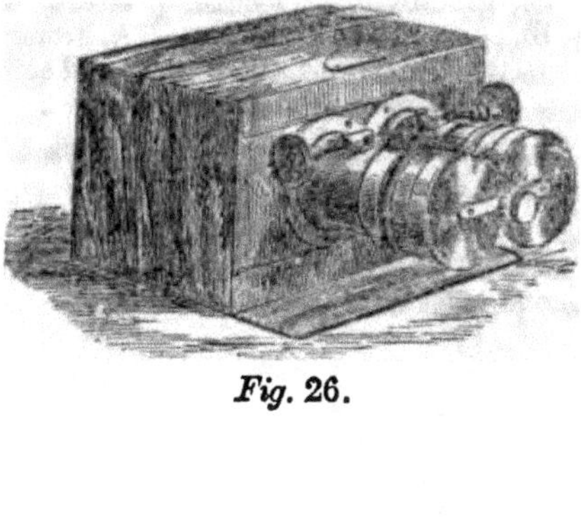

*Fig.* 26.

*Fig.* 27.

## DOUBLE LENS STEREOSCOPIC CAMERAS.

| | | £ | s. | d. |
|---|---|---|---|---|
| No. 1. | Mahogany French-polished sliding body Camera (*Fig.* 26), with single back and focussing glass, to take plate in back, size 6¾ by 3¼, with two compound Achromatic lenses, of coincident foci suited for Stereoscopic portraits or views . . | 4 | 10 | 0 |
| No. 2. | Very superior Spanish mahogany sliding body Camera (*Fig.* 27), with rising front and rack separation for lenses, shifting bar for connecting caps of lenses, one single back, to take plates 7¾ by 4¼, and loose frame for Stereoscopic size 6¾ by 3¼., ground glass focussing screen, and two of BLAND and Co.'s compound Achromatic lenses, fitted with Waterhouse's stops, and suited for Stereoscopic portraits or views . . . | 7 | 7 | 0 |

N.B. This Camera, with its lenses, is also adapted for two Carte de Visite pictures on the plate, 7¾ by 4¼.

It is necessary to state that the pictures taken by Nos. 1 and 2, require to be reversed when they are mounted, in order to obtain the true stereoscopic effect.

# BLAND AND CO.'S

## IMPROVED TOURISTS' STEREOSCOPIC CAMERAS.

*Fig.* 28.

| | | £ | s. | d. |
|---|---|---|---|---|
| No. 3. | BLAND and Co.'s improved Tourists' Binocular Stereoscopic Bellows body Camera (*Fig.* 28), with screw adjustment to back part of Camera for focussing; three double backs, each for holding two prepared plates, size 6¾ by 3¼, and one single back, for wet or dry process; ground glass focussing screen, very portable, packing into a mahogany case, outside dimensions 8¾ by 5 by 5½, price without lenses . . . . . | 6 | 10 | 0 |
| No. 3A. | Ditto, ditto, with two Achromatic view lenses . | 8 | 8 | 0 |
| No. 3B. | Or with two of BLAND and Co.'s Compound Achromatic Lenses, with Waterhouse stops, for portraits and views . . . . . | 12 | 0 | 0 |

*Fig.* 29.

*Fig.* 30.

Fig. 29 represents the Camera, with case of three double backs attached, which are not included in price of No. 4, but are included in No. 5.

| | | £ | s. | d |
|---|---|---|---|---|
| No. 4. | Improved Tourists' Stereoscopic Binocular Camera (*Fig.* 29), designed by Mr. C. D. Smith, of best Spanish French-polished mahogany, with Bellows body, rising front and separating rack adjustment, for increasing distances between lenses; simple arrangement for reversing lenses into body of Camera when travelling; one single back and focussing screen; size when shut up for travelling (*Fig.* 30) about $9\frac{3}{4}$ by $6\frac{1}{2}$ by $5\frac{1}{2}$, price without lenses, and lower case of backs . . . . . . . . . . | 5 | 15 | 0 |
| No. 4A. | Pair of Bland and Co.'s single Achromatic view lens, for above, extra . . . . . . . | 1 | 15 | 0 |

| | | £ | s. | d. |
|---|---|---|---|---|
| No. 4B. | Pair of BLAND and Co.'s compound Achromatic lenses, with Waterhouse's stops, for either porraits or views, extra . . . . . | 5 | 10 | 0 |
| No. 5C. | Improved Tourists' Stereoscopic Binocular Camera, as above, with addition of rack adjustment to body for focussing at back, WITH CASE, containing three double backs (*Fig.* 29), for use for dry processes, price without lenses . . | 8 | 8 | 0 |

N.B. The case containing the double backs can, by a very simple arrangement, be attached or detached from body of camera, as required.

Lenses for this camera same as described with the foregoing.

---

*Fig.* 31.

## BLAND & CO.'S CARTE DE VISITE CAMERAS.

| | | £ | s. | d. |
|---|---|---|---|---|
| No. 1. | Mahogany square sliding body French-polished Camera, with one single back and focussing screen for taking single Carte de Visite pictures, as per page 26, fig. 12, No. 1 . . . . . | 1 | 5 | 0 |
| No. 1A. | BLAND and Co.'s compound Achromatic Carte de Visite lens, with Waterhouse's stops for above, extra . . . . . . . . . | 2 | 15 | 0 |
| | Brass binding, for above, extra . . . . | 0 | 15 | 0 |

| | | £ | s. | d. |
|---|---|---|---|---|
| No. 2. | BLAND and Co.'s improved single lens Carte de Visite Camera (*Fig.* 31), arranged for taking two pictures. This Camera is of the sliding body form, with improved rack motion for focussing lenses from the front, and made of best Spanish mahogany, with long frame for containing the back and focussing screen . . | 3 | 10 | 0 |
| | Brass binding, for above, extra . . . . | 0 | 15 | 0 |
| No. 2A. | BLAND and Co.'s best Carte de Visite lens for above, with Waterhouse's stops . . . | 2 | 15 | 0 |

*Fig.* 32.

| | | | | |
|---|---|---|---|---|
| No. 3. | BLAND and Co.'s improved binocular Camera, as per fig. 32, for operating room, of best Spanish mahogany, with rack adjustment, focussing from front, rising front, one single back and focussing glass . . . . . . . . . . | 4 | 15 | 0 |
| | Brass binding, extra . . . . . . | 0 | 15 | 0 |

For price of lenses for above, see page 8, according to length of operating room.

Lenses of any other makers adapted to this or any other Carte de Visite Camera.

*Fig.* 33.

| | | £ | s. | d. |
|---|---|---|---|---|
| No. 4. | Bland and Co.'s improved Camera, arranged for Carte de Visite and Stereoscopic Pictures, consisting of a very superior Spanish mahogany Sliding Body Camera, with rising front and rackwork separation for lens (*Fig.* 33); shifting bar for connecting caps of lenses; one single back to take plates 7¾ by 4¼ inches for two Carte de Visite pictures at one exposure; ground glass focussing screen. This Camera has also a loose frame to take plates of ordinary stereoscopic size, with two of Bland and Co.'s Compound Achromatic Lenses, fitted with Waterhouse's diaphragms, and suited for two Carte de Visite portraits, or for stereoscopic portraits and views . . . . . . . | 7 | 7 | 0 |

# BLAND AND CO.'S

## IMPROVED DOUBLE LENS CARTE DE VISITE CAMERAS.—*Figs.* 34, 35.

*Fig.* 34.

*Fig.* 35.

| | £ | s. | d. |
|---|---|---|---|
| No. 5. Bland and Co's improved Carte de Visite Camera for the operating room, for two lenses to take four pictures by two exposures, long frame, holding back and ground glass, having horizontal and vertical motions, as per figs. 34 & 35 | 9 | 9 | 0 |
| Brass binding, extra . . . . . . | 1 | 10 | 0 |
| Swing Backs for Carte de Visite Camera, extra, from, each . . . . . . . . , | 1 | 5 | 0 |

For lenses suitable for above Camera, according to length of room, see page 8.

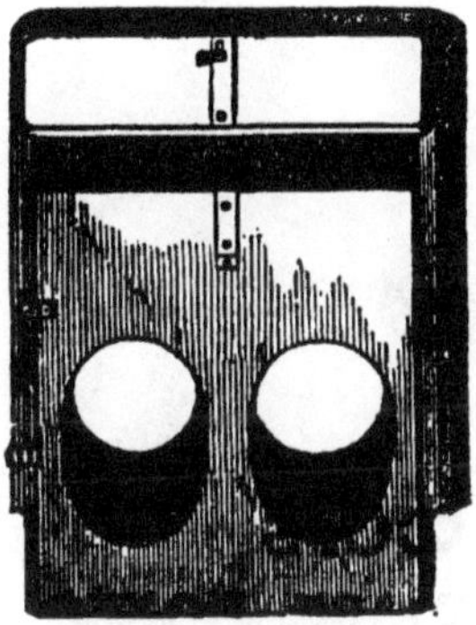

*Fig.* 36.

*Fig.* 37.

## BLAND AND CO.'S

# NEW INSTANTANEOUS SHUTTER.

Bland and Co.'s improved instantaneous Shutter, which admits of rapid exposure for fast moving objects, landscapes, &c.; also for use in taking portraits of children.

This Shutter has an arrangement for regulating the time of exposure at the will of operator, and can be adapted to the hood of lens of any camera.

Fig. 36 represents the front view of shutter adapted for stereoscopic Bi-Lens Camera.

Fig. 37 the back part sliding on to hoods of lenses, price from £1 1s. upwards.

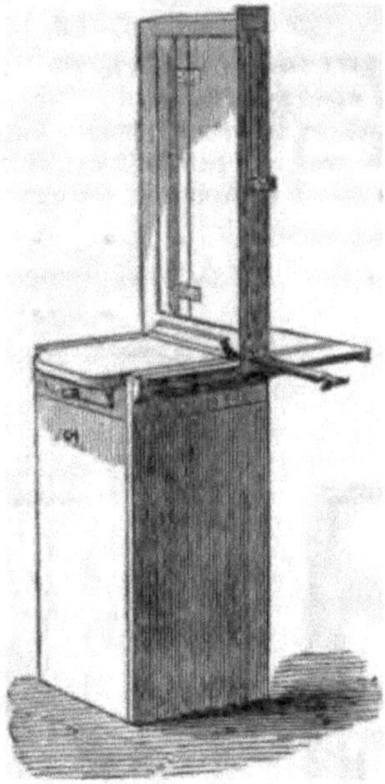

*Fig.* 38.

# BLAND AND CO.'S

## CHANGING BOXES, OR DARK BOXES,

*For transferring Dry Plates to Camera Backs in Open Air, &c.*
(*Fig.* 38.)

These boxes can be adapted to any sized Camera, but require the Camera back to be specially made for the purpose.

| | | £ | s. | d. |
|---|---|---|---|---|
| For Stereoscopic size, to hold 1 doz. plates | . . . | 2 | 5 | 0 |
| For size, 7 by 6 ,, | . . . | 2 | 10 | 0 |
| ,, 9 by 7 ,, | . . . | 3 | 0 | 0 |
| ,, 10 by 8 ,, | . . . | 3 | 7 | 6 |
| ,, 11 by 9 ,, | . . . | 4 | 0 | 0 |
| ,, 12 by 10 ,, | . . . | 4 | 10 | 0 |

The above prices do not include the Camera back. The prices of corresponding sizes of which are the same as single backs, see page 34 (*Fig.* 19).

The same construction of changing box can be applied to double backs, where two plates can be changed at one operation, at an additional expense.

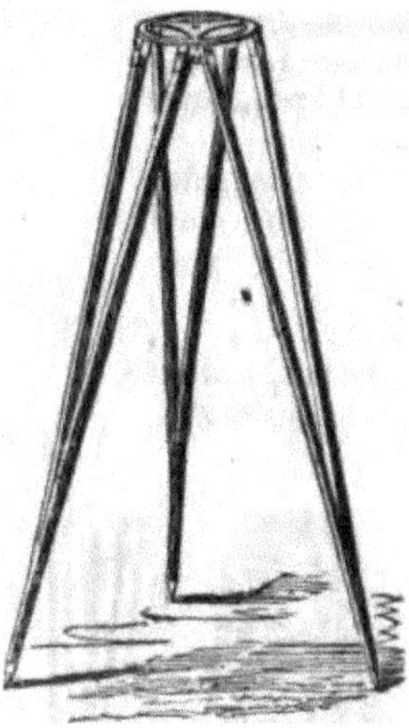

*Fig.* 39.

*Fig.* 40.

## CAMERA STANDS.

To ensure success in taking either portraits or views, it is absolutely essential that the Camera should be perfectly free from vibration; if this be not the case, it is obviously impossible to obtain a perfectly sharp impression. Lightness, with freedom from vibration, are combined in the Stands offered in the following list:—

| | | £ | s. | d. |
|---|---|---|---|---|
| No. 1. | Tripod Stand, with round iron top and bolt and screw. Double legs of ash for small Camera (*Fig.* 39) . . . . . . . | 0 | 7 | 6 |
| No. 2. | Ditto, ditto, superior make, round brass top, screw and bolt, and French-polished (*Fig.* 39) . | 0 | 10 | 0 |
| No. 3. | Ditto, ditto, with 4-inch triangular metal top (*Fig.* 40), with double legs and brass stretchers, bolt, screw, and nut . . . . . . . . . | 0 | 16 | 6 |
| No. 4. | Ditto, ditto, very strong, with 6-inch triangular brass top, with bolt and screw, double legs of ash, French-polished, and hinged at bottom with brass stretchers . . . . . . | 1 | 2 | 6 |
| No. 5. | Ditto, ditto, larger, with 8-inch triangular head for large-sized Camera . . . . . . . | 1 | 10 | 0 |

| | | £ | s. | d. |
|---|---|---|---|---|
| No. 6. | Very light, strong, and firm Folding Tripod Stand, with double legs of ash, jointed in centre, French-polished, with brass 4-inch triangular top, and bolt and screw . . . . . . | 1 | 1 | 0 |
| No. 7. | Ditto, ditto, strong, with large iron triangular head, with bolt and screw, very firm and portable, can be packed into an ordinary portmanteau . . . . . . . . . . | 1 | 7 | 6 |
| No. 8. | Ditto, ditto, with brass triangular top . . . | 1 | 10 | 0 |
| No. 9. | Light and portable Folding Tripod Stand, three legs, as per fig. 42, of new pattern and design, suitable for Stereoscopic Cameras . . . | 1 | 1 | 0 |

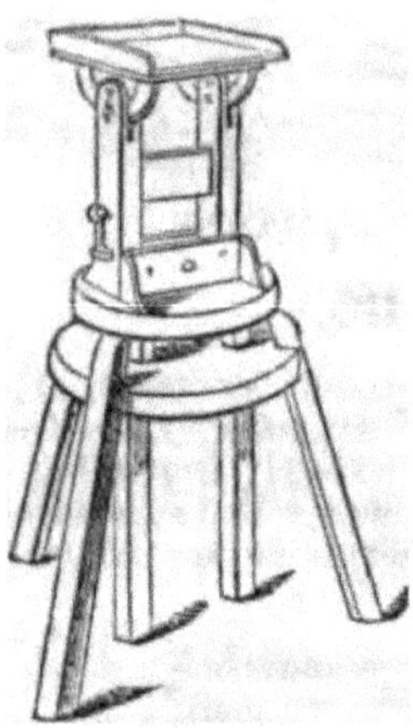

*Fig.* 41.

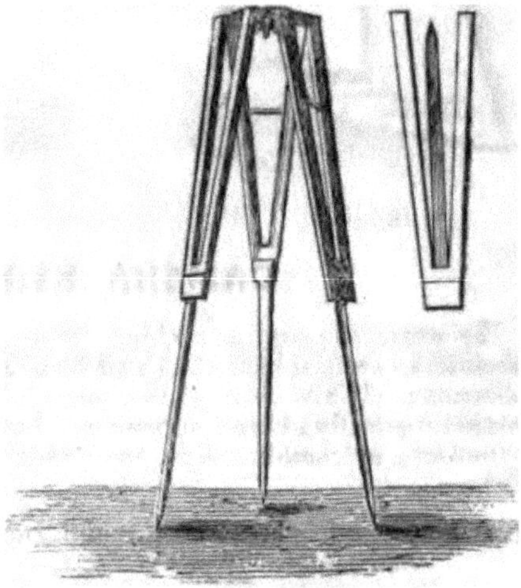

*Fig.* 42.

## CAMERA STANDS FOR OPERATING ROOM.

| | | £ | s. | d. |
|---|---|---|---|---|
| No. 10. | Table Camera Stand, in white wood, with every adjustment for raising or depressing Camera (*Fig.* 41) . . . . . . . . . . . | 1 | 1 | 0 |
| No. 11. | Ditto, ditto, in oak, very strong (*Fig.* 41) . . | 1 | 6 | 0 |
| No. 12. | Ditto, ditto, in oak, very strong and French-polished, with metal rack adjustment with handle, for raising or depressing Camera, and with horizontal and vertical motion to top of Stand . . . . . . . . . . . . | 5 | 5 | 0 |

| | | £ | s. | d. |
|---|---|---|---|---|
| No. 13. | Table Camera Stand, with Archimedean screw adjustment, in French-polished oak or mahogany, very firm and substantial, with all the most recent improvements and motions . . | 9 | 9 | 0 |

## HEAD RESTS,

*For enabling the Sitter to keep the Head in one position without fatigue.* (*Figs.* 43, 44, *and* 45.)

| | | £ | s. | d. |
|---|---|---|---|---|
| No. 1. | Head Rest of simplest form, with screw to attach to back of chair . . . . . . . | 0 | 2 | 0 |
| No. 2. | Ditto, ditto, with adjustments for raising, depressing, and placing the head-piece in any required position or inclination, with screw to attach to back of chair (*Fig.* 43) . . . | 0 | 5 | 0 |
| No. 3. | Bland and Co.'s Universal Head Rest, with means of adjustment for every position of the sitter, for attaching to chair (*Fig.* 45) . . | 1 | 2 | 6 |

*Fig.* 43.

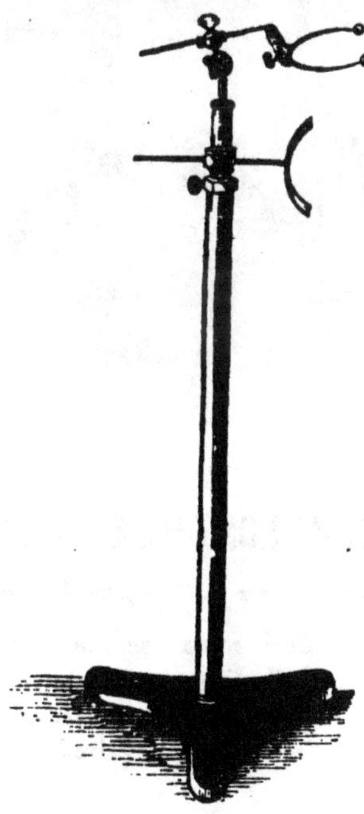

*Fig.* 44.

*Fig.* 45.

| | | £ | s. | d. |
|---|---|---|---|---|
| No. 4. | **Universal Head Rest, with heavy iron foot, and brass sliding tube, which enables this rest to be used either for standing or sitting posture, without hip rest (*Fig.* 44)** . . . . . | 2 | 15 | 0 |
| No. 5. | **Ditto, ditto, ditto, with hip rest attached, as in *Fig.* 44** . . . . . . . . . . | 3 | 0 | 0 |

# DARK TENT.

*Fig.* 46.

## BLAND AND CO.'S PORTABLE DARK TENT,

***For working the Collodion Process in the Open Country (Fig. 46).***

**A good substitute for a dark room has long been a desideratum to the photographer in Collodion, and we have much pleasure in submitting the present invention to the notice of photographers generally, as combining all that can be required for the purposes of open-air work.**

The Tent consists of a strong and roomy table, mounted on a firm Tripod Stand; from the top of the table at each corner rise four metal supports; these sustain a frame over which is stretched yellow calico. A black calico envelope covers the whole, and enables the operator to work with as great ease in the open country as he would in his own laboratory at home. The black envelope is furnished with a circular aperture at the top, for admitting yellow light to the interior of the tent; there is also a curved bar, which keeps the covering from touching the head of the operator while at work. The envelope is bound at its edge with strong webbing, and iron spikes are attached at intervals in order to secure it to the ground, and prevent the wind and light from getting into the tent.

When not in use, the rods that support the yellow calico chamber double inwards, and fall quite flat; the legs of the Tripod then fold up and are laid on the top; finally, the black calico envelope is folded up, and laid over these, immediately under the cover, which secures the whole, the table of the tent forming the containing box. These tents have been in use for a long time, and we can pronounce them to answer perfectly, and to fulfil all the conditions required in such an apparatus.

The extreme size of outside containing box of a tent, suitable for an operator 6 feet high, is 24 by 18 by 4 inches, forming a portable and compact case. (*Fig.* 47.)

*Fig.* 47.

| | £ | s. | d. |
|---|---|---|---|
| Bland & Co.'s portable Dark Tent, for working Collodion in the open air, complete (*Fig.* 46) . . . | 3 | 3 | 0 |

Larger sizes made to order.

# LAMPS FOR DARK ROOM.

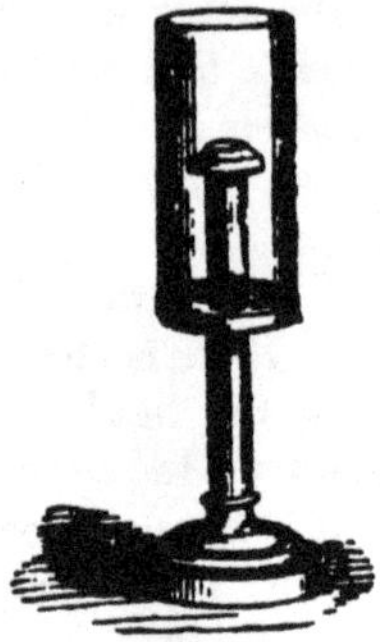

*Fig.* 48.

*Fig.* 49.

| | £ | s. | d. |
|---|---|---|---|
| Gas Jets, with metal chimney and gauze, with flexible tube, for burning off plates without smoke . each | 0 | 8 | 0 |
| Lanterns furnished with yellow glass shades, for use in dark room (*Fig.* 49) . . . . . . . . | 0 | 3 | 6 |
| Improved form of Photographic Lamp, where the ruby glass can be raised or depressed (*Fig.* 48) . . . | 0 | 7 | 6 |

## PORTABLE STILLS.

It is found very convenient frequently to have at hand the means of obtaining pure water at a trifling cost; this desideratum is acquired in a very economical way by the use of a small still, which can be placed over a common fire. (*Figs.* 50 & 51.)

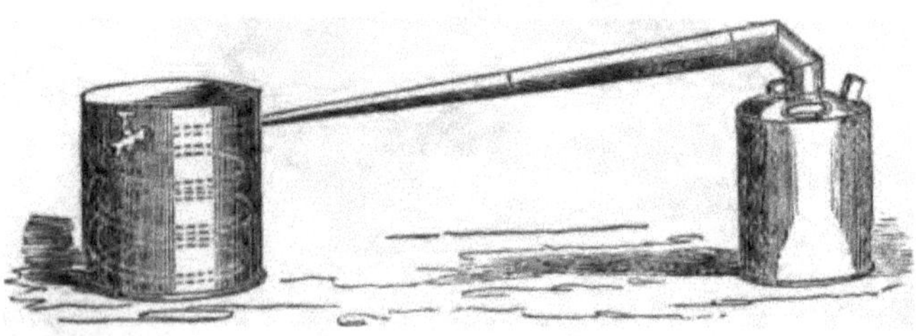

*Fig.* 50.

| | £ | s. | d. |
|---|---|---|---|
| Tin Still, to hold half a gallon, with worm tub complete, for use over the common fire (*Figs.* 50 & 51) . | 0 | 14 | 0 |
| Ditto, ditto, one gallon . . . . . . . . | 0 | 17 | 6 |
| Ditto, ditto, two ditto . . . . . . . . | 1 | 2 | 0 |

| | £ | s. | d. |
|---|---|---|---|
| Copper Still, half a gallon . . . . . . | 1 | 4 | 0 |
| Ditto, ditto, one ditto . . . . . . . | 1 | 13 | 6 |

*Fig.* 51.

## PORTABLE STILL,

*Packed for Travelling.*

*Fig.* 52. *Fig.* 53. *Fig.* 54.

## LEVELLING STAND,

*With adjusting Screws, for laying Plates with Albumen, and Developing and Fixing Collodion Pictures.*

| | | s. | d. |
|---|---|---|---|
| No. 1. size, for plates up to 5 by 4 inches | (*Fig.* 54) | 3 | 0 |
| 2. " " 7 by 6 " | (*Fig.* 52) | 4 | 0 |
| 3. " " 9 by 7 " | (*Fig.* 52) | 5 | 6 |
| 4. " " 12 by 10 " | (*Fig.* 53) | 6 | 6 |

*Fig.* 55.

## CIRCULAR SPIRIT LEVEL,

For accurately levelling Cameras, or Glass Plates for Developing (*Fig.* 55), each 3s.

*Fig.* 56.

*Fig.* 57.

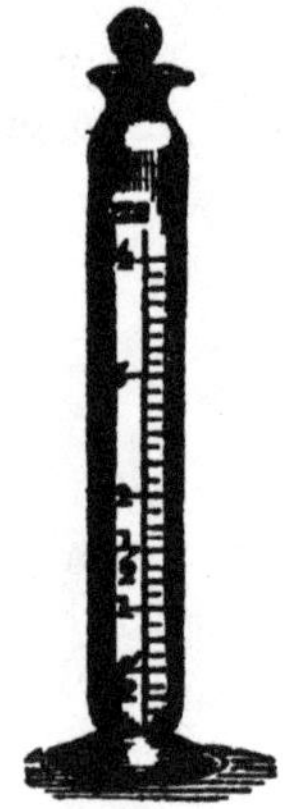

*Fig.* 58.

## COLLODION BOTTLES, POURERS, AND FILTERS.

The Collodion Bottles (*Fig.* 58), can be used either for mixing the plain Collodion with the Iodizer, or for receiving the turbid portion of Collodion when it has been flowed over the plate several times; from the shape of the bottle, it allows all particles to subside at the bottom, and enables the operator, after a short time, to pour away the clear collodion within a very short distance of the deposit without disturbing it.

| | | | £ | s. | d. |
|---|---|---|---|---|---|
| No. 1. Collodion Bottle or Pourer, plain | | . 1 oz. | 0 | 1 | 3 |
| No. 2. „ „ | graduated | „ | 0 | 2 | 0 |
| No. 3. „ „ | plain | . 2 oz. | 0 | 1 | 9 |
| No. 4. „ „ | graduated | „ | 0 | 2 | 6 |
| No. 5. „ „ | plain | . 4 oz. | 0 | 2 | 6 |
| No. 6. „ „ | graduated | „ | 0 | 3 | 6 |
| **Cometless Collodion Bottle** (*Fig.* 57) . . . | | | 0 | 4 | 0 |

The tube in the neck of this bottle can be removed and cleaned as frequently as used, and so particles of dry collodion prevented from being carried on to the plate.

Collodion Filters (*Fig.* 56), each, 7s. 6d. and 10s.

*Fig.* 59.

*Fig.* 60.

*Fig.* 61.

| | £ | *s.* | *d.* |
|---|---|---|---|
| **Drop Bottles** (*Fig.* 59), for adding small quantities of nitrate of silver solution to developing or other solutions, each . . . . . . . . . | 0 | 2 | 0 |
| **Developing Glasses.**—Nest of three for pouring developing solution on to plates (*Fig.* 61) . . . . . | 0 | 1 | 6 |
| **Argentometer,** for testing strength of silver bath, in case (*Fig.* 60) . . . . . . . . . | 0 | 3 | 6 |
| Ditto, with outer glass for holding solution to be tested, in case . . . . . . . . | 0 | 4 | 6 |

## SCALES AND WEIGHTS.

*Fig.* 62.

*Fig.* 63.

| | | £ | s. | d. |
|---|---|---|---|---|
| No. 1. | In Oak box metal pans (*Fig.* 62) with set of drachm, scruple, and grain weights | 0 | 2 | 6 |
| 2. | Ditto, ditto, larger | 0 | 5 | 0 |
| 3. | Ditto, superior beam and glass pans in box | 0 | 5 | 9 |
| 4. | Balance, with brass pillar and shifting glass pan mounted on mahogany box, with drawer (*Fig.* 63) | 1 | 10 | 0 |

---

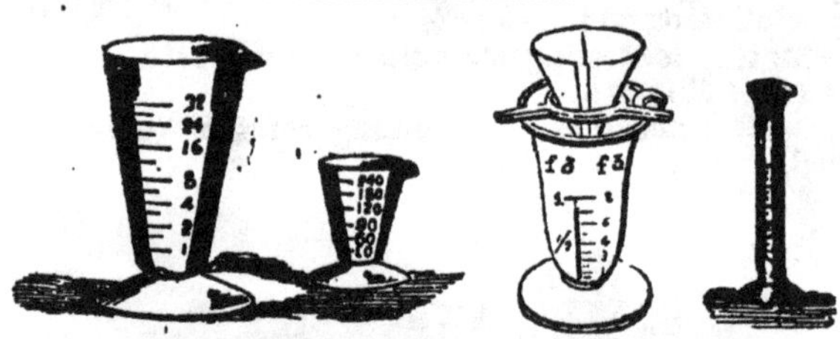

*Fig.* 64. *Fig.* 65. *Fig.* 66.

## GLASS GRADUATED MEASURES,

(*Figs.* 64, 65, 66),

Accurately divided, of either Cylindrical or Conical form.

| | s. | d. | | s. | d. |
|---|---|---|---|---|---|
| Contents 1 ounce, each | 0 | 10 | Contents 8 ounces, each | 2 | 6 |
| „ 2 „ | 1 | 0 | „ 10 „ | 3 | 0 |
| „ 4 „ | 1 | 6 | „ 20 „ | 3 | 6 |
| „ 6 „ | 2 | 3 | „ 40 „ | 6 | 6 |

| | | s. | d. |
|---|---|---|---|
| Minim measures (*Fig.* 66) | 60 drops . . | 1 | 0 |
| Ditto | 120 ,, . . | 1 | 3 |

Stirring Rods, of glass, each, 3d. and 4d.

Filter Rings or Supports, as on top of fig. 65, very useful for filtering small quantities of solution without a funnel, each, 3d., 4d., and 6d.

Glass Syringes, for taking up small quantities of liquids, plain, from 6d.; graduated, from 1s.

*Fig.* 67.

*Fig.* 68.

**Glass Spirit Lamps** (*Fig.* 68), each, 9s., 1s., 2s., and 3s.

**Glass Funnels** (*Fig.* 67), *Ribbed Inside, for Filtering Solutions.*

| | | s. | d. | | | s. | d. |
|---|---|---|---|---|---|---|---|
| No. 1. | 2 ins. diameter | 0 | 4 | No. 4. | 4 ins. diameter . | 0 | 7 |
| 2. | 2½ ,, | 0 | 5 | 5. | 5 ,, | 0 | 8 |
| 3. | 3 ,, | 0 | 6 | 6. | 6 ,, | 1 | 0 |

No. 7. 7 ins. diameter . 1s. 3d.

## GUTTA PERCHA FUNNELS.—(*Fig.* 67.)

3 in., 6d. 3½ in., 9d. 4½ in., 1s. 5 in., 1s. 3d.

## WEDGEWOOD WARE FUNNELS.—(*Fig.* 67.)

Funnels, Wedgewood, cream colour, ribbed inside :—

| | | s. | d. |
|---|---|---|---|
| No. 1. | 2 inches diameter . . . | 0 | 4 |
| 2. | 3½ ,, . . . . | 0 | 6 |
| 3. | 4 ,, . . . . | 0 | 8 |
| 4. | 5 ,, . . . . | 1 | 0 |
| 5. | 6 ,, . . . . | 1 | 6 |
| 6. | 6½ ,, . . . . | 1 | 10 |

## EBONITE FUNNELS.—(*Fig.* 67.)

| | | s. | d. | | | s. | d. |
|---|---|---|---|---|---|---|---|
| No. 1. | 1 oz. capacity . | 0 | 10 | No. 5. | 6 oz. capacity . | 1 | 9 |
| 2. | 2 „ | 1 | 0 | 6. | 8 „ | 2 | 3 |
| 3. | 3 „ | 1 | 3 | 7. | 10 „ | 2 | 6 |
| 4. | 4 „ | 1 | 6 | 8. | 16 „ | 3 | 8 |

**Filter Paper,** cut round, in packets of 100 each.

| | | s. | d. |
|---|---|---|---|
| No. 1. | 5½ inches diameter . . . . | 0 | 10 |
| 2. | 7½ „ . . . . | 1 | 0 |
| 3. | 9½ „ . . . . | 1 | 3 |
| 4. | 13 „ . . . . | 1 | 9 |

*Fig.* 69.

*Fig.* 70.

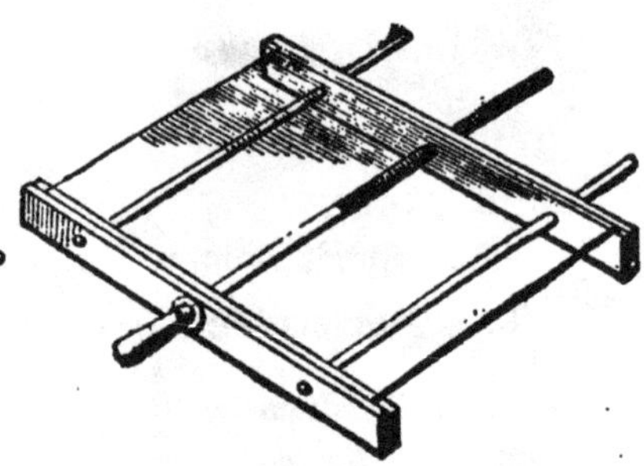

*Fig.* 71.

| | £ | s. | d. |
|---|---|---|---|
| **Pneumatic Plate Holder,** simple form (*Fig.* 70) . | 0 | 1 | 0 |
| Ditto, small, with lever (*Fig.* 69) . . . . . | 0 | 2 | 6 |
| Ditto, ditto, large, with lever (*Fig.* 69) . . . . | 0 | 3 | 6 |
| Globe Plate Holders, each . . . . . . . . | 0 | 4 | 6 |

**Plate Cleaner,** with Screw Adjustment, for cleaning Plates of various sizes, 4s. 6d. and 5s. 6d (*Fig.* 71).

Plate-cleaning liquid, per bottle, 6d. and 1s.

Leathers for cleaning glass plates, 1s. and 1s. 6d.

India-rubber Finger-stalls, each, 4d.

## COLLODION DIPPING BATHS.

*Fig.* 72.

## GUTTA PERCHA DIPPING BATHS,

*Inclined with Hingea Wood Back and Glass Dipper* (*Fig.* 72).

| | | £ | s. | d. |
|---|---|---|---|---|
| No. 1. size, for plates, | 4¼ by 3¼ | 0 | 2 | 9 |
| 2. „ | 5 by 4 | 0 | 4 | 0 |
| 3. „ | 6½ by 4¾ | 0 | 4 | 6 |
| 4. „ | 6 by 5 | 0 | 4 | 6 |
| 5. „ | 7¾ by 4¼ | 0 | 6 | 0 |
| 6. „ | 8½ by 6½ | 0 | 7 | 6 |
| 7. „ | 9 by 7 | 0 | 8 | 6 |
| 8. „ | 10 by 8 | 0 | 11 | 0 |
| 9. „ | 12 by 10 | 0 | 15 | 0 |
| 10. „ | 15 by 12 | 1 | 1 | 6 |
| 11. Stereoscopic | 6¾ by 3¼ | 0 | 4 | 3 |

## EBONITE BATHS.

### PATENT EBONITE BATHS.

| | £ | s. | d. | | £ | s. | d. |
|---|---|---|---|---|---|---|---|
| 5 by 3⅝ each | 0 | 4 | 3 | 12½ by 9½ each | 0 | 13 | 0 |
| 7¾ by 5¾ „ | 0 | 6 | 0 | 13 by 9½ „ | 0 | 13 | 6 |
| 9¾ by 7¼ „ | 0 | 8 | 6 | 13½ by 10½ „ | 0 | 14 | 6 |
| 11½ by 8½ „ | 0 | 10 | 6 | 14½ by 10½ „ | 0 | 15 | 0 |
| 12 by 8½ „ | 0 | 11 | 6 | 16½ by 13½ „ | 1 | 0 | 0 |

### PATENT EBONITE BATHS, WITH AIR-TIGHT TOPS.

| | £ | s. | d. | | £ | s. | d. |
|---|---|---|---|---|---|---|---|
| 5 by 3⅝ each | 0 | 8 | 0 | 12½ by 9½ each | 1 | 3 | 0 |
| 7¾ by 5¾ „ | 0 | 12 | 0 | 13 by 9½ „ | 1 | 4 | 0 |
| 9¼ by 7¼ „ | 0 | 15 | 0 | 13½ by 10½ „ | 1 | 5 | 0 |
| 11½ by 8½ „ | 1 | 0 | 0 | 14½ by 10½ „ | 1 | 6 | 0 |
| 12 by 8½ „ | 1 | 1 | 6 | 16½ by 12½ „ | 1 | 11 | 0 |

## PATENT EBONITE BATHS—STEREOSCOPIC.

| | s. | d. | | s. | d. |
|---|---|---|---|---|---|
| 8¾ by 3¾ ins. each . | 5 | 0 | Do. with air-tight top, each | 8 | 6 |

*Fig.* 73.

## GLASS DIPPING BATHS,

*Of Solid White Moulded Glass, fitted in Mahogany Stand, with Glass Dipper (Fig.* 73).

| | | | £ | s. | d. |
|---|---|---|---|---|---|
| No. 1. | for plates | 4¼ by 3¼ | 0 | 4 | 6 |
| 2. | " | 5 by 4 | 0 | 6 | 0 |
| 3. | " | 6½ by 4¾ | 0 | 7 | 6 |
| 4. | " | 6 by 5 | 0 | 7 | 6 |
| 5. | " | 7¾ by 4¼ | 0 | 8 | 6 |
| 6. | " | 9 by 7 | 0 | 10 | 6 |
| 7. | " | 10 by 8 | 0 | 15 | 0 |
| 8. | " | 12 by 10 | 0 | 18 | 6 |
| 9. | Stereoscopic | 6¾ by 3¼ | 0 | 6 | 6 |

## PORCELAIN BATHS,

*Without Stand and Dipper.*

| | | | £ | s. | d. |
|---|---|---|---|---|---|
| No. 1. | for plates | 4¼ by 3¼ | 0 | 2 | 0 |
| 2. | " | 5 by 4 | 0 | 2 | 9 |
| 3. | " | 6½ by 4¾ | 0 | 3 | 6 |
| 4. | " | 8½ by 6½ | 0 | 4 | 0 |
| 5. | " | 9 by 7 | 0 | 5 | 6 |
| 6. | " | 10 by 8 | 0 | 8 | 0 |
| 7. | " | 12 by 10 | 0 | 11 | 0 |
| 8. | " | 15 by 12 | 1 | 1 | 0 |
| 9. | Stereoscopic | 6¾ by 3¼ | 0 | 4 | 0 |

## WATERTIGHT GUTTA PERCHA BATHS,

*With Dipper and Hinged Back, for containing Solution when Travelling.*

| | | | £ | s. | d. |
|---|---|---|---|---|---|
| No. 1. | for plates | 5 by 4 | 0 | 8 | 0 |
| 2. | " | 6½ by 4¾ | 0 | 9 | 6 |
| 3. | " | 8½ by 6½ | 0 | 12 | 6 |
| 4. | " | 9 by 7 | 0 | 14 | 0 |
| 5. | " | 10 by 8 | 0 | 18 | 6 |
| 6. | " | 11 by 9 | 1 | 2 | 6 |
| 7. | " | 12 by 10 | 1 | 4 | 0 |
| 8. | " | 15 by 12 | 1 | 15 | 0 |
| | Stereoscopic | 6¾ by 3¼ | 0 | 8 | 6 |

## WATERTIGHT GLASS BATHS,

*With Dipper, mounted in Mahogany Cases, French-polished.*

| | | | £ | s. | d. |
|---|---|---|---|---|---|
| No. 1. | for plates | 5 by 4 | 0 | 17 | 6 |
| 2. | " | 6½ by 4¾ | 1 | 1 | 0 |
| 3. | " | 8½ by 6½ | 1 | 8 | 6 |
| 4. | " | 9 by 7 | 1 | 10 | 0 |
| 5. | " | 10 by 8 | 1 | 15 | 0 |
| 6. | " | 12 by 10 | 2 | 5 | 0 |
| 7. | " | 15 by 12 | 3 | 3 | 0 |
| 8. | Stereoscopic | 6¾ by 3¼ | 1 | 0 | 0 |

*Fig. 74.*

## BLAND AND CO.'S IMPROVED WATERTIGHT GLASS BATHS.

(*Fig*. 74.)

With accurately fitted Ground Glass Cover. The upper portion of the framework at top is hinged, and when the bath is in use, can

**be turned over, as in figure, and at once be put into its place when the bath is out of use; a shutter is placed at bottom lined with yellow glass, so that the bottom of bath can be examined as to its freedom from sediment; this contrivance will be found of great use in India, or tropical climates. Screwed and brass bound.**

| | | | £ | s. | d. |
|---|---|---|---|---|---|
| No. 1. | for plates | 5 by 4 | 1 | 0 | 0 |
| 2. | „ | 6¼ by 4¾ | 1 | 10 | 0 |
| 3. | „ | 9 by 7 | 2 | 0 | 0 |
| 4. | „ | 10 by 8 | 2 | 10 | 0 |
| 5. | „ | 11 by 9 | 2 | 15 | 0 |
| 6. | „ | 12 by 10 | 3 | 3 | 0 |
| 7. | „ | 15 by 12 | 4 | 4 | 0 |
| 8. | Stereoscopic | 6¾ by 3¼ | 1 | 10 | 0 |

---

## DIPPERS FOR COLLODION BATHS.

*Fluted Glass Dippers, in One Piece, allowing the Fluid to drain down from Back of the Plate.*

| | | | | s. | d. |
|---|---|---|---|---|---|
| No. 1. | length | 6 | inches each | 0 | 6 |
| 2. | „ | 8 | „ | 0 | 9 |
| 3. | „ | 9 | „ | 0 | 10 |
| 4. | „ | 11 | „ | 1 | 0 |
| 5. | „ | 13 | „ | 1 | 3 |
| 6. | „ | 16 | „ | 1 | 9 |

### PORCELAIN DIPPERS.

| | | | s. | d. |
|---|---|---|---|---|
| No. 1. | for plates | 4¼ by 3¼ | 0 | 8 |
| 2. | „ | 5 by 4 | 0 | 11 |
| 3. | „ | 6½ by 4¾ | 1 | 2 |
| 4. | „ | 8½ by 6½ | 1 | 6 |
| 5. | „ | 10 by 8 | 1 | 9 |
| 6. | „ | 12 by 10 | 2 | 0 |

### SILVER WIRE DIPPERS,

From 7s. 6d. upwards.

*Fig.* 75.

## PORCELAIN DISHES,

*For Sensitizing or Albumenizing Paper, and for Washing Paper Pictures, with Spout.*

| | | | Porcelain Pans, Shallow. | | | Porcelain Pans, Deep. | | |
|---|---|---|---|---|---|---|---|---|
| | | | £ | s. | d. | £ | s. | d. |
| No. 1. | for Paper | 5 by 4 | 0 | 0 | 9 | 0 | 0 | 11 |
| 2. | Stereoscopic | 6¾ by 3¼ | 0 | 1 | 0 | 0 | 1 | 3 |
| 3. | for Paper | 8 by 6 | 0 | 1 | 3 | 0 | 1 | 6 |
| 4. | „ | 9 by 7 | 0 | 1 | 6 | 0 | 1 | 9 |
| 5. | „ | 10 by 8 | 0 | 1 | 9 | 0 | 2 | 0 |
| 6. | „ | 11 by 9 | 0 | 2 | 6 | 0 | 2 | 9 |
| 7. | „ | 12 by 10 | 0 | 3 | 0 | 0 | 3 | 6 |
| 8. | „ | 13 by 11 | 0 | 4 | 0 | 0 | 5 | 0 |
| 9. | „ | 16 by 12 | 0 | 6 | 6 | 0 | 7 | 6 |
| 10. | „ | 16 by 13 | 0 | 7 | 0 | 0 | 8 | 6 |
| 11. | „ | 19 by 12 | 0 | 9 | 0 | 0 | 10 | 6 |
| 12. | „ | 20 by 16 | 0 | 15 | 0 | 0 | 17 | 6 |
| 13. | „ | 24 by 19 | 1 | 1 | 0 | 1 | 5 | 0 |

*Fig.* 76.

## WELL PORCELAIN SENSITIZING, DEVELOPING, OR FIXING DISHES.

These dishes are very convenient for sensitizing wet or dry collodion plates, or for their subsequent manipulation, as, from the construction of them, a very small quantity of solution is required. (*Fig.* 76.)

| | | | s. | d. |
|---|---|---|---|---|
| No. 1. | for plates | 6¾ by 3¼ | 2 | 6 |
| 2. | „ | 6½ by 5 | 3 | 6 |
| 3. | „ | 8½ by 6½ | 5 | 6 |
| 4. | „ | 9 by 7 | 6 | 6 |
| 5. | „ | 10 by 8 | 7 | 6 |
| 6. | „ | 11 by 9 | 9 | 0 |
| 7. | „ | 12 by 10 | 10 | 6 |

---

## GUTTA PERCHA WASHING TRAYS.

| | | | s. | d. |
|---|---|---|---|---|
| No. 1. | size, 8 by 6 by 1 | inch, inside measurement | 2 | 0 |
| 2. | „ 9 by 7 by 1¼ | „ | 3 | 0 |
| 3. | „ 10 by 8 by 1¼ | „ | 3 | 6 |
| 4. | „ 11 by 9 by 1½ | „ | 4 | 6 |
| 5. | „ 12 by 10 by 1½ | „ | 5 | 6 |
| 6. | „ 13 by 11 by 1½ | „ | 6 | 0 |
| 7. | „ 14 by 12 by 2 | „ | 8 | 6 |
| 8. | „ 16 by 12 by 2 | „ | 10 | 0 |
| Or in nests of three useful sizes, Nos. | | 1, 2, & 3 | 8 | 6 |
| „ | „ | 2, 3, & 4 | 11 | 0 |
| „ | „ | 4, 5, & 6 | 16 | 0 |

Larger sizes made to order, and mounted in wood cases.

## EBONITE TRAYS.

| | s. | d. | | | s. | d. |
|---|---|---|---|---|---|---|
| 5 by 3⅝ | 2 | 6 | ... | 11 by 9 | 5 | 3 |
| 7¾ by 8¾ | 3 | 0 | ... | 11½ by 9½ | 6 | 0 |
| 8 by 6 | 3 | 6 | ... | 12 by 10 | 6 | 6 |
| 9½ by 7½ | 4 | 6 | ... | 12½ by 10½ | 7 | 0 |
| | | | | 13 by 11 | 8 | 0 |

*Fig.* 77.

## GLASS DISHES.—(*Fig.* 77.)

The advantage possessed by these dishes is, that they are entirely unacted upon by the chemicals employed, and therefore can be used for different solutions one after another, without risk of the admixture which is so likely to take place when the pans are of porcelain.

| | | | | s. | d. |
|---|---|---|---|---|---|
| No. 1. | for stereoscopic plate | 7½ by 3¾ by 1, | each | 2 | 0 |
| 2. | size | 6 by 4½ by 1 | „ | 2 | 0 |
| 3. | „ | 8 by 6 by 1 | „ | 3 | 0 |
| 4. | „ | 9 by 7 by 1 | „ | 4 | 6 |
| 5. | „ | 10 by 8 by 1 | „ | 5 | 0 |
| 6. | „ | 11 by 9 by 1 | „ | 6 | 0 |
| 7. | „ | 12½ by 10½ by 1 | „ | 7 | 6 |

*Fig.* 78.

## ELLIOT'S NEW SYPHON WASHING TROUGH.—(*Fig.* 78.)

**Elliot's Syphon Washing Trough,** in porcelain, for washing prints. Very useful for Operators or Amateurs, as by the use of it any number of prints may be subjected to the action of a continuous stream of water for any time. The pan should be placed with the prints in it in a sink, and a small stream of water let flow into it at a position at right angles to the syphon, which gives the contents of the pan a rotatory motion. When the height of the water reaches the bend of the syphon, the water from the lower part of the pan passes away through the syphon, which is then self-acting as long as water is allowed to pass into the pan.

| | | | s. | d. |
|---|---|---|---|---|
| No. 1. | Diameter of the pan | . 14 inches, each . | 12 | 0 |
| 2. | " | . 17 " " . | 14 | 0 |
| 3. | " | . 19 " " . | 16 | 0 |

## DOXES FOR GLASS PLATES.

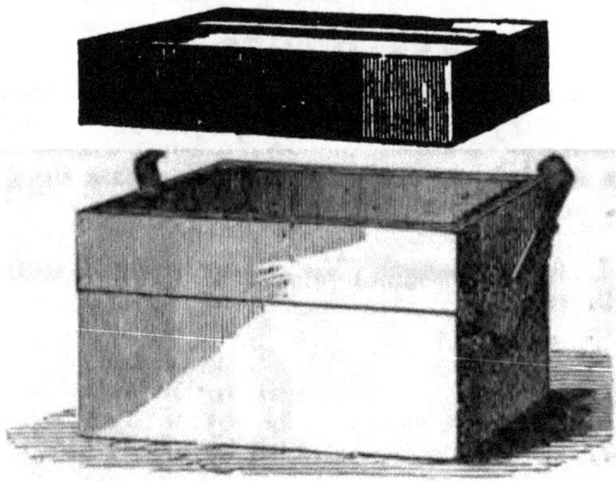

*Fig.* 79.

BLAND AND CO., AGENTS.

## KEENE'S PRESERVATIVE NON-CHEMICAL PLATE BOX (*Fig.* 79),

***For storing Sensitized Dry Plates, and for Plate Box purposes generally.***

The body of this box is composed of metal, from contact with which the plate is preserved by gutta percha grooves at the ends, and the same material placed at the top and bottom; the lid fits into a deep groove, and is fastened by a simple contrivance, which renders it both light tight and safe. Prepared plates are thus kept free from chemical influence, and may be preserved for the longest possible period. It is universally acknowledged perfect for the purpose, and the very favourable opinion passed upon it, at its introduction by, among others, the Editor of the PHOTOGRAPHIC NEWS, that it was an admirable and ingenious contrivance likely to come into general use, and *that nothing better could be desired for the purpose,* has since been fully endorsed by photographers both at home and abroad.

| | | | | s. | d. |
|---|---|---|---|---|---|
| No. 1. | for Stereoscopic plates | . | 6¾ by 3¼ . . | 6 | 0 |
| 2. | for plates . . . | . | 6½ by 4¾ . . | 6 | 6 |
| 3. | ditto . . . . | . | 7¼ by 4½ . . | 7 | 0 |
| 4. | ditto . . . . | . | 7 by 6 . . | 7 | 6 |
| 5. | ditto . . . . | . | 8½ by 6½ . . | 8 | 6 |
| 6. | ditto . . . . | . | 9 by 7 . . | 9 | 0 |
| 7. | ditto . . . . | . | 10 by 8 . . | 10 | 6 |
| 8. | ditto . . . | . | 12 by 10 . . | 11 | 6 |

*Fig.* 80.

## PLATE BOXES (*Fig.* 80),

*For holding Glass Plates, in White Wood.*

| | | | For 12 Plates. | | 24 Plates. | | 50 Plates. | |
|---|---|---|---|---|---|---|---|---|
| | | | s. | d. | s. | d. | s. | d. |
| No. 1. | for plates | 3¼ by 2¾ | 1 | 9 | 2 | 9 | 4 | 0 |
| 2. | ,, | 4¼ by 3¼ | 2 | 3 | 3 | 3 | 4 | 6 |
| 3. | ,, | 5 by 4 | 2 | 9 | 3 | 6 | 5 | 6 |
| 4. | ,, | 6½ by 4¾ | 3 | 3 | 4 | 0 | 6 | 6 |
| 5. | ,, | 6¾ by 3¼ | 3 | 3 | 4 | 0 | 6 | 6 |
| 6. | ,, | 6 by 5 | 3 | 3 | 4 | 0 | 6 | 6 |
| 7. | ,, | 7 by 6 | 3 | 9 | 4 | 6 | 7 | 6 |
| 8. | ,, | 8½ by 6½ | 4 | 0 | 5 | 0 | 8 | 0 |
| 9. | ,, | 7¾ by 4¼ | 3 | 9 | 4 | 6 | 7 | 6 |
| 10. | ,, | 7¼ by 4½ | 3 | 9 | 4 | 6 | 7 | 6 |
| 11. | ,, | 9 by 7 | 4 | 3 | 5 | 6 | 8 | 6 |
| 12. | ,, | 10 by 8 | 4 | 9 | 6 | 6 | 9 | 6 |
| 13. | ,, | 11 by 9 | 5 | 6 | 7 | 0 | 10 | 6 |
| 14. | ,, | 12 by 10 | 6 | 3 | 7 | 9 | 12 | 6 |
| 15. | ,, | 13 by 11 | 7 | 0 | 9 | 0 | 14 | 0 |
| 16. | ,, | 15 by 12 | 8 | 0 | 11 | 0 | 16 | 0 |
| 17. | ,, | 16 by 13 | 9 | 0 | 12 | 0 | 18 | 0 |

## PLATE BOXES (*Fig.* 80),

*In Mahogany.*

| | | | | | 12 Plates. | | 24 Plates. | |
|---|---|---|---|---|---|---|---|---|
| | | | | | *s.* | *d.* | *s.* | *d.* |
| No. 1. | for plates | 3¼ | by | 2¾ | 3 | 6 | 4 | 6 |
| 2. | ,, | 4¼ | by | 3¾ | 4 | 0 | 5 | 0 |
| 3. | ,, | 5 | by | 4 | 4 | 6 | 6 | 0 |
| 4. | ,, | 6½ | by | 4¾ | 5 | 3 | 7 | 6 |
| 5. | ,, | 6 | by | 5 | 5 | 3 | 7 | 6 |
| 6. | ,, | 6¾ | by | 3¼ | 5 | 3 | 7 | 6 |
| 7. | ,, | 7 | by | 6 | 5 | 6 | 8 | 0 |
| 8. | ,, | 7¼ | by | 4½ | 5 | 6 | 8 | 0 |
| 9. | ,, | 7¾ | by | 4¼ | 5 | 6 | 8 | 0 |
| 10. | ,, | 8½ | by | 6½ | 6 | 3 | 8 | 6 |
| 11, | ,, | 9 | by | 7 | 7 | 0 | 9 | 0 |
| 12. | ,, | 10 | by | 8 | 8 | 0 | 10 | 0 |
| 13. | ,, | 11 | by | 9 | 9 | 6 | 12 | 0 |
| 14. | ,, | 12 | by | 10 | 10 | 6 | 13 | 0 |

## PLATE BOXES IN METAL.

| | | | | | 12 Plates. | | 24 Plates. | |
|---|---|---|---|---|---|---|---|---|
| No. 1. | for plates | 3¼ | by | 2¾ | 2 | 3 | 3 | 9 |
| 2. | ,, | 4¼ | by | 3¼ | 2 | 6 | 4 | 6 |
| 3. | ,, | 5 | by | 4 | 2 | 9 | 5 | 0 |
| 4. | ,, | 6½ | by | 4¾ | 3 | 0 | 5 | 6 |
| 5. | ,, | 6 | by | 5 | 3 | 0 | 5 | 6 |
| 6. | ,, | 6¾ | by | 3¼ | 2 | 6 | 4 | 6 |
| 7. | ,, | 7 | by | 6 | 3 | 9 | 6 | 6 |
| 8. | ,, | 7¾ | by | 4¼ | 3 | 9 | 6 | 6 |
| 9. | ,, | 7¼ | by | 4½ | 3 | 9 | 6 | 6 |
| 10. | ,, | 8½ | by | 6½ | 5 | 0 | 9 | 0 |
| 11. | ,, | 9 | by | 7 | 6 | 0 | 10 | 6 |
| 12. | ,, | 10 | by | 8 | 7 | 0 | 13 | 0 |
| 13. | ,, | 11 | by | 9 | 8 | 0 | 14 | 6 |
| 14. | ,, | 12 | by | 10 | 9 | 6 | 16 | 0 |

## DRAINING BOXES.

New plate draining boxes for wet negatives, fitted with gutta-percha grooves and india-rubber cushions, to protect the negatives from injury during carriage, with draining chamber at bottom.

| | | | | | *s.* | *d.* |
|---|---|---|---|---|---|---|
| No. 1. | for 1 doz. plates | 6¾ | by | 3¼ . . | 7 | 6 |
| 2. | ,, | 6½ | by | 4¾ . . | 7 | 6 |
| 3. | ,, | 8½ | by | 6½ . . | 10 | 0 |
| 4. | ,, | 9 | by | 7 . . | 11 | 0 |
| 5. | ,, | 10 | by | 8 . . | 12 | 0 |

# PATENT PLATE GLASS FOR COLLODION PICTURES,

*Free from Specks, and with Edges roughed.*

The great discrepancy in prices of glass plates between this and former quotations, is in consequence of the manufacturers having recently greatly advanced their prices.

| Size | Per Dozen. s. | d. | Size | Per Dozen. s. | d. |
|---|---|---|---|---|---|
| Size 3¼ by 2¾ | 1 | 0 | Size 7¾ by 4¼ | 5 | 0 |
| 4¼ by 3¼ | 2 | 0 | 7¼ by 4½ | 5 | 0 |
| 5 by 4 | 2 | 9 | 8½ by 6½ | 8 | 6 |
| 6½ by 4¾ | 4 | 6 | 9 by 7 | 10 | 0 |
| 6 by | 4 | 6 | 10 by 8 | 13 | 6 |
| 6¾ by 3¼ | 3 | 3 | 11 by 9 | 16 | 0 |
| 7 by 6 | 5 | 9 | 12 by 10 | 21 | 0 |

## EXTRA WHITE PATENT PLATE.

| Size | Per Dozen. | | Size | Per Dozen. | |
|---|---|---|---|---|---|
| Size 2½ by 2 | 0 | 8 | Size 6¾ by 3¼ | 4 | 0 |
| 3¼ by 2¾ | 1 | 2 | 6½ by 4¾ | 5 | 6 |
| 4¼ by 3¼ | 2 | 3 | 6 by 5 | 5 | 6 |
| 5 by 4 | 3 | 6 | 8½ by 6½ | 10 | 0 |

## BEST POLISHED CROWN GLASS,

*Or Crystal Sheet.*

| Size | Per Dozen. | | Size | Per Dozen. | |
|---|---|---|---|---|---|
| Size 2½ by 2 | 0 | 3 | Size 6¾ by 3¼ | 1 | 3 |
| 3¼ by 2¾ | 0 | 5 | 6½ by 4¾ | 1 | 6 |
| 4¼ by 3¼ | 0 | 8 | 6 by 5 | 1 | 6 |
| 5 by 4 | 1 | 0 | 8½ by 6½ | 3 | 3 |

## BEST OPAL GLASS.

| Size | Per Dozen. | | Size | Per Dozen. | |
|---|---|---|---|---|---|
| Size 2½ by 2 | 0 | 10 | Size 6¾ by 3¼ | 5 | 6 |
| 3¼ by 2 | 2 | 0 | 6½ by 4¾ | 7 | 0 |
| 4¼ by 3¼ | 3 | 0 | 6 by 5 | 7 | 0 |
| 5 by 4 | 4 | 6 | 8½ by 6½ | 14 | 0 |

Diamonds for cutting glass plates, best patent kind, 16s. and 18s. each.

## CRYSTAL MEDIUM,

*Sold in Packets of Fifty, with Directions for Use.*

| | | s. | d. |
|---|---|---|---|
| Packet of fifty sheets | 1 by 1 inch | 2 | 0 |
| ditto | $2\frac{1}{4}$ by 2 " | 3 | 6 |
| ditto | $3\frac{1}{4}$ by $2\frac{3}{4}$ " | 7 | 6 |

## TRANSFER CLOTH,

| | | | |
|---|---|---|---|
| In packets of one dozen | $2\frac{1}{2}$ by 2 inch | 0 | 6 |
| ditto | $3\frac{1}{4}$ by $2\frac{3}{4}$ " | 0 | 9 |
| ditto | $4\frac{1}{4}$ by $3\frac{1}{4}$ " | 1 | 0 |
| ditto | $6\frac{3}{4}$ by $3\frac{1}{4}$ " | 1 | 6 |
| Or per yard | . . . . . | 3 | 0 |

## PHOTOGRAPHIC PAPERS.

As much of the success of the Calotype, waxed paper, and other paper processes, depends on the nature of the material on which the sensitive compound is spread, a careful selection of papers from the most eminent makers has been made, combining fineness of surface and evenness of texture, with a proper tenacity to allow of the necessary washings to which the paper is exposed in the various manipulations.

### Foreign Papers. (Per Quire.)

| | | | s. | d. |
|---|---|---|---|---|
| Canson's Paper, size $22\frac{1}{2}$ by $17\frac{1}{2}$ | | Negative | 2 | 9 |
| Do. | do. | Positive | 3 | 0 |
| Papier Saxe, size $22\frac{1}{2}$ by $17\frac{1}{2}$ | | Negative | 3 | 6 |
| Do. | do. | Positive | 4 | 0 |
| Papier Le Rive, size $22\frac{1}{2}$ by $17\frac{1}{2}$ | | Negative | 3 | 6 |
| Do. | do. | Positive | 4 | 0 |

### English Papers. (Per Quire.)

| | | | | s. | d. |
|---|---|---|---|---|---|
| Hollingworth's Paper, thin, | size | 22 by 18 | Negative | 4 | 0 |
| Do. | do. | do. | Positive | 4 | 0 |
| Whatman's | do. | 19 by 15 | Negative | 3 | 0 |
| Do. | do. | do. | Positive | 2 | 6 |
| Towgood's | do. | 19 by 15 | Negative | 2 | 6 |
| Do. | do. | do. | Positive | 2 | 6 |
| Do. | do. | 51 by 33 | for Solar Camera | 16 | 0 |
| Turner's Paper, | Small, size | 15 by $9\frac{1}{2}$ | Negative | 3 | 0 |
| Do. | Large | 19 by 15 | " | 6 | 0 |
| Do. | Extra large | 24 by 19 | " | 10 | 0 |
| Do. | Small | 15 by $9\frac{1}{2}$ | Positive | 1 | 3 |
| Do. | Large | 19 by 15 | " | 2 | 6 |

## Filtering Papers. (Per Quire.)

| | s. | d. |
|---|---|---|
| White Filtering Paper, free from iron or other impurities | 1 | 0 |
| Ditto, ditto, extra thick | 1 | 6 |
| Swedish Filtering Paper | 4 | 0 |
| Papier Joseph | 1 | 0 |

## Bland and Co.'s Prepared Papers,

*Prepared with great Care.*

| | £ | s. | d. | |
|---|---|---|---|---|
| Bland and Co.'s Waxed Paper for Negatives, size 17½ by 11½ | 0 | 7 | 0 | per quire. |
| Bland and Co.'s ditto . size 22½ by 17½ | 0 | 14 | 0 | „ |
| Bland and Co.'s Iodized Waxed Papers, size 17½ by 11½ | 0 | 15 | 0 | „ |
| Bland and Co.'s ditto . 22½ by 17½ | 1 | 10 | 0 | „ |
| Bland and Co.'s Iodized Calotype Paper, size 7 by 6 | 0 | 2 | 6 | per doz. |
| Bland and Co.'s ditto . 9½ by 7½ | 0 | 4 | 0 | „ |
| Bland and Co.'s ditto . 10 by 8 | 0 | 6 | 0 | „ |
| Bland and Co.'s ditto . 15 by 12 | 0 | 9 | 0 | „ |
| Bland and Co.'s Positive Papers, salted with Chloride of Sodium . 22½ by 17½ | 0 | 6 | 6 | per quire. |
| Ditto, with Chloride of Barium 22½ by 17½ | 0 | 6 | 0 | „ |
| Ditto, ditto Chloride of Ammonium | 0 | 6 | 0 | „ |

## Albumenized Papers.

The *superior excellence* of the Albumenized Papers, prepared and sold by Bland and Co., is acknowledged by their customers both at home and abroad, and is beyond dispute.

| | Per quire. s. | d. |
|---|---|---|
| Bland and Co.'s thin Negative Saxe Extra Albumenized paper, for Stereoscopic or Carte de Visite pictures, size 22½ by 17½ | 12 | 0 |
| Bland and Co.'s thin Negative Rive Extra Albumenized paper, for Carte de Visite or Stereoscopic pictures, size 22 by 17 | 12 | 0 |
| Bland and Co.'s Medium Positive Saxe Extra Albuminized paper, for Stereoscopic or Carte de Visite pictures, size 22½ by 17½ | 12 | 0 |
| Bland and Co.'s slightly Albumenized Positive Saxe paper, size 22½ by 17½ | 6 | 0 |
| Bland and Co.'s highly Albumenized Positive thick Saxe paper, for small or large pictures, size 22½ by 17½ | 10 | 0 |
| Bland and Co.'s highly Albumenized Medium Positive Rive paper, for small or large pictures, size 22 by 17 | 10 | 0 |

# WOOD BOARDS,

*For attaching Paper to whilst Spreading on Solutions.*

| | | | s. | d. |
|---|---|---|---|---|
| No. 1. | for paper | 7 by 6 . . . . . | 0 | 9 |
| 2. | „ | 9 by 7 . . . . . | 1 | 0 |
| 3. | „ | 10 by 8 . . . . . | 1 | 6 |
| 4. | „ | 11 by 9 . . . . . | 2 | 0 |

Glass Rods, for spreading solutions on to paper, each 3d., 4d., 6d., and 1s.

---

# CAMEL HAIR BRUSHES,

*For spreading Solutions on to Paper, made without Metal Binding.*

| | s. | d. | | s. | d. |
|---|---|---|---|---|---|
| $1\frac{1}{2}$ inches broad, each | 1 | 6 | 3 inches broad, each | 2 | 6 |
| 2 „ „ | 1 | 9 | 4 „ „ | 3 | 6 |
| $2\frac{1}{2}$ „ „ | 2 | 3 | 5 „ „ | 4 | 6 |

Thick round ditto, each 1s. and 1s. 6d.

---

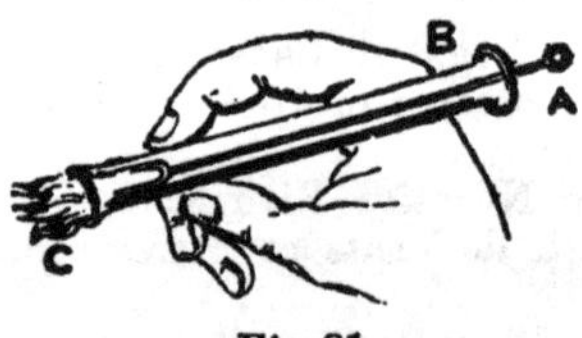


*Fig.* 81.

**Buckle's Brushes** (*Fig.* 81), for spreading solutions; each 1s. 6d. Glass tube, B; silver wire hook, A, which draws a piece of wool partly through the tube at C.

**Wood Clips,** for suspending sheets of paper, 1s. per doz.

*Fig.* 82.

## REVERSING OR PRINTING FRAMES.

These frames are so constructed that a uniform pressure may be obtained, thus ensuring perfect contact between the positive paper and negative plate. The back boards of these frames are so arranged that the progress of the picture may be watched without danger of shifting the papers.

## BLAND AND CO.'S IMPROVED PRESSURE FRAMES (*Fig.* 82),

With jointed backs for examination whilst printing, in Oak or French-polished Mahogany, of best kind and make.

| | | Oak. | | | | Mahogany. | | |
|---|---|---|---|---|---|---|---|---|
| | | £ | s. | d. | | £ | s. | d. |
| No. 1. size of glass | 9 by 7 ... | 0 | 11 | 6 | ... | 0 | 13 | 6 |
| 2. „ | 10 by 8 ... | 0 | 13 | 0 | ... | 0 | 16 | 0 |
| 3. „ | 11 by 9 ... | 0 | 15 | 0 | ... | 0 | 17 | 6 |
| 4. „ | 12 by 10 ... | 0 | 16 | 6 | ... | 0 | 19 | 0 |
| 5. „ | 13 by 11 ... | 0 | 18 | 6 | ... | 1 | 1 | 0 |
| 6. „ | 14 by 12 ... | 1 | 1 | 0 | ... | 1 | 5 | 0 |
| 7. „ | 16 by 13 ... | 1 | 5 | 0 | ... | 1 | 10 | 0 |
| 8. „ | 19 by 17 ... | 1 | 10 | 0 | ... | 1 | 18 | 0 |
| 9. „ | 25 by 23 ... | 2 | 5 | 0 | ... | 2 | 15 | 0 |

*Fig.* 88.

## PRESSURE FRAMES,

*Of Common Kind and Make, with Screws or Springs and Hinged Backboard (Fig. 88).*

| No. | | Size | EACH. £ | s. | d. |
|---|---|---|---|---|---|
| No. 1. | for pictures, | 7 by 6 | 0 | 7 | 6 |
| 2. | „ | 9 by 7 | 0 | 9 | 6 |
| 3. | „ | 10 by 8 | 0 | 12 | 0 |
| 4. | „ | 12 by 10 | 0 | 16 | 6 |
| 5. | „ | 14 by 12 | 1 | 1 | 0 |

## PRESSURE FRAMES,

*In White Wood, Common Kind, with Hinged Backs.*

| No. | | Size | EACH. £ | s. | d. |
|---|---|---|---|---|---|
| No. 1. | for plates, | 4¼ by 3¼ | 0 | 4 | 6 |
| 2. | „ | 6½ by 4¾ | 0 | 6 | 6 |
| 3. | „ | 8½ by 6½ | 0 | 8 | 6 |
| 4. | „ | 9 by 7 | 0 | 8 | 6 |
| 5. | „ | 12 by 10 | 0 | 14 | 0 |
| 6. | „ | 14 by 12 | 0 | 17 | 6 |
| 7. | „ | 16 by 14 | 0 | 19 | 0 |
| 8. | „ | 18 by 16 | 1 | 1 | 0 |
| 9. | „ | 22 by 18 | 1 | 8 | 6 |
| 10. | „ | Stereoscopic | 0 | 4 | 6 |

Commonest form of Stereoscopic Printing frame, 2s.

*Fig.* 84.

| | £ | s. | d. |
|---|---|---|---|
| **Double Zinc Dish for Waxing Paper** (*Fig.* 84), very convenient . . . . . . . . . | 0 | 10 | 0 |
| Ditto, ditto, with plated inner dish . . . . . | 1 | 1 | 0 |

**Horn Forceps,** for manipulating with waxed or other paper (*Fig.* 85), 9d. each

*Fig.* 85.

**Boxwood Forceps,** (*Fig.* 85), for same purpose, each 6d.

**Silver Wire Hooks,** for lifting sensitive plates from dishes, from 1s. each.

## VIGNETTE PLATES,

*For Portraits or Landscapes.* (*Fig.* 86.)

*Fig.* 86.

## VIGNETTE PLATES.—(*Fig.* 86.)

| No. | Size | | s. | d. | No. | Size | | s. | d. |
|---|---|---|---|---|---|---|---|---|---|
| No. 1. | size $2\frac{1}{2}$ by 2 | each | 0 | 6 | No. 6. | size $6\frac{1}{2}$ by $4\frac{3}{4}$ | ea. | 1 | 10 |
| 2. | „ $3\frac{1}{4}$ by $2\frac{3}{4}$ | „ | 0 | 9 | 7. | „ $8\frac{1}{2}$ by $6\frac{1}{2}$ | „ | 2 | 2 |
| 3. | „ $4\frac{1}{4}$ by $3\frac{1}{4}$ | „ | 1 | 0 | 8. | „ 9 by 7 | „ | 2 | 6 |
| 4. | „ 5 by 4 | „ | 1 | 6 | 9. | „ 10 by 8 | „ | 3 | 0 |
| 5. | Carte de Visite | „ | 1 | 0 | 10. | „ 12 by 10 | „ | 4 | 6 |

Double for stereoscopic pictures, each 2s. 4d.

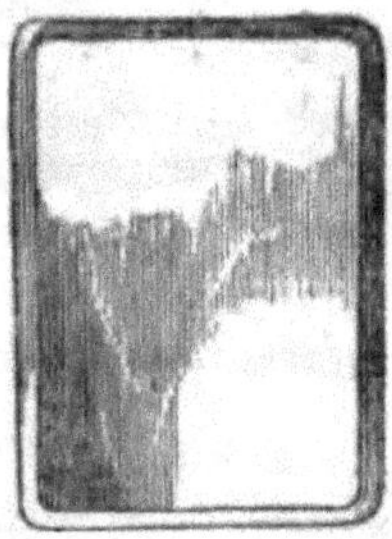

*Fig.* 87.

*Fig.* 88.

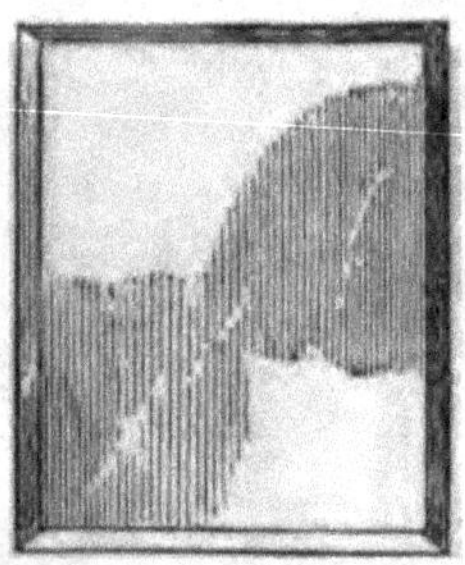

*Fig.* 89.

*Fig.* 90.

## GLASS CUTTING OR SHAPING PLATES,

*With Bevelled and Polished Edges* (*Figs.* 87, 88, 89, 90).

These plates are for placing over the positive paper prints before mounting, and are of four patterns—Oval, Square, Dome, and Cushion (*Figs.* 87, 88, 89, 90), being held firmly on to the picture. When the best position of the picture is obtained, a sharp-pointed knife is run along the outer-polished edge of the shape; the *picture is then* ready to be placed on card-board.

| | | | | s. | d. |
|---|---|---|---|---|---|
| No. 1. | for pictures | 2½ by 2 | each | 0 | 6 |
| 2. | " | 3¼ by 2¾ | " | 0 | 6 |
| 3. | " | 4¼ by 3¼ | " | 0 | 9 |
| 4. | " | 5 by 4 | " | 1 | 0 |
| 5. | " | 6½ by 4¾ | " | 1 | 4 |
| 6. | " | 8½ by 6½ | " | 1 | 6 |
| 7. | " | 10 by 8 | " | 2 | 3 |
| 8. Carte de Visite | | | , | 0 | 9 |

*** The above prices are the same for any shape, as in figures above.

Cutting-knives for using with above, each, 1s.

*Fig.* 91.

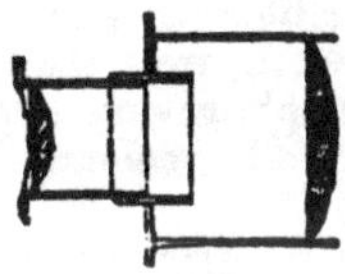

*Fig.* 92.

| | £ | s. | d. |
|---|---|---|---|
| Photographic Visuometer (*Fig.* 91), for enabling the tourist to judge of the effect of a landscape, folding for the pocket . . . . 3s. 6d. and | 0 | 4 | 6 |
| Focussing Glass or Eye-piece, for obtaining a perfectly sharp and distinct picture on the focussing screen (*Fig.* 92) . . . . . . 7s. 6d. and | 0 | 10 | 0 |
| Instrument to count Seconds, with Alarum . . . | 2 | 5 | 0 |
| Ditto, ditto, without Alarum . . . . . | 1 | 1 | 0 |

## PHOTOGRAPHIC COLOURS,

*For Colouring Photographs on Plate or Collodion.*

| | | | |
|---|---|---|---|
| No. 1. Box, containing 7 colours, with gold and silver shells, brushes, &c. . . . . . . . . | 0 | 6 | 0 |
| No. 2. Ditto, containing 14 colours, gold and silver shells, and an assortment of brushes . . | 0 | 8 | 0 |
| No. 3. Ditto, containing 21 colours, ditto . . . | 0 | 12 | 0 |

Elastic Bottle for removing dust from plate, No. 1, 2s.; No. 2, 2s. 9d.; No. 3, 3s. 6d.

# NEWMAN'S

## INSTRUCTIONS FOR COLOURING PHOTOGRAPHS

IN

*Oil Colours, Water Colours, Photographic Colours, &c.*

**WITH VALUABLE INFORMATION ON COLOURING, SIZING, VARNISHING, ETC. ETC.**

FOURTH EDITION, BOUND IN CLOTH, PRICE 2s. 6d.

---

## NEWMAN'S PHOTOGRAPHIC COLOURS (POWDER).

These colours are prepared by a *peculiar process*, meeting every want of the photographer. They adhere with ease and fulness to the plate; while, from their transparency, *they colour without hiding* the photograph, giving a pure, brilliant, *life-like effect*, unattainable by any other colours.

---

**THE SILVER DAGUERREOTYPE PLATE,**
**THE GLASS COLLODION PLATE,**
**PORTRAITS, LANDSCAPES, &c., TAKEN ON THE PAPER.**

---

THE FOLLOWING ARE SOME OF THE PRINCIPAL COLOURS:—

| | | |
|---|---|---|
| Flesh, Fair, 1 2 | Golden Yellow | Satin White |
| Ditto, Dark, 1 2 | Distance | 3 Greys |
| Carmine | Peach | Silver Grey |
| Carnation | White | 3 Browns |
| Horizon | Black | Rose |
| Lavender | 3 Blues | Permanent Scarlet |
| Crimson | 4 Greens | Claret |
| Plum | Orange | White (Solarization) |
| 3 Complexions | Pink | Background |
| Lips | Puce | &c., &c., &c. |
| 3 Yellows | Damask | |

In Small Bottles, sealed and tied over, price 1s. each.

---

Newman's Positive Colouring Varnish, 1s. and 1s. 6d. per Bottle.

Newman's Positive Colouring Varnish, for Non-Inverted Positives, 1s. and 1s. 6d. per Bottle.

Newman's Preparation, for Sizing Salted and Albumenized Paper, 1s. and 1s. 6d. per Bottle.

## PHOTOGRAPHIC BRUSHES.

| | | s. | d. |
|---|---|---|---|
| Nos. 1 and 2, Small Camel Hair | per dozen | 1 | 6 |
| Ditto, No. 3. | ,, | 2 | 0 |
| Sables in Quill | each 4d., 6d., to | 1 | 0 |
| Miniature Brushes | per dozen | 4 | 0 |
| Sables in Albata, very fine | ,, 4s. to | 6 | 0 |
| Camel Hair Dusters | each | 0 | 3 |
| Bound Camel Hair, for Chemicals | 6d., 9d., and | 1 | 0 |
| Ditto, with silver wire | each | 1 | 6 |
| Flat Brushes, for Chemicals | up to 4 inches, per inch | 0 | 9 |
| Ditto, in tufts | 4 inches, per inch | 1 | 0 |
| Ditto, 6 Quills in handle | each | 1 | 6 |
| Ditto, ditto, large | ,, | 2 | 0 |
| Ditto, in Tin, half to six inches | at per inch | 0 | 9 |
| Round Camel Hair in Tin | each 4d. to | 2 | 6 |

(ALL POLISHED HANDLES.)

| | | | |
|---|---|---|---|
| Stumps | each 4d. and | 0 | 6 |
| Gold Shells | each 6d. and | 1 | 0 |
| Silver or Alumina Shells | each | 0 | 6 |

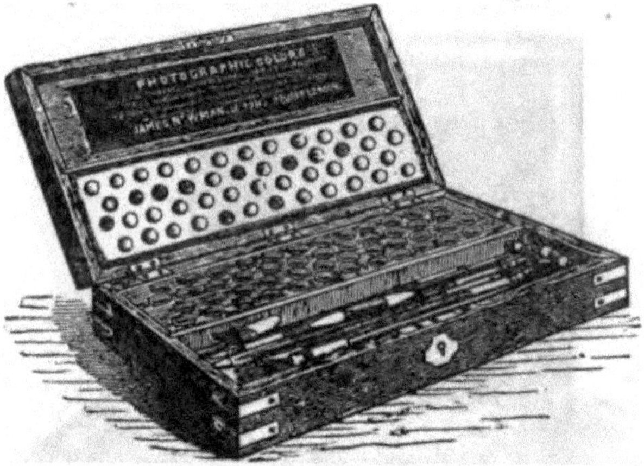

*Fig.* 98.

**Lock Mahogany Box,** with Velvet Palette, Brushes,

| | | £ | s. | d. |
|---|---|---|---|---|
| Stumps, Shells, &c. | 36 Colours | 2 | 2 | 0 |
| Ditto | 24 ,, | 1 | 11 | 6 |
| Ditto | 18 ,, | 1 | 5 | 0 |
| Ditto | 12 ,, | 1 | 0 | 0 |
| Ditto | 9 ,, | 0 | 10 | 6 |

| | £ | s. | d. |
|---|---|---|---|
| **Slide Boxes,** containing any number of Colours, with Brushes, Stumps, Shells, &c. . . . . . | | | |
| **Albata and Brass-bound Dove-tailed Mahogany Boxes,** with extra reserve of Brushes, Stumps, &c., for hot climates, from . . . . . . . | 2 | 2 | 0 |

# PHOTOGRAPHIC COLOURS.

## SUPERFINE WATER COLOURS.

*Newman's Mahogany Boxes, arranged with Extra Colours, especially for Photographic Portraiture, with Slabs, Sable & Camel Hair Brushes, &c.*

| | | | s. | d. | s. | d. |
|---|---|---|---|---|---|---|
| **Mahogany Slide Boxes,** | 12 | Half-Cakes . | 7 | 0 | 9 | 0 |
| Ditto | 18 | " . | 10 | 6 | 13 | 0 |
| Ditto | 24 | " . | 14 | 0 | 18 | 0 |
| Ditto | 12 | Whole Cakes . | 12 | 0 | 16 | 0 |
| Ditto | 18 | " . | 20 | 0 | 24 | 0 |
| Ditto | 24 | " . | 24 | 0 | 30 | 0 |

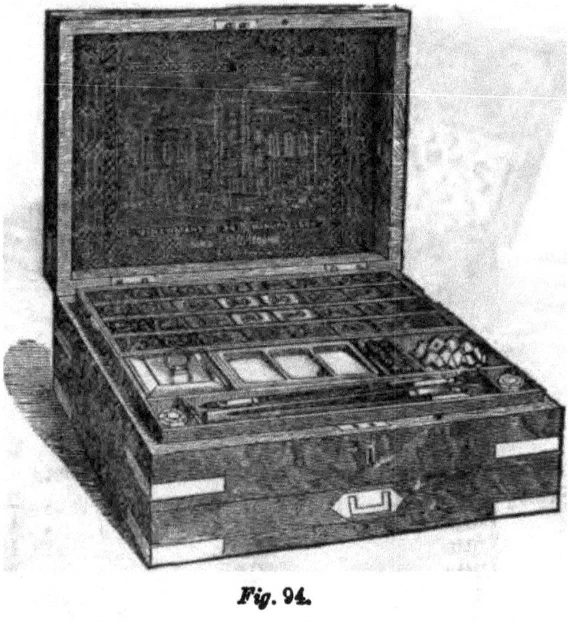

*Fig. 94.*

| | | | s. | d. | s. | d. |
|---|---|---|---|---|---|---|
| **Mahogany Lock Box,** with Sable and Camel Hair Brushes, Slabs, &c. | 12 Half-Cakes | . | 10 | 6 | 12 | 6 |
| Ditto | 18 ,, | . | 14 | 0 | 18 | 0 |
| Ditto | 24 ,, | . | 18 | 0 | 25 | 0 |
| Ditto | 12 Whole Cakes | . | 16 | 0 | 20 | 0 |
| Ditto | 18 ,, | . | 22 | 0 | 28 | 0 |
| Ditto | 24 ,, | . | 31 | 6 | 42 | 0 |
| **Handsome Best Box,** with Water Glasses, Sable, and Camel Hair Pencils, Drawer, Slabs, Body-Colour, and | 12 Cakes | . | 31 | 6 | 35 | 0 |
| Ditto | 18 ,, | . | 40 | 0 | 48 | 0 |
| Ditto | 24 ,, | . | 45 | 0 | 63 | 0 |

*Fig.* 95.

## MOIST WATER COLOURS.

| | | | s. | d. | s. | d. |
|---|---|---|---|---|---|---|
| **Japanned Box,** with selected list of the Improved Moist Colours for Photographic portraiture, and Brushes | 10 Half-Cups | . | 10 | 6 | 12 | 6 |
| Ditto | 12 ,, | . | 12 | 0 | 15 | 0 |
| Ditto | 16 ,, | . | 15 | 0 | 20 | 0 |
| Ditto | 18 ,, | . | 17 | 0 | 22 | 0 |
| Ditto | 10 Whole Cups | . | 15 | 0 | 20 | 0 |
| Ditto | 12 ,, | . | 18 | 0 | 25 | 0 |
| Ditto | 16 ,, | . | 25 | 0 | 35 | 0 |
| Ditto | 18 ,, | . | 31 | 6 | 40 | 0 |

The higher prices in the second column are for extra and more expensive but necessary Colours and Brushes.

# OIL COLOURS.

*Boxes, with Oil Colours, especially selected for Photographic Portraiture, with Palette, Sable & Hog-Hair Brushes, Oils, Varnishes, Palette Knife, Softener, &c.*

| | | | £ | s. | d. |
|---|---|---|---|---|---|
| **Japanned Boxes,** with folding Palette, Brushes, &c. | | | | | |
| Varnishes, Oils, &c., &c. | 12 Tubes | . . . . | 1 | 8 | 0 |
| Ditto long | 12 „ | . . . . | 1 | 8 | 0 |
| Ditto | 16 „ | . . . . | 1 | 15 | 0 |
| Ditto | 20 „ | . . . . | 2 | 6 | 0 |
| Ditto | 27 „ | . . . . | 3 | 10 | 0 |
| Ditto | 30 „ | and Double Bottom for Millboards, *very complete* . | 4 | 4 | 0 |

*The larger the Boxes, in Oil or Water Colours, the more complete the selection of Brushes, Oils, Varnishes, Slabs, Dippers, &c.*

*Fig.* 96.

*Fig.* 97.

# STEREOSCOPES AND STEREOSCOPIC PICTURES.

Stereoscopes are of two kinds, namely, the Reflecting Stereoscope of Professor Wheatstone (*Fig.* 98), and the Lenticular or refracting one of Sir David Brewster (*Figs.* 96 & 99). They both possess the power, as their name implies, of exhibiting objects properly prepared as solids; that is to say, precisely as we see them in nature, having three dimensions—length, breadth, and thickness.

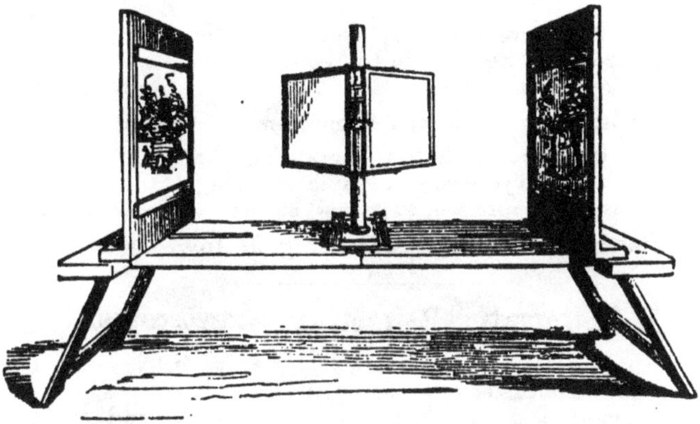

(*Fig*. 98.)

The Reflecting Stereoscope (*Fig*. 98) is best adapted to the display of large pictures and views; while the Lenticular one is most suited for the exhibition of portraits, architectural subjects, still life, groups of statuary, and such objects which do not suffer by being reduced to pictures of small size.

One of the most beautiful applications of photography is, the taking of pictures fitted for the Stereoscope; in fact, this is the only really correct means by which we can obtain them.

**Reflecting Stereoscope** for large views (*Fig*. 98) £3 3s. & £4 4s.

(*Fig*. 99.)

| | | *s.* *d.* | | *s.* *d.* |
|---|---|---|---|---|
| No. 1. | Refracting stereoscope in japanned tin | | | 2 6 |
| No. 2. | Ditto, ditto (Fig. 96) in mahogany or rosewood . . . . . . | 5 0 | to | 7 6 |

| | | s. | d. | | s. | d. |
|---|---|---|---|---|---|---|
| No. 3. | Ditto, ditto, with improved Prismatic eye-pieces (Fig. 99), in rosewood, mahogany, or other woods . . . . | 7 | 6 | to | 21 | 0 |
| No. 4. | Ditto, ditto, with mirror reflectors . | 10 | 0 | to | 25 | 0 |
| No. 5. | Ditto, ditto, with top, containing the Prismatic eye-pieces, capable of being raised or depressed, to suit all sights . | 16 | 0 | to | 30 | 0 |

Stands for stereoscopes, as per Fig. 97, from 12s. each.

## Achromatic Refracting Stereoscopes.

| | | £ | s. | d. | | £ | s. | d. |
|---|---|---|---|---|---|---|---|---|
| No. 1. | Achromatic stereoscope, plain mounting, . . . . . | 1 | 15 | 0 | and | 2 | 0 | 0 |
| No. 2. | Ditto, ditto, ornamental wood or leather . . . . . | 2 | 2 | 0 | and | 2 | 10 | 0 |
| No. 3. | Ditto, ditto, plain mounting and stand . . . . . | 2 | 12 | 6 | and | 3 | 3 | 0 |
| No. 4. | Ditto, ditto, ornamental wood and stand . . . . . | 3 | 3 | 0 | and | 4 | 4 | 0 |

## Patent Revolving or Magazine Stereoscopes.

| | | £ | s. | d. | | £ | s. | d. |
|---|---|---|---|---|---|---|---|---|
| No. 1. | Magazine stereoscope, to hold and exhibit 25 transparent glass, or 50 paper slides . . | 4 | 4 | 0 | to | 8 | 8 | 0 |
| No. 2. | Ditto, ditto, with achromatic lenses . . . . . . | 5 | 5 | 0 | to | 10 | 10 | 0 |

Stereoscopic slides for refracting stereoscopes, 9d., 1s., and 1s. 6d. each.

Ditto, on glass, 4s. 6d., 6s., and 7s. 6d. each.

Large views on paper, for reflecting stereoscope, from per pair, 7s. 6d.

## CARTE DE VISITE ALBUMS.

Albums for holding Carte de Visite pictures in a variety of mounting, and beautifully bound and finished, of sizes to contain 10, 25, 50, 80, and 100 pictures, price, according to number to contain and finish; from 5s. to 25s.

and many of the most delicate lines, which add the deepest beauty to a picture, are altogether lost unless the ROLLING MACHINE be used.

In the words of the PHOTOGRAPHIC NEWS of the 14th March, 1862, and the PHOTOGRAPHIC TIMES of the 1st of June, 1862 (from which many of these remarks are borrowed):—

"Until the trial is actually made, it is difficult to believe the difference in a print which can be produced by the mere change of surface. Of course, this improvement in appearance results from rolling by any good machine, possessing a perfectly burnished plate, and giving a very powerful pressure."

"This rolling and finishing is now absolutely necessary to render a print marketable, and fit for competition; and it is only right our readers should know which of the many now offered to photographers is the BEST, MOST EFFICIENT, and CHEAPEST."

These observations are applicable to all photographs, but especially to *cartes de visite*, and portraits generally; the "character" and "expression" of the countenance frequently depending altogether on those extremely delicate lines and finely-toned shades, which cannot be traced till the ROLLING MACHINE has done its work.

It will be obvious that, in a matter of such vital importance, no photographer can afford to have an inferior article, while no purchaser wishes to give an extravagant price even for a good one. The machines made by I. D. WADDY are at the same time perfect in material, exquisite in workmanship, and moderate in price. A steel plate, very highly polished, is passed, by the action of cog-wheels, between two cylinders, which are approximated by means of regulating screws so as to secure immense power of compression.

Directions for their use, and for their more perfect preservation from accident, or injury, are given by the maker with every machine. We feel that we can confidently recommend these Improved Rolling Machines, because every thing is done to ensure their excellence. Made by experienced workmen, from the most perfect materials, under the eye of the manufacturer, who has introduced all the latest improvements, and yet has retained that simplicity of construction so indispensable to regular and hard work, and carefully tested before they are allowed to leave the factory, may safely bear the guarantee which the maker invariably supplies.

At the same time, the prices are remarkably low, and could not, indeed, have been fixed at such a moderate figure, if Mr. Waddy had not possessed great advantages in the extensive works at which these machines are made. Artists in all parts of the world, therefore, may rely that these neat and compact, but strong and perfect, little rollers, will travel with perfect safety, and will do their work in such a style as to afford the purchaser the satisfaction of beholding *the realization* of his brightest hopes.

## PARTICULARS, SIZES, AND PRICES OF

# WADDY'S ROLLING MACHINES & PRESSES.

*Fig.* 100.

DOUBLE GEARED MACHINE, WITH FLY WHEEL AND CONNECTED PRESSURE SCREWS.

Size of Plate 18×12, £7; 21×15, £8 15s.; 24×18, £11. (*Fig.* 100.)

*Fig.* 101.

DOUBLE GEARED AND FLY WHEEL.

This is the Machine for which there is the largest demand.
Size of Plate 18×12, £5 5s.; 21×15. £7; 24×18, £9. (*Fig.* 101.)

SINGLE GEAR MACHINE.

Size of Plate 18×12, £4 15s; 21×15, £6 6; 24×18, £8 5s.

All the above Machines are supplied with burnished steel plates and mahogany boards.

Metal tables, planed on both sides, may be had, if preferred, in place of wood, as under:—

18 by 12, 5s.—21 by 15, 7s.—24 by 18, 9s. Extra.

*Fig.* 102.

| SMALL MACHINE FOR CARTES DE VISITE (*Fig.* 102). | £ | s. | d. |
|---|---|---|---|
| Rollers two inches in diameter and four inches long . | 1 | 10 | 0 |
| SMALL MACHINE FOR CARTES DE VISITE (*Fig.* 102), BUT WITH PLATE. | | | |
| Size of Plate $7\frac{1}{4}$ by $3\frac{3}{4}$ . . . . . . . . | 1 | 15 | 0 |
| AMATEUR'S MACHINE. | | | |
| Size of Plate 9 by 6 . . . . . . . . | 2 | 15 | 0 |

These two Machines are supplied with burnished steel plate and planed metal table.

*⁎* In ordering, be sure to give the price, and thus avoid mistake.

BLAND & CO., 153, Fleet Street, London.

## Stoppered Bottles for Chemicals.

| Green Glass (narrow mouth). | s. | d. | White Glass (narrow mouth). | s. | d. | White Glass (wide mouth). | s. | d. |
|---|---|---|---|---|---|---|---|---|
| 5 oz. capacity | 0 | 5 | 1 oz. | 0 | 4 | 1 oz, | 0 | 5 |
| 10 „ | 0 | 6 | 2 | 0 | 6 | 2 | 0 | 7 |
| 15 „ | 0 | 7 | 4 | 0 | 8 | 4 | 0 | 9 |
| 20 „ | 0 | 8 | 5 | 0 | 9 | 8 | 0 | 11 |
| 40 „ | 0 | 10 | 10 | 0 | 10 | 10 | 1 | 0 |
| 80 „ | 1 | 0 | 20 | 1 | 3 | 20 | 1 | 6 |

Glass Carboy, for distilled water, to hold 2 gallons, bound with wicker work, 4s. 6d.

# PURE CHEMICALS AND PREPARATIONS

*Used in the Photographic Processes.*

| | | | s. | d. |
|---|---|---|---|---|
| Acid, Acetic, Beaufoy's | | per lb. | 1 | 0 |
| „ Glacial, for paper processes | | per oz. | 0 | 9 |
| „ „ for Collodion | per lb. 5s., | „ | 0 | 4 |
| „ Citric | per lb. 4s., | „ | 0 | 4 |
| „ Formic | | „ | 0 | 4 |
| „ Gallic | | „ | 1 | 3 |
| „ Nitric, sp. gr. 1·450 | per lb. 2s. | „ | 0 | 2 |
| „ Pyrogallic | per oz. 6s., | per dram | 0 | 10 |
| „ Sulphuric | | per lb. | 0 | 3 |
| „ pure | | „ | 1 | 6 |
| „ Tannic | | per oz. | 1 | 0 |
| Alcohol | per pint 4s. | „ | 0 | 3 |
| „ Absolute, sp. gr. ·800 | „ 7s. 6d. | „ | 0 | 6 |
| Ammonia, sp. gr. ·880 | „ 1s. 6d. | „ | 0 | 2 |
| Ammonium, Bromide | | „ | 2 | 6 |
| „ Chloride | | „ | 0 | 3 |
| „ Iodide | | „ | 2 | 6 |
| Barium, Chloride | per lb. 2s. | „ | 0 | 2 |
| „ Iodide | | „ | 3 | 0 |
| Baryta, nitrate | per lb. 2s. | „ | 0 | 2 |
| Benzole | | per pint | 2 | 0 |
| Bromine | | per oz. | 2 | 6 |
| Cadmium, Bromide | | „ | 3 | 0 |
| „ Iodide | | „ | 2 | 6 |
| Calcium, Bromide | | „ | 3 | 6 |
| „ Iodide | | „ | 3 | 6 |
| Charcoal, Animal | | „ | 3d. & | 6 |
| Chloroform | | „ | 0 | 8 |
| Collodions, Ponting's, see page 93 | | | | |
| „ Keene's „ 95 | | | | |
| „ Thomas's „ 96 | | | | |
| „ Ramsden's „ 94 | | | | |
| „ Bland and Co.'s, Negative | | per pint | 12 | 6 |
| „ „ Positive | | „ | 9 | 0 |
| Cotton Wool | | per oz. | 0 | 3 |
| Dextrine | per lb. 1s. 6d. | „ | 0 | 2 |
| Diamond Polish for cleaning plates | per bottle 6d. and | | 1 | 0 |
| Æther, Sulphuric, sp. gr. ·724 | per lb. 7s. | per oz. | 0 | 6 |
| „ „ ·750 | „ 6s. | „ | 0 | 5 |
| „ „ Methylated Spirit | | | | |
| „ sp. gr. ·720 | per lb. 3s. | per oz. | 0 | 3 |
| Glycerine | „ 6s. | „ | 0 | 6 |

| | | s. | d. |
|---|---|---|---|
| Gold Chloride, in 15 gr. tubes ¼ dram, each | | 2 | 6 |
| " " ½ " | | 4 | 6 |
| " " 1 " | | 8 | 6 |
| " and Soda, non-deliquescent, neutral, 15 grs. | | 2 | 6 |
| Iodine, pure (variable) | per oz. | 1 | 6 |
| Iron Iodide | " | 2 | 6 |
| " Protosulphate . . . per lb. 1s. | " | 0 | 1 |
| Kaolin (China Clay) . . . " 1s. | " | 0 | 1 |
| Lead, Nitrate | " | 0 | 2 |
| Mercury, Distilled . . . per lb. 3s. 6d. | " | 0 | 3 |
| " Bichloride | " | 0 | 5 |
| Naphtha | per pint | 1 | 6 |
| Potash, Bichromate | per oz. | 0 | 3 |
| " Nitrate . . . per lb. 1s. | " | 0 | 1 |
| Potassium, Bromide | " | 2 | 0 |
| " Cyanide . . in 1 lb. bottles, 4s. | " | 0 | 4 |
| " Iodide | " | 1 | 6 |
| Plate Cleaning Solution | per bottle 6d. & | 1 | 0 |
| Silver, Nitrate, see page 91. | | | |
| Soda, Acetate . . . per lb. 2s. | per oz. | 0 | 2 |
| " Hyposulphite | per lb. | 0 | 8 |
| " Phosphate | per oz. | 0 | 2 |
| Sodium, Chloride | " | 0 | 2 |
| " Fluoride | " | 1 | 0 |
| Solution for Iodizing Waxed Paper | per pint | 4 | 0 |
| " rendering Waxed Paper sensitive | " | 8 | 0 |
| Sugar of Milk | per oz. | 0 | 3 |
| Tannin | " | 1 | 0 |
| Test Paper, Blue Litmus | per book | 0 | 2 |
| " Red | " | 0 | 2 |
| Tripoli | per oz. | 0 | 3 |
| Uranium, Nitrate | " | 2 | 0 |
| Varnish Amber in Chlorform | " | 0 | 10 |
| " Benzoin, see page 91 | " | 1 | 0 |
| " Bristol Hard (Ponting's), see page 94, 5 oz. 1s. 6d. 10 oz. 2s. 6d. | per pint | 4 | 6 |
| " Crystal Varnish, see page 91, per pint, 4s. | per oz. | 0 | 4 |
| " Black Jet | per bottle 6d. & | 1 | 0 |
| " Newman's Positive Colouring see page 78 . . . " | 1s. & | 2 | 6 |
| " Newman's Penetrating, see page 78 " | 1s. 6d. & | 3 | 0 |
| " Sohnèe Freres . . . " | | 2 | 0 |
| Water, distilled | per gallon | 0 | 8 |
| White Wax | per lb. | 3 | 0 |

## NITRATE OF SILVER.

These prices are for Cash only, which must accompany the order, as Credit cannot be given.

| | Ordinary Commercial. | Fused. | Pure re-crystallized. |
|---|---|---|---|
| | s. d. | s. d. | s. d. |
| 1 oz. and under 5 | 4 0 | 4 3 | 4 6 |
| 5 " 10 | 3 9 | 4 0 | 4 3 |
| 10 " 25 | 3 8 | 3 10 | 4 0 |
| 25 " 50 | 3 7 | 3 9 | 3 10 |

| | s. | d. |
|---|---|---|
| Nitrate of Silver Bath, prepared for Positive or Negative process, inclusive of bottles . . . per pint | 7 | 6 |
| Nitrate of Silver Bath, 60 grs. to the oz. of distilled water, for sensitizing albumenized paper . . . per oz. | 0 | 7 |

---

### BLAND & CO.'S
## LIQUID JET,

FOR APPLYING TO THE BACK OF COLLODION POSITIVES,

GIVING GREAT BRILLIANCY AND LUSTRE TO THE PICTURES.

**This peculiar Preparation is not liable to crack under any circumstances of age or exposure.**

Price 6d. per 4-ounce bottle; 8-ounce ditto 1s.

---

### BLAND & CO.'S
## CRYSTAL VARNISH,

FOR POSITIVE PICTURES.

This preparation does not require the plate to be warmed; it dries in a few moments.—Price 4d. per ounce.

---

### BLAND & CO.'S
## BENZOIN VARNISH,

FOR PROTECTING THE FINISHED NEGATIVE.

1s. *per Ounce.*

This varnish does not require the plate to be warmed, but dries instantly, leaving a perfectly hard, transparent coating on the picture.

# DRY COLLODION PLATES,

## BY DR. NORRIS'S PATENT PROCESS.

AGENTS,

## BLAND & CO.,

OPTICIANS TO THE QUEEN,

**153, Fleet Street, London, E. C.**

## PRICE LIST OF
# DRY COLLODION PLATES.

## DR. NORRIS'S PATENT PROCESS.

| Size | | £ | s. | d. |
|---|---|---|---|---|
| 4¼ by 3¼ | inches, per dozen . . . | 0 | 5 | 0 |
| 5 by 4 | „ „ . . . | 0 | 6 | 8 |
| 6½ by 4¾ | „ „ . . . | 0 | 10 | 0 |
| 6¾ by 3¼ | „ „ . . . | 0 | 8 | 9 |
| 7 by 6 | „ „ . . . | 0 | 14 | 0 |
| 8½ by 6½ | „ „ . . . | 0 | 18 | 0 |
| 9 by 7 | „ „ . . . | 1 | 1 | 0 |
| 10 by 8 | „ „ . . . | 1 | 6 | 8 |
| 12 by 10 | „ „ . . . | 2 | 0 | 0 |

## PRICE LIST OF DR. NORRIS'S

NEGATIVE PORTRAIT AND RAPID LANDSCAPE PLATES.

| Size | | £ | s. | d. |
|---|---|---|---|---|
| 4¼ by 3¼ | inches, per dozen . . . | 0 | 5 | 9 |
| 5 by 4 | „ „ . . . | 0 | 8 | 0 |
| 6¾ by 3¼ | „ „ . . . | 0 | 10 | 0 |
| 6½ by 4¾ | „ „ . . . | 0 | 11 | 6 |
| 7 by 6 | „ „ . . . | 0 | 16 | 0 |
| 8½ by 6½ | „ „ . . . | 1 | 1 | 0 |
| 9 by 7 | „ „ . . . | 1 | 3 | 6 |
| 10 by 8 | „ „ . . . | 1 | 10 | 6 |
| 11 by 9 | „ „ . . . | 1 | 18 | 0 |
| 12 by 10 | „ „ . . . | 2 | 6 | 0 |

All other Sizes to order, up to 36 by 24 inches.

The Plates are securely packed in Cases impervious to light or moisture. Every Package is accompanied with full and lucid *directions for* exposing, developing, fixing, &c.

# PONTING'S COLLODIONS,

FOR NEGATIVE AND POSITIVE PICTURES.

AGENTS FOR LONDON,

## BLAND AND CO.,

OPTICIANS TO THE QUEEN,

153, Fleet Street, London, E.C.

---

## PONTING'S UNCHANGEABLE COLLODIONS.

The Manufacturer has the gratification to announce that he has been awarded the **only Medal given for Collodion by the Jury of the International Exhibition,** thus endorsing the favourable opinion so long expressed by the Photographic Public.

---

### Jurors' Reports, Class 14.

(No. 3043.) BLAND & Co., *as Wholesale Agents, exhibit the* only Collodion *to which a* MEDAL *was awarded, that of* Mr. PONTING, *of Bristol* (3136). *This Collodion, on trial by the* Jury, *fully bore out the reputation it has obtained amongst Practical Photographers, as extremely* rapid, *and giving very delicate details, full of* half tone *and* brilliancy. *The* stability *of this* Collodion *is a feature to which the* Jurors *call* especial attention. *At the period when the trial was made, the* Sensitive Collodion *had been prepared* many months; *and as some of the Members had been in the habit of using the same preparation, they were enabled by their individual experience to confirm and endorse the* results of the trial *then made, as to the* high character *for* SENSITIVENESS *and* STABILITY *of this* Collodion.

---

## Ponting's Iodized Collodion for Negatives.

This preparation has been so many years before the public, and has met with such constantly increasing favour both at home and abroad, that it will be unnecessary to say anything about it.

Sold in stoppered bottles, 5 oz. 4s., 10 oz. 7s. 6d., 20 oz. 15s., 40 oz. 30s.

---

## Ponting's Bromo-Iodized Collodion for Negatives.

Specially prepared for Instantaneous Pictures and for quick Portraiture.

This combination being made upon the same principles as the above, like it, retains its sentiveness for years, and is, probably, the most rapid in action of any yet introduced, producing very fine soft pictures, full of detail; and though it suffers under the disadvantage of requiring two developments, first with iron, and afterwards with pyrogallic, yet the important gain of a short exposure, together with the clean and easy working properties, imparted by the use of bromine, will no doubt make it a favourite, both with the professional man and the amateur.

Mr. H. P. Robinson, of Leamington, writes of this Collodion: "Your Bromo-Iodized Collodion is the best I have ever used; it will take intensity, which no other Bromo-Iodized Collodion ever would that I have used before."

This, likewise, answers admirably for dry plates. Prices and sizes same as above.

## Ponting's Bromo-Iodized Collodion for Positives.

This, like the two foregoing preparations, is unchangeable. Possessing extreme rapidity, it produces first-class pictures of extreme delicacy and beauty, and has met with a large share of public favour.

Sold in corked bottles, 5 oz. 2s. 6d., 10 oz. 5s., 20 oz. 10s.

The manufacturer has now had nearly ten years of large experience in the preparation of Collodion, and can safely guarantee that these preparations possess in an eminent degree the highest qualities of good Collodion; while they are rich in cotton, they likewise have a brightness and fluidity which produce a smooth and even film free from spots, of great strength and tenacity' allowing the various operations connected with the production of a picture to be conducted without fear of rupture of the film. To this must be added, the remarkable qualities of keeping indefinitely, combined with the highest degree of sensitiveness, properties possessed alone by Collodions of his manufacture.

## Bristol Hard Varnish for Collodion Negatives.

This Varnish, the result of a number of careful experiments, extending over several years, is confidently recommended to photographers as both the best and cheapest of its kind. It stands the wear and tear of printing a large number of copies better than any other, and does not stick in the hottest sun.

Sold in bottles, 5 oz. 1s. 6d., 10 oz. 2s. 6d., 20 oz. 4s. 6d.

MANUFACTORY, 32, HIGH STREET, BRISTOL.

# RAMSDEN'S COLLODIONS.

AGENTS,

## BLAND & CO.,

PHOTOGRAPHIC INSTRUMENT MAKERS TO THE QUEEN.

153, Fleet Street, London, E.C.

Ramsden's New Negative Collodion, for Carte de Visite and Stereoscopic pictures, 4 oz. 2s. 6d., 10 oz. 5s. 6d., 20 oz. 11s.

# KEENE'S COLLODIONS.

AGENTS,

## BLAND & CO.,

PHOTOGRAPHIC INSTRUMENT MAKERS TO THE QUEEN,

153, Fleet Street, London, E.C.

### KEENE'S (original) FOTHERGILL OR DRY PROCESS COLLODION,

Universally acknowledged unequalled for all Preservative and Dry Processes; peculiarly adapted for use in hot climates, and an excellent Wet Process Collodion, particularly for Views and Copying purposes. This Collodion is so well known that further comment is considered unnecessary.—Pints (16 oz.), 11s. 6d.; half-pints, 6s.; quarter-pints, 3s. 6d., in separate solutions, or Iodized.

It may be used twelve or twenty-four hours after being Iodized, but will be found to work best for the Dry Processes a few weeks, and is by some preferred even months after.

Full directions for the Fothergill process are given with each bottle.

### KEENE'S (Cadmium) WET PROCESS COLLODIONS

Are specially prepared for the Wet Process, and possess the following characteristics:—Extreme sensitiveness, uniformity, structureless film, extraordinary keeping properties, delicate detail without flatness, and vigour without harshness; and embrace all the requirements for Instantaneous, Carte de Visite, and Portrait and View purposes of every description. They consist of the Normal Collodion, with different Iodizers, to meet the varied requirements of Photographers, viz:—

CADMIUM IODIZED.—Highly sensitive, gives full intensity, and well adapted for use in dull weather, or with a good diffused light, where much contrast is desired.

**CADMIUM BROMO-IODIZED.**—Giving more detail, and the best for general purposes, whether Instantaneous, Carte de Visite, or View. N.B. This is the Collodion supplied to agents, and recommended to amateurs, and those not requiring one of a special character; it works well under all circumstances, is very uniform, long keeping, and sensitive.

**EXTRA BROMO-IODIZED.**—Containing the Iodide and Bromide in equivalent proportions; more particularly adapted for View Photography, under extreme circumstances of light and heat, and other special purposes.

The Normal Collodion can also be had with usual, or any special Iodizer, and in separate solutions to order.—Price; same as Dry Process Collodion; and ⅛-size 1s. 10d. each.

---

## KEENE'S EXTRA SENSITIVE (Bromo-Iodized) POSITIVE COLLODION.

A first-class article at a moderate price, and should be in the hands of every Professional Photographer.—Two-oz. bottles 1s.; 4-oz. 2s.; 8-oz. 4s. each ready Iodized; and pints (16 oz.) separate solutions, 8s.

BLAND & CO., 153, Fleet Street, London.

---

# THOMAS'S COLLODIONS.

AGENTS,

## BLAND & CO.,

OPTICIANS TO THE QUEEN,

153, Fleet Street, London, E.C.

Thomas's Negative Collodion, with Potassium Iodizer, per pint 16s. ½-pint 8s. 6d., 4-oz. 4s.

Thomas's Negative Collodion, with Cadmium Iodizer, pints 16s., ½-pints 8s. 6d., 4-oz. 4s.

Thomas's Negative Collodion, with Bromo-Cadmium Iodizer, pints 16s., ½-pints 8s. 6d., 4-oz. 4s.

Thomas's Negative Collodion and Bromo-Potassium Iodizer, pints 16s., ½-pints 8s. 6d,, 4-oz. 4s.

Thomas's Positive Collodion and Iodizer, pints 16s., ½-pints 8s. 6d., 4-oz. 4s.

BLAND & CO., 153, Fleet Street, London.

*Fig.* 103.

*Fig.* 104.

*Fig.* 105.

## PASSE PARTOUTS.—(*Fig.* 105.)

**No. 1.**

Black or brown ground, bronze bevil, oval, dome, or cushion shape.

| Size | | £ | s. | d. |
|---|---|---|---|---|
| 2½ by 2 | per doz. | 0 | 1 | 6 |
| 3¼ by 2¾ | „ | 0 | 2 | 0 |
| 4¼ by 3¼ | „ | 0 | 2 | 6 |
| 5 by 4 | „ | 0 | 4 | 6 |
| 6½ by 4¾ | „ | 0 | 6 | 6 |
| 8½ by 6½ | „ | 0 | 8 | 6 |

**No. 2.**

White ground, buff bevil, oval, dome, or cushion shape.

| Size | | £ | s. | d. |
|---|---|---|---|---|
| 2½ by 2 | per doz. | 0 | 2 | 0 |
| 3¼ by 2¾ | „ | 0 | 2 | 10 |
| 4¼ by 3¼ | „ | 0 | 3 | 9 |
| 5 by 4 | „ | 0 | 6 | 0 |
| 6½ by 4¾ | „ | 0 | 8 | 0 |
| 8½ by 6½ | „ | 0 | 13 | 0 |

**No. 3.**

Porcelain bevil, dark ground, oval, dome, or cushion shape.

| Size | | £ | s. | d. |
|---|---|---|---|---|
| 2½ by 2 | per doz. | 0 | 2 | 6 |
| 3¼ by 2¾ | „ | 0 | 3 | 0 |
| 4¼ by 3¼ | „ | 0 | 3 | 9 |
| 5 by 4 | „ | 0 | 5 | 9 |
| 6½ by 4¾ | „ | 0 | 8 | 0 |
| 8½ by 6½ | „ | 0 | 14 | 0 |

**No. 4.**

Gold ground, gold bevil, oval, dome, or cushion.

| Size | | £ | s. | d. |
|---|---|---|---|---|
| 2½ by 2 | per doz. | 0 | 4 | 6 |
| 3¼ by 2¾ | „ | 0 | 5 | 6 |
| 4¼ by 3¼ | „ | 0 | 7 | 0 |
| 5 by 4 | „ | 0 | 12 | 0 |
| 6½ by 4¾ | „ | 0 | 15 | 6 |
| 8½ by 6½ | „ | 1 | 10 | 0 |

### No. 5.

Bristol board, smooth or rough, with extra large margin, white bevil, oval, dome, and cushion shape.

| Size | | £ | s. | d. |
|---|---|---|---|---|
| $2\frac{1}{2}$ by 2 . | per doz. | 0 | 2 | 9 |
| $3\frac{1}{4}$ by $2\frac{3}{4}$ . | ,, | 0 | 4 | 0 |
| $4\frac{1}{4}$ by $3\frac{1}{4}$ . | ,, | 0 | 5 | 0 |
| 5 by 4 . | ,, | 0 | 7 | 0 |
| $6\frac{1}{2}$ by $4\frac{3}{4}$ . | ,, | 0 | 9 | 6 |
| $8\frac{1}{2}$ by $6\frac{1}{2}$ . | ,, | 0 | 14 | 0 |
| Ditto, extra | ,, | 0 | 17 | 0 |

### No. 6.

White ground, gold bevil, oval, dome, and cushion shape.

| Size | | £ | s. | d. |
|---|---|---|---|---|
| $2\frac{1}{2}$ by 2 . | per doz. | 0 | 1 | 6 |
| $3\frac{1}{4}$ by $2\frac{3}{4}$ . | ,, | 0 | 2 | 3 |
| $4\frac{1}{4}$ by $3\frac{1}{4}$ . | ,, | 0 | 2 | 9 |
| 5 by 4 . | ,, | 0 | 4 | 6 |
| $6\frac{1}{2}$ by $4\frac{3}{4}$ . | ,, | 0 | 6 | 9 |
| $8\frac{1}{2}$ by $6\frac{1}{2}$ . | ,, | 0 | 9 | [illegible] |

### No. 7.

Tinted ground, two gold bevils, extra margin.

| Size | | £ | s. | d. |
|---|---|---|---|---|
| $2\frac{1}{2}$ by 2 . | per doz. | 0 | 8 | 0 |
| $3\frac{1}{4}$ by $2\frac{3}{4}$ . | ,, | 0 | 8 | 6 |
| $4\frac{1}{4}$ by $3\frac{1}{4}$ . | ,, | 0 | 10 | 0 |
| 5 by 4 . | ,, | 0 | 13 | 6 |
| $6\frac{1}{2}$ by $4\frac{3}{4}$ . | ,, | 0 | 19 | 0 |
| $8\frac{1}{2}$ by $6\frac{1}{2}$ . | ,, | 1 | 6 | 0 |

### No. 8.

Bristol board, with extra large margin, tinted bevil, white ground, and tinted stamped rim.

| Size | | £ | s. | d. |
|---|---|---|---|---|
| $3\frac{1}{4}$ by $2\frac{3}{4}$ . | per doz. | 0 | 7 | 6 |
| $4\frac{1}{4}$ by $3\frac{1}{4}$ . | ,, | 0 | 9 | 6 |
| 5 by 4 . | ,, | 0 | 14 | 0 |
| $6\frac{1}{2}$ by $4\frac{3}{4}$ . | ,, | 1 | 0 | 0 |
| $8\frac{1}{2}$ by $6\frac{1}{2}$ . | ,, | 1 | 10 | 0 |
| Ditto, extra | ,, | 1 | 13 | 6 |

### No. 9.

Tinted ground, gold bevil, and white embossed rim.

| Size | | £ | s. | d. |
|---|---|---|---|---|
| $3\frac{1}{4}$ by $2\frac{3}{4}$ . | per doz. | 0 | 8 | 0 |
| $4\frac{1}{4}$ by $3\frac{1}{4}$ . | ,, | 0 | 10 | 0 |
| 5 by 4 . | ,, | 0 | 14 | 0 |
| $6\frac{1}{2}$ by $4\frac{3}{4}$ . | ,, | 1 | 0 | 0 |
| $8\frac{1}{2}$ by $6\frac{1}{2}$ . | ,, | 1 | 10 | 0 |
| Ditto, extra | ,, | 1 | 14 | 0 |

### No. 10.

White ground, gold bevil and fillet, and white embossed ground.

| Size | | £ | s. | d. |
|---|---|---|---|---|
| $3\frac{1}{4}$ by $2\frac{3}{4}$ . | per doz. | 0 | 8 | 6 |
| $4\frac{1}{4}$ by $3\frac{1}{4}$ . | ,, | 0 | 10 | 6 |
| 5 by 4 . | ,, | 0 | 15 | 0 |
| $6\frac{1}{2}$ by $4\frac{3}{4}$ . | ,, | 1 | 1 | 0 |
| $8\frac{1}{2}$ by $6\frac{1}{2}$ . | ,, | 1 | 11 | 6 |
| Ditto, extra size | ,, | 1 | 15 | 6 |

### No. 11.

Bristol bevil, white ground, and white embossed rim.

| Size | | £ | s. | d. |
|---|---|---|---|---|
| $3\frac{1}{4}$ by $2\frac{3}{4}$ . | per doz. | 0 | 7 | 6 |
| $4\frac{1}{4}$ by $3\frac{1}{4}$ . | ,, | 0 | 9 | 6 |
| 5 by 4 . | ,, | 0 | 14 | 0 |
| $6\frac{1}{2}$ by $4\frac{3}{4}$ . | ,, | 1 | 0 | 0 |
| $8\frac{1}{2}$ by $6\frac{1}{2}$ . | ,, | 1 | 9 | 0 |
| *Ditto, extra size* | ,, | 1 | 13 | 0 |

### No. 12.

Best London make, with glass gilt bevilled edge, extra lines, and bound with gold.

| Size | | £ | s. | d. |
|---|---|---|---|---|
| $3\frac{1}{4}$ by $2\frac{3}{4}$ . | per doz. | 0 | 6 | 0 |
| $4\frac{1}{4}$ by $3\frac{1}{4}$ . | ,, | 0 | 9 | 0 |
| 5 by 4 . | ,, | 0 | 11 | 6 |
| $6\frac{1}{2}$ by $4\frac{3}{4}$ . | ,, | 0 | 16 | 6 |
| $8\frac{1}{2}$ by $6\frac{1}{2}$ . | ,, | 1 | 2 | 6 |
| 9 by 7 . | ,, | 1 | 12 | 6 |

## Stereoscopic Passe Partouts.

| | £ | s. | d. |
|---|---|---|---|
| Stereoscopic Passe-partouts, dark ground, and gold line for positives or negatives on glass, per dozen | 0 | 4 | 0 |
| Ditto, ditto, ornamental, per dozen . . . 7s. and | 0 | 9 | 0 |
| Card Mounts for mounting Stereoscopic paper pictures, in packets of 3 dozen, assorted tints | 0 | 1 | 0 |
| Enamelled Stereoscopic Card Mounts, per gross | 0 | 6 | 6 |
| Ditto, ditto, per dozen | 0 | 0 | 8 |
| Card Mounts, stout, for Carte de Visite pictures, per gross | 0 | 12 | 0 |
| Ditto, ditto, per dozen | 0 | 1 | 6 |
| Card Mounts for large Photographs :— | | | |
| Size 11½ by 9 per dozen | 0 | 3 | 0 |
| 14½ by 10½ „ | 0 | 4 | 9 |
| 22 by 18½ „ | 0 | 11 | 0 |

## ORMOLU FRAMES (*Fig.* 104),

*With Mats, Glasses, and Rings.*

| | | s. | d. |
|---|---|---|---|
| For pictures 2½ by 2 | each | 0 | 10 |
| „ 3¼ by 2¾ | „ | 1 | 3 |
| „ 4¼ by 3¼ | „ | 1 | 8 |
| „ 5 by 4 | „ | 2 | 3 |
| „ 6½ by 4¾ | „ | 3 | 6 |

## PAPIER MACHE FRAMES (*Fig.* 103),

*With Dome, Oval, or Cushion Mats, Glasses, and Suspension Ring.*

| | | s. | d. |
|---|---|---|---|
| For pictures 2½ by 2 | each | 1 | 9 |
| „ 3¼ by 2¾ | „ | 2 | 6 |
| „ 4¼ by 3¼ | „ | 3 | 3 |
| „ 5 by 4 | „ | 3 | 9 |

## Outer Frames for Passe Partouts.

*For Passe Partouts of Sizes given.*

No. 1. Imitation rosewood, or Renaissance pattern.

| | | £ | s. | d. |
|---|---|---|---|---|
| 2½ by 2 | per doz. | 0 | 3 | 6 |
| 3¼ by 2¾ | „ | 0 | 3 | 9 |
| 4¼ by 3¼ | „ | 0 | 4 | 0 |
| 5 by 4 | „ | 0 | 5 | 9 |
| 6½ by 4¾ | „ | 0 | 7 | 6 |
| 8½ by 6½ | „ | 0 | 11 | 0 |
| Ditto, extra | „ | 0 | 15 | 0 |

No. 2. Gilt Frames.

| | | £ | s. | d. |
|---|---|---|---|---|
| 2½ by 2 | per doz. | 0 | 7 | 0 |
| 3¼ by 2¾ | „ | 0 | 8 | 6 |
| 4¼ by 3¼ | „ | 0 | 10 | 0 |
| 5 by 4 | „ | 0 | 12 | 0 |
| 6½ by 4¾ | „ | 0 | 13 | 0 |
| 8½ by 6½ | „ | 0 | 15 | 0 |

No. 3.
Rustic oak, very ornamental, square shape.

| | | £ | s. | d. |
|---|---|---|---|---|
| 2½ by 2 . | per doz. | 0 | 7 | 9 |
| 3¼ by 2¾ . | ,, | 0 | 8 | 6 |
| 4¼ by 3¼ . | ,, | 0 | 9 | 0 |
| 5 by 4 . | ,, | 0 | 13 | 6 |
| 6½ by 4¾ . | ,, | 0 | 16 | 6 |
| 8½ by 6½ . | ,, | 1 | 2 | 0 |

No. 4.
Rustic oak, very ornamental, oval or cushion shape.

| | | £ | s. | d. |
|---|---|---|---|---|
| 2½ by 2 . | per doz. | 0 | 12 | 0 |
| 3¼ by 2¾ . | ,, | 0 | 12 | 6 |
| 4¼ by 3¼ . | ,, | 0 | 13 | 6 |
| 5 by 4 . | ,, | 0 | 19 | 0 |
| 6½ by 4¾ . | ,, | 1 | 1 | 0 |
| 8½ by 6½ . | ,, | 1 | 12 | 0 |

No. 5.
Oval black Frames, polished.

| | | £ | s. | d. |
|---|---|---|---|---|
| 2½ by 2 . | per doz. | 0 | 11 | 6 |
| 3¼ by 2¾ . | ,, | 0 | 12 | 6 |
| 4 by 3¼ . | ,, | 0 | 15 | 6 |
| 5 by 4 . | ,, | 1 | 2 | 6 |
| 6½ by 4¾ . | ,, | 1 | 10 | 6 |
| 8½ by 6½ . | ,, | 2 | 10 | 0 |

No. 6.
German stone paste Frames.

| | | £ | s. | d. |
|---|---|---|---|---|
| 2½ by 2 . | per doz. | 0 | 8 | 0 |
| 3¼ by 2¾ . | ,, | 0 | 8 | 6 |
| 4¼ by 3¼ . | ,, | 0 | 9 | 0 |
| 5 by 4 . | ,, | 0 | 12 | 6 |
| 6½ by 4¾ . | ,, | 0 | 14 | 6 |
| 8½ by 6½ . | ,, | 0 | 16 | 6 |

*Fig.* 106.

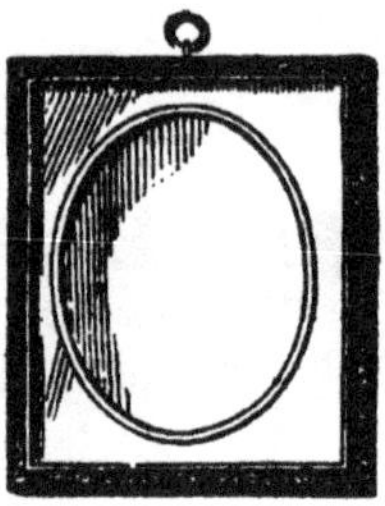

*Fig.* 107.

## MOROCCO CASES, TRAYS, &c.

No. 1.
Common cotton velvet cases, with embossed leather top, with mats, glasses, and preservers.

| | | £ | s. | d. |
|---|---|---|---|---|
| 2½ by 2 . | per doz. | 0 | 2 | 6 |
| 3¼ by 2¾ . | ,, | 0 | 4 | 6 |
| 4¼ by 3¼ . | ,, | 0 | 7 | 6 |
| 5 by 4 . | ,, | 0 | 15 | 0 |
| 6½ by 4¾ . | ,, | 1 | 4 | 0 |

No. 2.
Common cotton velvet cases, with embossed leather top, gilt rim to edges, with mats, glasses, and preservers.

| | | £ | s. | d. |
|---|---|---|---|---|
| 2½ by 2 . | per doz. | 0 | 3 | 0 |
| 3¼ by 2¾ . | ,, | 0 | 5 | 0 |
| 4¼ by 3¼ . | ,, | 0 | 8 | 3 |
| 5 by 4 . | ,, | 0 | 16 | 6 |
| 6½ by 4¾ . | ,, | 1 | 7 | 0 |

### No. 3.

Morocco leather cases, embossed silk velvet inside, gilt line on inside edges, mats, glasses, and preservers, very good quality.

| | | £ | s. | d. |
|---|---|---|---|---|
| 2½ by 2 . | per doz. | 0 | 6 | 6 |
| 3¼ by 2¾ . | ,, | 0 | 9 | 0 |
| 4¼ by 3¼ . | ,, | 0 | 15 | 0 |
| 5 by 4 . | ,, | 1 | 7 | 0 |
| 6½ by 4¾ . | ,, | 2 | 2 | 0 |
| 8½ by 6½ . | ,, | 4 | 10 | 0 |

### No. 4.

Best English Morocco leather cases, lined with rich silk velvet, gilt line on inner edge, with mats, glasses, and preservers, of best quality.

| | | £ | s. | d. |
|---|---|---|---|---|
| 2½ by 2 . | per doz. | 0 | 8 | 0 |
| 3¼ by 2¾ . | ,, | 0 | 12 | 0 |
| 4¼ by 3¼ . | ,, | 0 | 18 | 0 |
| 5 by 4 . | ,, | 1 | 9 | 0 |
| 6½ by 4¾ . | ,, | 2 | 10 | 0 |
| 8½ by 6½ . | ,, | 5 | 10 | 0 |

### No. 5.

Lace band cases, of very superior finish, with best mats, glasses, and preservers.

| | | £ | s. | d. |
|---|---|---|---|---|
| 2½ by 2 . | per doz. | 0 | 17 | 6 |
| 3¼ by 2¾ . | ,, | 1 | 5 | 0 |
| 4¼ by 3¼ . | ,, | 1 | 13 | 0 |
| 5 by 4 . | ,, | 2 | 17 | 6 |
| 6½ by 4¾ . | ,, | 3 | 17 | 6 |

### No. 6.

Double morocco cases, for holding two pictures, of best quality, gilt rims, mats, glasses, and preservers.

| | | £ | s. | d. |
|---|---|---|---|---|
| 2½ by 2 . | per doz. | 0 | 9 | 0 |
| 3¼ by 2¾ . | ,, | 0 | 13 | 0 |
| 4¼ by 3¼ . | ,, | 1 | 0 | 0 |
| 5 by 4 . | ,, | 1 | 16 | 0 |

### No. 7.

Carte de Visite cases, with silk velvet lining, gilt edges inside, fitted with mats, glasses, &c.

| | £ | s. | d. |
|---|---|---|---|
| Per doz. . . . . | 0 | 10 | 0 |
| With clasp . . . | 0 | 14 | 0 |
| American Union Carte de Visite Case . . . | 1 | 4 | 0 |

### No. 8.

American Union cases, resembling carved ebony, with snaps and hinges, and best silk velvet linings, without mats or glasses.

| | | £ | s. | d. |
|---|---|---|---|---|
| 2½ by 2 . | per doz. | 0 | 16 | 0 |
| 3¼ by 2¾ . | ,, | 1 | 0 | 0 |
| 4¼ by 3¼ . | ,, | 1 | 10 | 0 |

## Mats and Preservers.

### No. 1.

Gilt mats, chased or plain, oval, dome, or cushion.

| | | £ | s. | d. |
|---|---|---|---|---|
| 2½ by 2 . | per gross | 0 | 3 | 0 |
| 3¼ by 2¾ . | ,, | 0 | 4 | 6 |
| 4¼ by 3¼ . | ,, | 0 | 7 | 6 |

### No. 2.

Superior gilt mats, chased and beaded, with burnished edges, oval, dome, or cushion.

| | | £ | s. | d. |
|---|---|---|---|---|
| 2½ by 2 . | per gross | 0 | 10 | 0 |
| 3¼ by 2¾ . | ,, | 0 | 15 | 0 |
| 4¼ by 3¼ . | ,, | 1 | 0 | 0 |

**No. 3.**
**Gilt Mats, oval, dome, or cushion, best frosted.**

| | | £ | s. | d. |
|---|---|---|---|---|
| 2½ by 2 . | per gross | 0 | 14 | 0 |
| 3¼ by 2¾ . | " | 1 | 1 | 0 |
| 4¼ by 3¼ . | " | 1 | 10 | 0 |
| 5 by 4 . | " | 2 | 5 | 0 |
| 6½ by 4¾ . | " | 3 | 3 | 0 |
| 8½ by 6½ . | " | 7 | 0 | 0 |

**No. 4.**
**American stamped Mats (thin), oval, dome, or cushion.**

| | | £ | s. | d. |
|---|---|---|---|---|
| 2½ by 2 . | per doz. | 0 | 0 | 7 |
| 3¼ by 2¾ . | " | 0 | 0 | 10 |
| 4¼ by 3¼ . | " | 0 | 1 | 8 |

**No. 5.**
**American stamped Mats, stout.**

| | | £ | s. | d. |
|---|---|---|---|---|
| 2½ by 2 . | per doz. | 0 | 2 | 0 |
| 3¼ by 2¾ . | " | 0 | 3 | 0 |
| 4¼ by 3¼ . | " | 0 | 5 | 0 |
| 6½ by 4¾ . | " | 0 | 8 | 0 |

**No. 6.**
**American Excelsior Mats.**

| | | £ | s. | d. |
|---|---|---|---|---|
| 2½ by 2 . | per doz. | 0 | 3 | 0 |
| 3¼ by 2¾ . | " | 0 | 5 | 0 |
| 4¼ by 3¼ . | " | 0 | 8 | 0 |
| 6½ by 4¾ . | " | 0 | 14 | 0 |

## Preservers.

**Good English.** per gross.

| | £ | s. | d. |
|---|---|---|---|
| 2½ by 2 | 0 | 3 | 0 |
| 3¼ by 2¾ | 0 | 4 | 6 |
| 4¼ by 3¼ | 0 | 7 | 0 |
| 5 by 4 | 0 | 15 | 0 |
| 6½ by 4¾ | 1 | 14 | 0 |
| 8½ by 6½ | 4 | 10 | 0 |

**Best English.** per doz.

| | £ | s. | d. |
|---|---|---|---|
| 2½ by 2 | 0 | 0 | 4 |
| 3¼ by 2¾ | 0 | 0 | 6 |
| 4¼ by 3¼ | 0 | 0 | 9 |
| 5 by 4 | 0 | 2 | 0 |
| 6½ by 4¾ | 0 | 4 | 0 |

**Best American.** per doz.

| | £ | s. | d. |
|---|---|---|---|
| 2½ by 2 | 0 | 0 | 8 |
| 3¼ by 2¾ | 0 | 0 | 10 |
| 4¼ by 3¼ | 0 | 1 | 8 |
| 5 by 4 | 0 | 2 | 6 |
| 6½ by 4¾ | 0 | 3 | 9 |

## Morocco Frames or Trays (*Fig.* 107).

**No. 1.**
**Morocco Trays, common, with glasses, mats, and preservers.**

| | | £ | s. | d. |
|---|---|---|---|---|
| 2½ by 2 . | per gross | 0 | 8 | 6 |
| 3¼ by 2¾ . | " | 0 | 12 | 0 |
| 4¼ by 3¼ . | " | 0 | 16 | 0 |

**No. 2.**
**Best Morocco Trays, lined with silk velvet, gilt rim, mats, glasses, and preservers.**

| | | £ | s. | d. |
|---|---|---|---|---|
| 2½ by 2 . | per doz. | 0 | 1 | 3 |
| 3¼ by 2¾ . | " | 0 | 2 | 0 |
| 4¼ by 3¼ . | " | 0 | 3 | 6 |
| 5 by 4 . | " | 0 | 6 | 0 |
| 6½ by 4¾ . | " | 0 | 10 | 6 |

No. 3.

**American Union Trays, without mats or glasses.**

| | | | £ | s. | d. |
|---|---|---|---|---|---|
| 2½ by 2 | . . | per doz. | 0 | 7 | 0 |
| 3¼ by 2¾ | . . | „ | 0 | 8 | 6 |
| 4¼ by 3¼ | . . | „ | 0 | 12 | 6 |

Lockets and Brooches for Photographs, in great variety, from 1s. 6d. each.

---

# ESTIMATES

OF

# Complete Sets of Photographic Apparatus,

## FOR THE COLLODION PROCESSES ONLY.

| | | £ | s. | d. |
|---|---|---|---|---|
| No. 1. | **Complete Set of Photographic Apparatus,** for taking positive portraits and views up to 4¼ by 3¼ inches, in wood case, complete, with tripod stand . . . . . . . . . . | 3 | 0 | 0 |

This apparatus is of the most simple kind, and consists of a compound achromatic lens (tested); walnut camera and back; 2 plate holders, and focussing screen; mahogany tripod stand; scales and weights; porcelain pan; gutta percha bath and dipper; filtering paper; glass funnel; graduated measure; 1 dozen plates in box; and bottles containing 6 oz. of nitrate of silver bath, 3 oz. positive collodion, 1 pint of developing solution, 1 oz. cyanide potassium, 1 oz. of Bland and Co.'s transparent varnish, with full directions for use.

| | | £ | s. | d. |
|---|---|---|---|---|
| No. 2. | **Complete Set of Photographic Apparatus,** for taking portraits up to 6½ by 4¾, the contents of box being the same as No. 1, only in larger quantities. . . . . . . . . | 5 | 5 | 0 |
| No. 3. | **Complete Set of Photographic Apparatus,** for taking portraits and views 4¼ by 3¼ inches; consisting of a sliding body camera, in walnut wood:—1 single back, for plates 4¼ by 3¼ inches, fitted with compound achromatic lens of superior construction; reversing frame; glass plates in | | | |

| | | £ | s. | d. |
|---|---|---|---|---|
| | box; gutta percha bath and dipper; porcelain pan; levelling stand; scales and weights; glass graduated measure; filtering paper and funnel; positive paper, for printing; camera tripod stand; and chemicals, consisting of 1 oz. nitrate of silver, ½ drachm pyrogallic acid, 1 oz. glacial acetic acid, 4 oz. iodized collodion, hyposulphite of soda, 1 oz. varnish; the whole packed in case, with lock and handle . . . . . . | 5 | 0 | 0 |
| No. 4. | **Complete Set of Photographic Apparatus,** for portraits 4¼ by 3¼ inches, same as No. 3, but with best French-polished mahogany camera, and compound achromatic lens, of Bland & Co.'s own make, in which the chemical and optical foci are warranted to coincide; chemicals, stand, &c., complete . . . . . . . . | 6 | 12 | 6 |
| No. 5. | **Complete Set of Photographic Apparatus,** consisting of sliding body camera of superior construction, with dark slide and loose frames for plates 5 by 4 inches, and 4 by 3 inches; compound achromatic lens, with Waterhouse's Diaphragms, of Bland and Co.'s own make, the chemical and optical foci being perfectly coincident; glass plates, plate boxes; gutta percha bath and dipper; washing pan; levelling stand; reversing frame; glass measures; scales and weights, with glass pans; with all the necessary chemicals, papers, tripod stand, &c., packed in case, complete, with lock and key . . . | 9 | 7 | 6 |
| No. 6. | **Complete Set of Photographic Apparatus,** consisting of sliding body camera, best make; dark slide with three loose frames for plates 6 by 5 inches, 5 by 4 inches, and 4 by 3 inches, fitted with compound achromatic lens, with Waterhouse's Diaphragms, of Bland and Co.'s own make, the chemical and optical foci being absolutely coincident; glass plates; 3 plate boxes; gutta percha bath and dipper; 2 washing pans; levelling stand; reversing frame; glass measures; scales and weights; funnel; filter ring; supply of positive paper; bibulous paper; tripod stand, with brass top; with all requisite chemicals, in stoppered bottles, and materials; the whole packed in case, with lock and key . | 13 | 10 | 0 |

| | | £ s. d. |
|---|---|---|
| No. 7. | **Complete Set of Apparatus for Collodion pictures,** 8½ by 6½ inches, 6 by 5 inches, and 5 by 4 inches; comprising mahogany sliding body camera, of best construction, with one dark slide, and three loose frames for glass plates, ground focussing glass, &c., fitted with double combination achromatic lens of Bland and Co.'s own manufacture, in which the chemical and optical foci are perfectly coincident, with Waterhouse's Diaphragms, with rack and pinion adjustment; 1 dozen plates, 8½ by 6½ inches in box; 1 dozen plates, 6 by 5 inches, in box; 1 dozen plates, 5 by 4 inches, in box; gutta percha bath and dipper; 2 washing pans; levelling stand; reversing frame; glass measures; scales and weights; with a full supply of all the necessary chemicals, tripod stand, &c. complete, packed in stout case, with lock and key . . . . . . . . . . | 27 0 0 |

**Stereoscopic Sets** estimated for, according to the kind of Camera selected.

---

## ESTIMATES

OF

## Complete Sets of Photographic Apparatus,

### FOR THE PAPER PROCESSES ONLY.

| | | £ s. d. |
|---|---|---|
| No. 1. | **Complete Set of Photographic Apparatus,** for taking pictures by the calotype or waxed-paper process, 6 by 5 inches; consisting of mahogany camera, fitted with single achromatic lens, 1¾ inches diameter, mounted in brass front; single dark slide for prepared paper; porcelain dish; preparing board; glass rod; reversing frame; 1 quire of photographic paper; 1 quire of bibulous ditto; set of scales and weights; 1 oz. measure; minim ditto; tripod stand; and all the necessary chemicals, &c., in stoppered bottles; the whole packed in case with lock and key . . . . . . . . . . . | 5 5 0 |

£ s. d.

No. 2. **Complete Set of Photographic Apparatus,** for taking pictures by the calotype or waxed-paper process, 7 by 6 inches, consisting of mahogany camera, fitted with single achromatic view lens, 2¼ inches diameter, mounted in brass front; single dark slide for prepared paper; ground focussing glass; 2 porcelain dishes; board for the preparation of paper; 2 glass rods; reversing or printing frame; tripod stand for supporting the camera; 2 quires of photographic paper; 2 quires of bibulous ditto; scales and weights; glass measures; funnel; with all the necessary chemicals, &c.; the whole packed in case, with lock and key . . . . . . 6 6 0

No. 3. **Complete Set of Photographic Apparatus,** for taking pictures 9 by 7 inches, by either the calotype or waxed-paper process, comprising mahogany camera, fitted with single achromatic view lens, 2⅝ inches diameter, mounted in brass front; 1 double back for prepared paper, ground focussing screen; tripod stand for supporting camera; 2 porcelain dishes; preparing board; 2 glass rods; reversing or printing frame, for obtaining positives; 2 quires of photographic paper; 2 quires of bibulous ditto; scales and weights; glass measures and funnels; with all the necessary chemicals, complete; the whole packed in case, with lock and key . . . . 9 9 0

No. 4. **Portable Photographic Apparatus,** consisting of a folding camera of best construction, with ground focussing glass; 1 double back for prepared paper; fitted with single achromatic lens, 2¼ inches diameter, mounted in brass front, sliding adjustment for foreground and sky, adapted for taking pictures by the calotype or waxed-paper process, 7 by 6 inches; tripod stand for supporting the camera; 2 porcelain washing pans; preparing board; 2 glass rods; reversing frame; glass graduated measures and funnels; 2 quires of photographic paper; 1 quire of albumenized ditto; 1 quire of bibulous ditto; scales and weights, with glass pans; and a full supply of chemicals; the camera and lens packed in leather sling case, for convenience of carriage; the chemicals and other apparatus in case, with lock and key . . . . . . . . . . 12 0 0

| | | £ s. d. |
|---|---|---|
| No. 5. | **Portable Photographic Apparatus,** comprising folding camera of best construction; ground focussing glass; 1 double back for prepared paper, 9 by 7 inches; fitted with single achromatic view lens, 2⅝ inches diameter, mounted in brass front, with adjustment for foreground and sky; tripod stand, for supporting the camera; preparing board; 2 glass rods; 1 ounce glass graduated measure; minim ditto; 2 glass funnels; 2 porcelain pans for washing paper; reversing or printing frame; set of scales and weights, with glass pans; 3 quires of photographic paper; 2 quires of albumenized ditto; 2 quires of bibulous ditto, with a full supply of chemicals, &c. The camera, with back and lens, packed in leather sling case, for convenience of carriage; the chemicals and other apparatus in strong case, with lock and key . . . | 15 0 0 |
| No. 6. | **Portable Photographic Apparatus,** consisting of folding camera of best construction; ground focussing glass; 1 double back for prepared paper, 11 by 9 inches fitted with single achromatic view lens, 3 inches diameter, mounted in brass front with rack-work adjustment; sliding front to camera, for adjusting proportion of foreground and sky; tripod stand for supporting the camera; 2 porcelain pans for washing paper; preparing board; 2 glass rods; glass graduated measures: glass funnels; reversing or printing frame; set of scales and weights, with glass pans; 3 quires of photographic paper; 3 quires of albumenized ditto; 3 quires of bibulous ditto; with a full supply of chemicals for the calotype or waxed-paper process; the camera and lens packed in leather sling case, for convenience of carriage; the chemicals and other apparatus in strong case, with lock and key . . . | 20 0 0 |

# ESTIMATES

FOR

# Complete Sets of Photographic Apparatus,

FOR COLLODION PORTRAITS AND VIEWS BY PAPER PROCESSES, OR FOR COLLODION PORTRAITS AND VIEWS.

---

| | | £ | s. | d. |
|---|---|---|---|---|
| No. 1. | **Complete Set of Photographic Apparatus,** for taking portraits by the collodion process, 4¼ by 3¼ inches, and views or landscapes 6 to 5 inches, on either collodion, calotype, or waxed paper; comprisisg a sliding body French-polished mahogany camera, with 1 single back for paper or glass, and 1 single back, with loose frames, for collodion plates; fitted with compound achromatic lens of Bland and Co.'s own make, which is adapted for either portraits or views; tripod stand; scales and weights; levelling stand; gutta percha bath and dipper; 1 dozen glass plates in box, 4¼ by 3¼ inches; 1 dozen ditto in box, 3¼ by 2¾ inches; reversing or printing frame; 2 glass graduated measures; 2 funnels; glass rods; preparing board; 2 porcelain washing pans; 1 quire of photographic paper; 1 quire of albumenized ditto; 1 quire of bibulous ditto; and a supply of chemicals, both for collodion and calotype or waxed paper process; the whole packed in case, with lock and key . . . . . . | 10 | 0 | 0 |
| No. 2. | **Complete Set of Photographic Apparatus,** for taking portraits on collodion 5 by 4 inches, and views or landscapes 7 by 6 inches, on either collodion, calotype, or waxed paper; consisting of mahogany French-polished sliding body camera, with 1 single back for paper or glass, 7 by 6 inches, and 1 single back for collodion plates; 2 loose frames 5 by 4 inches, and 4 by 3 inches; fitted with compound achromatic lens, | | | |

| | | £ | s. | d. |
|---|---|---|---|---|
| | of Bland and Co.'s own make, which is adapted for either portraits or views; tripod stand; scales and weights; levelling stand; gutta-percha bath and dipper; 1 dozen glass plates in box, 5 by 4 inches; 1 dozen ditto in boz. 4 by 3 inches; reversing frame; 2 glass graduated measures; preparing board; 2 pans for washing; 1 quire of photographic paper; 1 quire of albumenized ditto; 1 quire of bibulous ditto; 2 glass funnels; and a good supply of chemicals in stoppered bottles, consisting of nitrate of silver, iodide of potassium, gallic acid, acetic acid, varnish, hyposulphite of soda, iodized collodion, pyrogallic acid, chloride of sodium, cyanide of potassium, nitrate of silver bath, &c.; the whole packed in case complete, with lock and key . . . . . . . . . . | 13 | 10 | 0 |
| No. 3. | Ditto, ditto, same as above, but with portable folding camera, of best construction, with one double back for paper, and one single back for collodion plates . . . . . . . | 14 | 10 | 0 |
| No. 4. | **Complete Set of Photographic Apparatus,** for taking portraits on collodion 6 by 5 inches, and views or landscapes 6 by 7 inches, on collodion, calotype, or waxed paper; comprising a mahogany French-polished sliding body camera, with one single back for paper or glass, 9 by 7 inches, and one single back, with two loose frames, for collodion plates, 6 by 5 inches, and 5 by 4 inches, fitted with compound achromatic lens of Bland and Co.'s own make, which is adapted for both portraits and views; tripod stand; scales and weights; levelling stand; gutta-percha bath and dipper; 1 dozen glass plates, 6 by 5 inches, in box; 1 dozen ditto, 5 by 4 inches, in box; reversing frame; 2 glass graduated measures; preparing board; glass rods; 2 porcelain washing pans; 2 quires of photographic paper; 2 quires of albumenized ditto; 2 quires of bibulous ditto; 2 glass funnels; and a good supply of chemicals required in both processes; the whole carefully packed in case, with lock and key . . . . | 17 | 17 | 0 |

| | | £ | s. | d. |
|---|---|---|---|---|
| No. 5. | **Complete Set of Photographic Apparatus** (No. 4), with portable, folding camera, of best construction, with one double back for paper, and one single back for collodion plates . . | 18 | 10 | 0 |
| No. 6. | **Complete Set of Photographic Apparatus,** for taking portraits on collodion plates 8½ by 6½ inches, and views or landscapes 11 by 9 inches, on either collodion, calotype, or waxed papers; comprising mahogany sliding body camera, French-polished, with one single back for glass or paper, 11 by 9 inches, and one single back for glass plates, with two loose frames 8½ by 6½ inches, and 6 by 5 inches; fitted with compound achromatic lens, of Bland and Co.'s own make, which is adapted for either portraits or views; tripod stand; scales and weights; levelling stand, gutta percha bath and dipper; 1 dozen plates in box, 8½ by 6½ inches; 1 dozen ditto, 6 by 5 inches, in box; reversing frame; 2 glass graduated measures; preparing board; 2 glass rods; 2 pans for washing; 3 quires of photographic paper; 3 quires of albumenized ditto; 3 quires of bibulous ditto; 2 funnels; and an ample supply of all the requisite chemicals for both processes, in stoppered bottles; the whole packed in strong case, with lock and key . . | 30 | 0 | 0 |
| No. 7. | Ditto, ditto, same as above, but with portable folding camera of best construction, with one double back for paper, and one single back for collodion plates . . . . . . . | 31 | 15 | 0 |

**Estimates given for Complete Sets,** *for any single Process, or combination of Processes, not enumerated in the above List.*

# INDEX.

CPSIA information can be obtained
at www.ICGtesting.com
Printed in the USA
LVHW040358200422
716646LV00005B/313

9 783752 594522